More Kinnakeet Stories

Bernie Lewis

Other Books by Bernie Lewis

Kinnakeet Stories

The Long Branch You've Never Seen

Local Heroes:
Winchester, Virginia 2000-2010

More
Kinnakeet Stories

More Short Stories Inspired By The Coast Of North Carolina

Bernie Lewis

Dedication

As always, for my family. My great supporters.

To all those who read my stories and offered feedback, those who bought my books, and all lovers of good beach stories—you inspire me.

Table Of Contents

Introduction

The time since the publication of the first *Kinnakeet Stories* book has been magical.

The response to this book far exceeded my expectations and imagination. The outpouring of compliments, support, and encouragement has been truly inspiring. Readers have offered new story ideas along with comments about their favorite, and sometimes least favorite, stories. They have all encouraged me to share more stories in a second book, so here it is.

My love of Kinnakeet is even greater now than it was at the time of writing the stories in the first book. With each day and week spent in this special place there are new experiences and new learnings. The village, like Hatteras Island, is always changing. I consider it a privilege to walk the streets, the beaches, and through the dunes of this very unique place.

The stories in this second collection come from a variety of places. Some from the interactions with, and suggestions of, readers of the first book. Many from the game I like to play of "What If?" I like to imagine things that have happened, or could have happened in Kinnakeet, and let my mind just run with it. So we have stories here of a shipwreck, a ghost ship, a surfing lesson, and a message in a washed up bottle found on the beach.

The first story is a tribute to the spirit of Ray Stallings. The Hatteras and Ocracoke Island community lost this very special man in November 2024. Like many others who had the pleasure of meeting and knowing him, a piece of him will live on inside me forever.

All photographs in these pages were captured on Hatteras Island.

Walking Ray

When he arrived in Kinnakeet in 1948 he introduced himself as Ray Collins. By a year later everyone knew him as Walking Ray.

Ray walked everywhere. By choice. He told anyone who asked that he knew how to drive a car, but added, "I don't need one." Everything he wanted or needed was in walking distance. If it wasn't in Kinnakeet he could walk to Buxton, Frisco, or even Nags Head. When a local would pass him, carrying his knapsack, on Route 12 going in either direction, and offer a ride, he politely refused. He professed that he preferred to walk. And walk he did, even in the rain and wind that sometimes made it hard to stay on the road, much of which was still unpaved.

Most of the time he walked on the beach. He usually walked barefoot in the sand because he loved the feel of "the natural earth" under his feet. He was often on the ocean side of the island at sunrise, and the sound side at sunset. He always said the unique beauty of each sunrise and sunset was, "The greatest work of art on planet earth."

There was much speculation about Ray. Even after the war there were not many strangers who made their way to Kinnakeet, and very few found a reason to stay. The village was still very much a fishing and boat building community. Tourism picked up over the next few years, but outsiders weren't ready for the harsh conditions that living on a wind-swept coastal barrier island presented. The often-rough ferry ride across Oregon Inlet was enough to keep most people away.

Where he'd come from, who he really was, and especially, why he was in Kinnakeet, were frequent topics of conversation. Ray would say little about any of this, though he was always friendly as he deferred these lines of inquiry.

He didn't mind the questions, or the rumors. He walked for reasons beyond words. The island, with its windswept dunes and restless waves, spoke to him in ways people never could, and rarely understood. Each step was a conversation with this little piece of the earth. Each mile was a meditation. He would only say that he thought Kinnakeet was a lovely piece of the world and suited his needs perfectly.

Ray was a tall man. Thin, as you'd expect someone to be who walked all the time. His most outstanding physical features were his china blue eyes and his big feet. Some people speculated they could be a size 14EE, always housed in boots, when he wasn't barefoot. The fact that he arrived in military issue boots led people to say he was a veteran, which most men his age were just three years after the war ended. On his job application he listed his age as 33. That he wore an old olive-colored gabardine army rain jacket when the weather was wet reinforced the impression of military service. Of course, those jackets were in ready supply at any Army-Navy Surplus store.

The several Kinnakeeters who served in the Coast Guard, and the few who were in the Navy, said they'd never heard of him. That led to the assumption that he must have served in the Army. Perhaps he'd seen things there that he just didn't want to talk about, as many veterans had.

Ray lived in a rented house and got a job the second day he was in town at Robinson's General Store, which was just opening. Years later, Clint Robinson would say that Walking Ray was the best hire he ever made. The man showed up every day, in any weather. He didn't let petty things like tropical storms or washed-out roads keep him from opening the store on time, always with a smile on his face and a friendly greeting to everyone who stopped by.

Like all Kinnakeeters, Ray lived frugally. He ate most of his meals at home, except the snack he would pack to eat for lunch at the store. On the rare occasion he ate a meal at one of the two local cafes he would always pick up the check for another table, often a family. He quickly developed a reputation as being generous with everyone he met, especially children. Some said the expression, "He'd give you the shirt off his back" must have originated about Ray.

As people got to know him, everyone was impressed with the extent of his knowledge. He knew the stars and constellations, he knew history, he knew music. His favorite musical period was the Baroque. His favorite composer was J.S. Bach. His neighbors often heard choral works blaring out from records played on the turntable and speaker he'd managed to get from the store. His beautiful tenor voice accented the Saint Matthew Passion, and in December, the Christmas Oratorio. In German.

Because of his walking habit Ray was considered an eccentric. Because of his brain he was considered a genius. Over time, people began to see the thing he knew the most about was Hatteras Island. Its history, its geography, but mostly its biology. The flora and the fauna.

When he talked about it, and it was something he was always ready to discuss, he said the island spoke a language he understood—resilience, movement, respect. The plants and animals of the island were survivors, just like the people who he now considered his friends.

He invited people to join him on his walks along the road, the beaches, and through the dunes. Eventually they did. Initially one or two brave souls would join him on a Sunday afternoon or early summer morning. After the first couple years he was leading regular walks with 10 or 15 people tagging along, some of them children. While enthusiastic, they often asked him to keep his walks down to three or four miles, instead of his preferred eight to ten.

Ray always picked up trash as he walked on the roads or the beach and insisted his companions do the same. Whether this was the discards of insensitive humans, or naturally occurring debris from storms and tides, he was an ecologist well ahead of his time.

During the group walks, Ray shared his knowledge of the land and its life-giving properties with his friends. He pointed out the various grasses in the dunes – the American Beach Grass, the sea oats, and the Saltmeadow Cordgrasses that thrive at the back of the dunes. He talked to them about the live oaks, the Eastern Red Cedars, and the Yaupon with its bright red berries. Many knew of the latter. Yaupon had been used to make tea on the island for many years. Though most agreed it was not a particularly tasty drink.

His favorite flower, which he never failed to point out along the paths, was the Joe Bell. They grew in abundance in the wild, as well as around his house. He'd transplanted a few Black-eyed Susans to join them.

His favorite creatures were the blue herons, often encountered along the sound, the white-tailed deer, and the ghost crabs.

Ray encouraged his walkers to not only observe, but to listen as they walked. He claimed the ocean, the wind, and the land itself, was alive and had stories to tell, if only people would listen to them. He often led them to the wooden remnants of an old shipwreck on the beach, or steel fragments from a tanker or cargo ship torpedoed off the coast during the war, and asked them to put their hand on the remains and listen with their soul to the story the wreck had to tell. He would do the same with seashells and the occasional dead fish. Especially sharks and dolphins.

One summer day he announced to his assembly of walkers that he was going to walk to the end of Hatteras Island the next day. His plan was to spend the night under the blanket of stars, then walk back the next day. He invited all to join him. No one was ready for such an undertaking of 12 miles each way.

The next morning, he made the trek alone. He carried only a canteen of water, a blanket, some bread and cheese wrapped in cloth, and the small notebook that accompanied him everywhere. He walked to the end of Route 12, then the two miles down the packed sand of Pole Road to where the island met Pamlico Sound. Ocracoke Island was in clear view, just a couple miles across the inlet. He had the place to himself. He thought he was in heaven.

He spent much of the night tracing constellations with his finger and talking to the thousands of stars, many of which he could name. He listened to them when they answered back. The next day he walked back to Kinnakeet, feeling richer than ever.

As Walking Ray became a fixture and a local legend, his absence from the store and the roadways generated notice and often concern. He would disappear for up to three days at a time, though Clint informed anybody who inquired at the store that Ray had asked for the time off. When he was spotted again, he informed the concerned man or woman that he'd needed something that wasn't available locally and had gone to Nags Head or maybe Kill Devil Hills to get it.

One of Ray's best friends was Reverend Paul Weeks, the minister of the Methodist church. He lived a few doors down from Ray and made his acquaintance early on. They bonded over their shared interest in music. On occasion, the Reverend would sit on the small porch of Ray's house and listen with him to the cantatas and oratorios of Handel or Bach. After many invitations, Ray began to attend Sunday services. He always sat in the back of the sanctuary and resisted invitations to other church activities.

However, when it came time to sing a hymn, Ray's voice rang out, unmistakable and strong. This led to suggestions, and a near insistence, that he join the choir. He declined these offers, always politely, but did agree to an occasional solo section or verse, always sung from his position in the back row of the church pews. These were greeted with universal praise and compliments.

Reverend Weeks occasionally joined Ray on walks during the week. In discussions about religion with the Reverend, Ray referred to himself as, "A naturalist rather than a Methodist." He enjoyed the atmosphere of the church, certainly the singing of hymns, and the opportunity to share an experience with people who had become his friends. However, he insisted that God spoke to him more clearly when he was outside, in the beauty of His creation, than in a church building. He always insisted the Reverend not take offense, as he found his sermons interesting and was certain they were extremely helpful and inspiring to many of the congregants.

The speculation about Ray's military career was clarified one afternoon in 1954 when a man entered the store, spotted Ray, and immediately shouted out, "Ray, you old son-of-a-gun!" He rushed Ray and embraced him in a bearhug. Ray returned the embrace then introduced "My good friend Buck" to Clint and the handful of store patrons.

Buck acknowledged the introduction, then brashly announced, "I hope all of you know what a great hero you have here among you."

Ray instantly tried to hush his buddy by shaking his head and putting his hand over Buck's mouth. Buck would not be deterred. He brushed Ray's hand away and addressed the audience.

"This man saved my life while we were in the Army over in Belgium, at Bastogne in '44. He personally shot three Germans who had taken me and two others from our squad prisoner. He dragged me back to our lines, then went back and brought the other two back. All this under the worst weather conditions you can imagine and intense fire from the Germans. It was absolute hell that day."

Ray grit his teeth, shook his head, and tried again to silence Buck. "Let's go big guy. That's enough." He grabbed his arm and tried to pull him toward the front door. Buck was not ready to be silenced. He pulled free.

"He was awarded a silver star, his second one, for that little engagement, but it should have been the medal of honor. That was after a whole bunch of other stuff he did to save our asses while we were pushing our way through France. He spoke both French and German, and one night tricked a German patrol walking past our hiding place into thinking we were another German patrol unit. Saved our asses big-time that day."

Buck put his arm around Ray's shoulder and pulled him close. When Ray tried to move him toward the door, Buck stood his ground. "Hey, let me finish," he said. "They need to hear this."

Ray shook his head and grimaced, then stepped away and straightened a row of peanut butter jars on a shelf while Buck motioned for everyone in the store to gather around.

"He got two field promotions, to Lieutenant then Captain, along the way. He got two purple hearts in addition to the silver stars, and a whole bunch of other commendations before the war was over." He paused and stepped over to hug Ray again. "There's quite a few of us who never would have made it home without this guy risking his own life, several times, for the rest of us."

The flush across Ray's cheeks brightened as he grabbed Buck's arm again, this time more forcefully, and dragged him through the aisle to the front door. Buck managed to turn back and exclaim, "Nice to meet you all!" before Ray got him out the door. They stood and talked in the parking lot for the better part of an hour.

Ray never spoke about what the patrons in the store heard that afternoon. However, most of the rest of Kinnakeet talked about it for the next several days.

The group walks continued, and the number of locals interested in longer walks grew. On mild weather days Ray often led the group to Buxton or Frisco, mostly walking on the beach to avoid the increasing traffic on the road. In addition to his vast knowledge of the plant and animal life along the route, he also shared details of some of the older buildings and the human histories that went with them. On a cold blustery day in April 1958, he led the 25 person Kinnakeet contingent on a walk to the dedication of the Cape Hatteras National Seashore at the Hatteras Lighthouse.

As tourism on Hatteras Island increased, Ray began offering walking tours to visitors. The local motels and vacation rental agencies that sprung up all over the island were sources of frequent referrals.

Family groups especially loved to spend an afternoon with Walking Ray as he led them along the sound and through the dunes, pointing out the plants and animals that they would have missed if they spent all their time on the beach. Bags of collected trash were part of their education about the island's ecology and the impact of human visitors.

One day in 1978, the best-selling author, Beth Gray, stopped in Kinnakeet on the last leg of her cross-country trip. As she travelled in a VW microbus from San Francisco, she gathered stories of "interesting characters" who represented the uniqueness of the American culture. She planned to interview the keeper of the Cape Hatteras Lighthouse as the last potential subject for her book.

She stopped for lunch at the Froggy Dog, and after mentioning her quest to the person seated next to her, was informed that since the National Park Service took over management of the lighthouse, and the automation of the light in 1950, there was no longer a traditional lighthouse keeper. She was told instead she *had* to interview Walking Ray. She was intrigued with what she heard about Ray and found him that afternoon at Robinson's General Store.

Ray was initially reluctant to be interviewed. It took some persuasion, but he agreed to tell his story after Beth assured him it was a wonderful opportunity to tell America about the natural wonders of Kinnakeet and Cape Hatteras as part of the story. Ray set limits on what he would and would not talk about, especially his life before coming to Kinnakeet.

They spent much of the next two days together. Mostly they walked the beaches of the ocean and the sound. Ray educated Beth about the formation of the island, its on-going changes over time, and the glories of the surviving plant and animal life. He insisted Beth join him in picking up trash as they walked. Beth recorded his stories and responses to her questions on her cassette tape recorder, filling up eight, 60-minute tapes.

At the conclusion of the second day, Beth pronounced herself exhausted from the walking but thrilled with the story she was going to tell. When the book came out a year later the story of Walking Ray, and his love of Hatteras Island, was the lead chapter. The legend grew.

Age began to catch up with Ray in the 1980s, as one would suspect it would for a person who walked everywhere. His feet and joints ached much of the time. His group walks became shorter, though he still walked everywhere in and around Kinnakeet.

After his retirement from the ministry in 1986, Reverend Weeks and Ray began to spend more time together. On the porch in the evening, or on early morning walks along the beach, they talked about the increasing realities of ageing, the changes the island was undergoing as a result of tourism, and the importance of friendship. Occasionally, the topics of life, death, and religion took center stage. Ray never mentioned any biological family, always referring to his friends in Kinnakeet as his family.

Eventually, instead of walking, Ray began riding in the cars of visitors so he could continue the process of guiding them around the area and talking with them about his beloved island's history and ecology.

His time at the store decreased due to the pain. With much encouragement from his network of friends, in 1989, at the age of 74, he obtained a driver's license. To no one's surprise, he passed the test on his first attempt. Soon after, he purchased a used Ford F-150 pickup with four-wheel drive.

While he preferred to ride in other's vehicles, he began offering island tours and transportation services in his truck. For a small fee, to offset his lost income from the store, he transported customers to any point on the island, or with a ride on the ferry, across the inlet to Ocracoke.

Most of his customers wanted a ride on the beach, or to be taken to areas accessible only by four-wheel drive. His favorite place to take shell collectors or fishermen was the end of the island, where he'd once spent a glorious night he would never forget. He joked that he should now be called "Rolling Ray," but his many friends in Kinnakeet would never accept this.

One of the topics he enjoyed talking to visitors about was the evolution of driving on the island, going back to the time of his arrival in 1948. At that time, driving meant steering around dunes and gullies along rutted sand that was often just at the edge of the waves. No license was required back then, and pavement didn't come to the Kinnakeet area until 1953.

Ray never wore shoes while driving, claiming they only made his pain worse. He joked that if anyone saw him wearing shoes he was probably at a funeral. But he insisted he wouldn't be wearing them at his.

He still enjoyed time out of the vehicle while his customers walked the beach or collected shells. He walked short distances to feel the sand between his toes, collect a little trash, and listen to the earth as it spoke to him.

Walking Ray's unexpected death in his sleep, in 1994, came as a shock to the entire Kinnakeet and Hatteras Island community. Disbelief was the dominant feeling expressed, followed by sadness. It was hard to believe this kind man, the local legend who had touched so many, was gone.

The love for Ray, and his far-reaching reputation, was such that a funeral home in Nags Head provided their services free of charge. In accordance with his long-standing request, Ray's body was cremated.

Reverend Paul Weeks gave the eulogy at a memorial service in the Methodist Church. The service was broadcast to the crowd of 150 Kinnakeeters and others in the surrounding yard who were unable to find room to sit or stand inside the building.

Reverend Weeks reminded the mourners that Ray had no doubt taken more steps on Hatteras Island than anyone since the days when the island was populated only by Native Americans. He added that Ray had certainly driven and ridden more miles on the beaches, and gotten to know more visitors to the island, than anyone else. Everyone who had the pleasure of meeting Ray, the visitors and locals alike, knew Ray as a man of great intelligence and kindness, and considered him a friend.

The Reverend told of Ray's wish to be remembered as a man who respected the planet and who loved Hatteras Island. He hoped those who knew him might think of him occasionally as they respectfully walked the island's roads, the beaches, and the dunes. Perhaps they might hear him speak to them in some way or another as they listened to the voices of the island, the wind, and the waves.

Later that afternoon, Walking Ray's friends spread his ashes over the dunes of Kinnakeet and watched while the earth gratefully accepted them.

Ocean Rescue

"I'm sure you're going to like this one. It has just about everything on your wish list," Catherine said as she climbed out of the driver's side of the SUV while Jenny Kaye exited the passenger side. "It's the oldest and smallest of the five we're going to look at today, but it has been updated quite a bit." Jenny immediately noticed and liked the natural cedar shake siding on the saltbox building.

As they walked the few steps to the house on the sand driveway, Catherine continued. "The oldest part of the house dates to the early 1900s. It's been added to and remodeled several times over the years, of course, as any oceanfront house that has stood this long would have to be. You'll be surprised at what good condition it's in." She paused as she opened the lockbox and extracted the key. Before unlocking the door, she finished her pitch. "The current owner wanted it listed as a historical building, so he did the research to trace its lineage. It was originally built by a shipwreck survivor who decided to settle here. He lived in the house for 26 years. It's named Ocean Rescue."

Catherine opened the door and flicked a light switch, then allowed Jenny to walk inside ahead of her. As they entered the first floor she continued.

"As you can see, this part is now used as a storage area, which is nice to have. At one point it was a garage, as well, and could always be returned to that. And, you'll notice, all the storage shelves are at least a couple of feet above the floor, in case of flooding, which is always possible this close to the water. But as you'll see as we move up, there are large dunes between the house and the beach which provide wonderful protection." After a quick look around, Jenny followed Catherine up the stairs.

"This floor was originally the top floor," Catherine continued, "but now is used as the primary living space with this lovely living room, and one bedroom here," she pointed down a short hallway, "and the other bedrooms are up on the next floor. I'll let you look around for a little bit, then meet you on the deck, right through here." Catherine slid open a set of vertical blinds, revealing sliding glass doors that led to the deck.

"But before I do, let me point out the original flooring, at least most of it is, this beautiful fireplace, and this unique wall." She walked to the wall that separated the living space from what must be the bedroom on the other side. She pointed to two halves of an old barrel that were sticking out about a foot from the obviously timeworn wooden boards that made up the wall.

"This is the most unique feature of this wonderful old house. As you can see, this barrel was split vertically in half, and each half embedded in the wall. This wall has been preserved through the several remodelings. If you look closely, you can still read the writing on the barrels."

Jenny leaned in and examined the black lettering on the aged wooden pieces wrapped in rusted metal bands. On the left barrel she could make out, "Portside Barrel Company." On the right barrel were the faded numbers 41122. She ran her hand over the roughness of the barrel and the smoother lettering. "That really is unique. I love it," she said. She took a moment to ponder what the barrel might have held in its earlier days, and what its history might have been, but then turned back to the room.

For a couple of minutes, Jenny opened drawers and cabinet doors in the kitchen, checked out the relatively new refrigerator and oven, then ran her hand over the six-seat oak table that had been left behind in the dining area. She walked through the empty bedroom, opened the door to the closet, flushed the toilet, ran water in the bathroom sink, took a quick look at the laundry room and half-bath, then returned to the living room area. She took a moment to enjoy the view of the ocean and cloud-streaked blue sky, and tried to imagine the placement of her sofa, chairs, and tables in the room. The barrel pieces caught her eye again before she stepped out to the deck to join Catherine.

"Isn't this view wonderful?" Catherine exclaimed as she stared out to the calmness of the ocean less than two hundred yards away. "It's about low tide now, so in a few hours the water will be quite a bit closer. There is a wonderfully wide beach here and the water has never breached the dunes, even in the big storms... that we know of."

Jenny barely heard the words as she soaked in the warmth and inhaled the salt air. She watched a fishing boat of some kind slowly work its way south. Five minutes later, they were on the wrap-around deck of the upper level, admiring the even better view.

The location of the house was a big plus, on the very northern edge of Kinnakeet, just before the national seashore. Jenny could see only one house to the north, about a quarter mile away, and several, starting about an equal distant away, lined up to the south. They had just walked through the second small living area, two medium-sized bedrooms, and one-and-a-half bathrooms. There was also a small room facing the back of the house with a large window which Jenny visualized as an office.

"All the windows and glass doors in the house were updated about five years ago," Catherine said. "They are certified to withstand winds up to 100 miles an hour. And, as you can see, the building itself is very sound. And, barring a direct hit from a hurricane, it will stand for another hundred years or more. New roofing was installed five years ago. There have been a few pieces of siding replaced in the last few years, that's to be expected, but otherwise, this is an exceptionally fine beach property. Don't you agree?"

Jenny did agree. The house was very close to what she was hoping to find for her "let's start over" home. The year since Paul announced he was leaving her for his business associate, who was blond, beautiful, and 22 years younger than she, had been difficult. Living in the same town, sorting through friends, belongings, retirement and saving accounts, had been ghastly. She'd cried a bucket, or two, of tears. But that was over now. At least the house had sold quickly. Their daughter, Kelli, had been emotionally supportive of her while maintaining a superficial relationship with her father.

They looked at the other four houses on Catherine's list that day, but by the late afternoon Jenny had made up her mind. The asking price for Ocean Rescue was at the top of her price range, but the quaintness of the house, combined with the location, made it what her heart wanted. The opportunity to wake up each morning to that view, go to bed each night listening to the ocean, and in-between explore her long-postponed plans to put her college English degree to use and return to writing fiction in some form, was exactly what she wanted. Assuming the pre-closing home inspection didn't uncover any major faults.

Two days later she had a signed contract, $2,000.00 below the asking price, with a 21-day due diligence period. With Catherine's help, she engaged the services of Anthony Zander, who she was assured was one of the top home inspectors in the county. She returned to her rented townhouse in Richmond but agreed to meet with Anthony at the house on the afternoon of his inspection 13 days later.

When she pulled up at 3:55 p.m. on the appointed day and parked behind Anthony's pickup, she was more excited than on the day she had first visited the house. She had high hopes, but some realistic anxiety that the old house could be hiding some significant flaws, possibly even some structural issues. She knew that would not be surprising for a house of this age with multiple modifications.

She met Anthony inside and he asked her to wait for a few minutes while he finished a couple of last things. She stood on the mid-level deck with crossed fingers and imagined herself sitting here in the mornings for much of the year, drinking coffee and eating breakfast, while watching the sun rise and the birds and dolphins play. Twenty-five minutes later, he joined her and gave her the quick summary.

"There's no bad news to give you about this house. It has good bones, the modifications over the years have been done well. The electricity and plumbing are up to code. The heat and AC are in good shape. The roof is good for a few more years, I didn't find any evidence of recent leaks. The appliances all work, and the fireplace should be fine after the chimney is cleaned. I'll give you all the details in my written report which I'll email to you within 48-hours. But," he paused for a second while he took off his cap and scratched his balding head, "there is one thing I want to show you, if you'll walk with me to the first floor." Jenny's heart skipped a beat, but she told herself to relax, took a deep breath, and fell in behind him.

Once they stepped off the stairway into the storage area, Anthony had her stand in front of the wall and face the steps, just inside the stairway. He showed her how the wall was actually not immediately next to the stairway, as it first appeared, but sat out about three feet from it. There was a sort of optical illusion created by the slight slope of the ceiling in that particular section of the room and the wall she was looking at.

He stood on the first step of the stairway and shined his flashlight into the small cracks between the boards making up the wall that lined that side of the stairs. As he explained, she could not see the light because the wall she was looking at was not the same wall.

"I can't really explain what's going on here," he said, once he rejoined her, "but there are two best guesses. The first, is that when this house was originally built, the builders left this space next to the stairwell accidentally. That's possible, since builders here on the island back when this house was built weren't all professional builders, but typically had other jobs and built houses on the side, often with recruited laborers with little or no building experience. There could have been a design flaw, or maybe they built this wall first then realized the stairwell needed to be three feet closer to the outside wall. Maybe they just covered it up with the second wall next to the stairwell. I can't explain why they would do that, but you never know." He paused to look again at the wall and shook his head.

"And the second guess?" Jenny asked, her curiosity peaked.

"That one's a little more interesting," Anthony said. "It could be that this was intentionally built as a hidden, or secret room. It's a little small to hide a person or persons for more than a brief time, but it could easily hide other things." He paused again. "But the problem with that theory is that there's no door, or other way to get into the room. Of course, if it's a secret room you wouldn't want an obvious door, but I spent a few minutes looking for ways to get into the space and couldn't find anything. The boards seem to be tight and solid, as far as I can tell." He shook his head and took a couple steps back toward the center of the room and examined the wall again. "I guess I'd have to go with guess number one."

As they walked out of the building, Anthony offered some final words of advice. "I wouldn't knock down that wall because everything down there is supporting the weight of the structure above. And remember, that top floor just added a whole lot of weight to what was there when the house was originally built. I would just leave that little mystery alone."

Jenny decided that was probably good advice. At least for the time being. However, she was drawn to the idea of an intentionally hidden room, and it added to the appeal of the house.

She got through closing eight days later, celebrated with a delightful lobster dinner at Captain Tom's Wharf, and started the moving-in process the next week.

She made the small bedroom on the top floor her office, and after the settling in process, decided it was time to write. She had no illusions of being, or becoming, a great writer, but wanted to see what she could recall from her earlier writing days and the several workshops she'd attended once Kelli had gone off to college.

However, the first few days were frustrating. She tried to pull up from the depths of her memory the several ideas she'd had over the last few years for both novels and short stories. She made a couple of attempts to fill the empty computer screen in front of her but kept stalling out after a page or two. None of the ideas excited her the way they should to propel her through the challenging work of writing. She found herself spending her "writing time" sitting on one of the decks, absorbed in the sight, sound, and smell of the ocean in front of her, with every story idea eventually washing away with the tide.

On the eighth writing day, when early November gale force winds discouraged her from her deck time, she found herself in the storage room staring at the mystery room wall. Flashlight in hand, she examined every crack and crevice in the wall and pushed on every board, hoping to discover a secret opening. Nothing. She repeated the process twice over the next five days. Her frustration grew with each failed experience.

As she headed back up the stairs after her last discouraging effort, her attention waned, and her foot slipped off the first step. She landed hard on the stairs with her head on the fourth step. She paused for a moment before trying to get up to check herself for major injuries. After determining there were no apparent broken bones, and maybe just some banged up knees, she gripped the edge of the third step to support herself as she prepared to push herself back on her feet. Instead of meeting the supporting board at the edge of the step near the wall, her fingers slid into an empty space under the step and touched what felt like a metal object.

She froze for a moment, then adjusted her position so she could reach farther into the space. Her fingers found what felt like some sort of metal latch. There was no way to get her face where she could investigate the space, so she continued to explore by feel. She tried to grasp, push, and pull every way she could while attempting to construct a mental image of what her fingers were feeling.

After a few moments, she felt her index finger slide into a circular ring of metal slightly larger around than her finger. She tried pushing and pulling, and within seconds felt the object move and heard a metal 'clank' at the same time. A moment later she heard, from the direction of the mystery wall, what sounded like a creaking noise.

While she was hesitant to let go of what she imagined was the ring opening a latch of some kind, she knew she had to explore the sound from the wall. In her excitement, she forgot about her potential injuries, and bounded to her feet at the foot of the stairs and turned the corner to face the wall.

She immediately saw that a small section of the wall, at the very bottom, in the middle, perhaps three feet square, had opened just an inch or two. She grasped at once that this was obviously the door to the mystery space. Because it was so low on the wall, she and Anthony had both missed it since one would have to be on their knees with their face close to the floor to properly examine the boards there.

After taking a deep breath to try to calm herself, she carefully lowered herself to her knees, ignored the flashes of pain, and wedged her fingers into the opening. As she pulled the door toward her, she heard the creak of old, rusty hinges, and knew that was the sound she'd heard earlier.

With flashlight in hand, she lowered her face to investigate the opening. The light shining into the space revealed a metal safe, seemingly black in color, except for the lighter colored round dial with numbers on it facing the opening. The dial was set so that the number zero was at the top, just below the little arrow, with the last number of 50 just to the left. The safe was a bit smaller than the doorway, but she was unable to tell how far back it extended toward the stairway.

She switched the flashlight to her left hand and reached in to touch the safe with her right. She quickly confirmed that the safe was metal, probably either cast iron or steel. She tried to push it, first backward, then to the left. The fact that it wouldn't move even slightly told her it was indeed very heavy and would be extremely difficult to get out of the space where it rested. It could even be bolted to the floor.

She sat back for a moment to slow her racing heart rate, take another deep breath, and give herself a minute to assess the situation.

Now that she'd discovered the door to the secret room and the safe, the next objective was to open the safe. She decided she'd try to do this leaving the safe where it was rather than try to remove it from the room. Moving the safe would require help and disclosing her find to someone else, something she was not anxious to do at this point. She could reach the knob on the dial and the small handle to pull the door open while laying on her stomach in front of the safe.

A memory flashed into her brain of the toy safe she had as a child that had a combination lock on it. To open it, she turned the knob right to one number, then left to another, then right to the final number. From what she'd seen on television, this was the way these old safes typically worked. But she figured she'd probably have to research that.

She also remembered that when she wasn't worried about someone else breaking into her safe, she'd leave the dial just one or two numbers from the last combination number so she could make just a small turn of the dial and quickly and easily open the safe door. Maybe she wasn't the only one who used this shortcut. It was worth a try.

She got back into position with the flashlight on the floor shining onto the safe and reached for the knob on the dial. She turned it slowly to the right, stopping at each of the next several numbers to give the handle a tug with her left hand. Nothing. She did the same thing, turning the dial to the left, after returning the dial to the zero starting point. Again, nothing.

She sat back again, this time in a full sitting position to get off her knees. While staring at the safe she tried to review her options.

The first one was to try to figure out the combination. That would probably be very difficult, but at least worth some effort before giving up and admitting defeat.

Option number two was to talk to a locksmith about the safe and how to get into it. Presumably, the lock could be drilled out and the door opened, but that would mean bringing in someone else and having them here when the lock was drilled. Maybe she could have the drilling done and ensure the door would open, but have the locksmith leave before actually opening the door. However, that would mean disclosing the hidden room and destroying the safe, both of which she'd rather not do. She may want to return whatever was in the safe to its more-than-a-century-long resting place.

The third possibility she came up with was to simply give up. Let the mystery remain and enjoy the fantasies about what the original builder of the house needed to hide away that would be worth building the secret room with the elaborate door latch system. At least she knew it wasn't the skeletal remains of his serial murder victims, but something that could be placed inside a small safe. So ... maybe just their skulls.

She decided to take a break. She took a picture of the front of the safe with her cell phone camera, then left the wooden door slightly open and retreated up the stairs, feeling the discomfort in her knees with each step.

For the next couple of hours, she learned what she could from the internet about old safes. There were quite a few that looked like "her" safe, but few were that small. She had no manufacture's name to go by. She learned that the right-left-right three-number combination scheme was typical for safes of the late

19th and early 20th century. She hoped to find some embedded "safety" combination that might have been used back in that day, something like 1-2-3, or 10-20-30, that would open the safe in case the set combination was lost, but there didn't seem to be anything of that nature. She learned that combinations could be reset once the door was open.

When she Googled "How to unlock an old safe," the links boiled down to 1. Contact the manufacturer, 2. Engage the services of a locksmith, 3. Explosives. There was also an exceedingly long and detailed procedure that involved using a stethoscope and charting the number and locations of "clicks" heard when turning the dial certain ways. But even after reading through the 23 steps involved, the author acknowledged there were many things that could go wrong along the way and professional locksmiths were most likely to be able to make this technique work.

The rest of the day she thought about the situation and tried to get into the head of the long-dead house builder to come up with possible combinations for the safe. Just before bedtime she came up with the idea that perhaps he would use the street address of the house. She quickly realized it was unlikely in the early 1900s that houses out this far from the main part of the village would be given street numbers. There wasn't even a real street then. However, she had nothing else to go on, and maybe some later homeowner had installed the safe. So, she traipsed down the stairs in her nightgown, got on her bruised knees in front of the safe, then on her belly, and worked on various combinations of 23142. She tried 23R-14L-2R – no good. Then, 2R-31L-42R – no. Next, 23R-1L-42R – no luck. She was disappointed, but knew it was a longshot anyway.

She slept little that night but came up with nothing productive to add to her three options. She thought about the house builder, and that if he died suddenly or unexpectedly, he would have no chance to set the combination to something easy for someone else to guess, or leave the combination written down somewhere.

However, if he knew he was going to die, and had no one he wanted to pass the safe and its contents on to, he could either write the combination down somewhere it would be found, set an easy combination, or enjoy leaving it to a combination that made sense only to him, and force whoever found the secret room and the safe to have it drilled open. No way to tell. And, apparently, no subsequent owner of the house had found the room and opened the safe. But then it struck her, maybe they had, and simply removed whatever was there and locked everything up again. The safe could be empty.

The next day she made two trips to the safe, and tried every number combination she could think of that someone might use if they wanted to make the safe accessible to someone after their death. She tried 1-2-3, 10-20-30, 48-49-50, and about 30 other guesses. No luck.

After this failure, she decided to give safe cracking a break and return to her other frustrating project— writing. For the better part of two days, she sat in her office, and then on one of the decks, trying to come up with a good story to tell. Frequently, her mind drifted back to the safe, but she had decided to employ the "empty mind" technique of not thinking about a problem and allowing the solution to come to her when the universe was ready to reveal it. It had worked for her before.

Two days later, as a storm kept her away from her decks, she was wandering around the second floor living room area with a cup of coffee in hand, when she was drawn to the two barrel halves sticking out of the wall. She studied them for a few seconds, for probably the 20th time since she'd moved in, then ran her hand over the wooden planks and metal bindings. Her eyes focused first on the words printed on the left barrel—Portside Barrel Company, then on the numbers—41122 printed on the right barrel.

Immediately it struck her. The numbers could work as the combination to the safe! The original builder, she assumed, had constructed the mystery room, and put the safe in it, and had made sure the barrels were embedded in the wall of this room, with the numbers facing out! Brilliant!

Twenty seconds later she was on her belly in front of the safe. With the flashlight shining on the dial, she began trying the numbers. First, she tried 41-1-22 and pulled the handle. Nothing. Then 41-12-2. Nope. Then 4-11-22.

When she pulled the handle, the heavy door squeaked as it moved toward her.

She heard herself give an excited squeal and felt the adrenaline rush. She averted her eyes from the safe and sat back to catch her breath. She began talking to herself.

She wanted to go into this with the proper frame of mind. She must be prepared for disappointment. After all, the safe could be empty. Probably was. Whatever was originally stored there had likely been removed many years ago. Or she might find some kind of "Ha-Ha, Fooled You," note inside. It could also have contents that were of some value over 100 years ago but be worthless now. She hadn't spent much time trying to guess what was inside the safe, and now took three slow, deep, breaths before lowering herself again to look inside.

The first thing she saw was a medium-sized canvas bag, tied with a string around the top. Behind it was a similar bag. Resting beside the bags was an envelope.

She reached for the first bag and immediately felt its weight. From the position she was in, lying on her stomach, it took both hands to pull the bag from the safe. It fell to the floor with a clanging sound. She guessed it might weigh five pounds or more and was quite bulky. She pulled it out of the way, then reached for the second bag and dragged it to the front of the safe. With another considerable thump it dropped the six inches to the floor.

It was hard, but she made herself grab the envelope and pull it out before sitting back and turning her attention to the bags.

She decided it was time for another pause and a couple of deep breaths before opening the bags. She noticed her hand was shaking, then realized her whole body was too.

She closed her eyes, took three deep breaths, and instructed herself to relax. Fifteen seconds later she felt ready, or at least a little more relaxed, and untied the first bag. She pulled the top open and looked inside. What she saw almost made her faint. When she gathered herself and put her hand inside, she pulled out a handful of gold coins.

As she held them up to her eye, she realized they were American $10.00 and $20.00 coins with the familiar Liberty Head on the front and a stylized eagle on the back. When she looked for a date on them, she discovered the ones in her hand were dated 1904 or earlier. They didn't look new, but they were obviously in good condition, some better than others.

She set the coins on the floor beside her and took out another handful. There were more $20 than $10 coins this time, but the date range on them was about the same, with the oldest dated 1891.

After putting all the coins back in the bag, her still shaking hand spilling a couple on the ground, she untied the second bag and found another stash of $20 and $10 gold coins with the same date range. After returning these coins to the bag, she lifted one bag in each hand. While she was no expert at estimating weight, she figured they'd weigh between five and ten pounds each. She could weigh them on the bathroom scale upstairs later.

Her mind was racing, but she tried to recall what she knew about the price of gold. A couple of years ago this came up in a conversation with Kelli. She didn't remember why, but she did recall being surprised when Kelli told her gold was worth about $1600.00 an ounce. Of course, she knew it could be more or less now.

She knew nothing about the value of old gold coins but had to believe that coins this old would be worth substantially more to a collector than the weight of the gold they contained.

As these thoughts raced through her head, it dawned on her she had uncovered a real buried treasure. Buried in an old safe, in a secret room, in an old house, rather than in the sand. But none-the-less, still a buried treasure.

Since the date of the newest coins was well past the heyday of pirates patrolling the shipping lanes off the Outer Banks, it was unlikely this was a pirate's cache. She figured it was, more likely, the house builder's life savings. But then she quickly realized that wouldn't make sense, since the house was built in the early 1900s, the builder supposedly lived there for many years, and the most recently minted coins were from 1904.

Her eyes returned to the envelope she'd pulled from the safe, and she immediately guessed that the contents of the envelope would explain the origin of the coins and the reason they were left in the safe. She quickly examined the outside of the envelope, and after seeing no writing on it, ripped it open. Inside were three folded pages of paper with handwritten script. She briefly closed her eyes, took two deep breaths, then began reading.

If you're reading this, it means you found the money. Good for you. I wrote this letter to explain a couple things.

My name is Benjamin Pugh. I am 51 years old and may not be much longer for this life. I built this house as a much younger man and have enjoyed living here. Here is where the money came from and how this house came to be built.

I was on the crew of the schooner Amelia Pearl out of Providence Rhode Island. In the fall of 1905, we were returning home from Savannah with a load of lumber. The ship's Captain, Aaron Gaskill, was trying to speed home to earn a bonus and chose to try to get around a hurricane by taking us close to shore rather than a few more miles out to sea which would have brought us into port a day or two late and cost him some money. Our whole crew tried to talk him out of it but couldn't.

As we feared, the storm was right on top of us just before midnight on September 5th. It was horrible. The wind and surf pounded us, and the sea swept the deck. Before long, the foremast and mainmast were gone to the waves that were taller than the ship. We were taking on more water than we could possibly bail. Just after that we ran aground on a shoal. When the ship began to break apart, we knew we had to abandon her.

The crew was so angry with Capt. Gaskill that they confronted him and, while I was still bailing, one of them shot him. My crewmate, Oskar, who I believe did the deed, said to me that if we were all going to die because of the Capt.'s stupidity, at least the Capt. should die first. When I got to the Capt.'s quarters to tell everyone we had to go now, they were loading money from the safe into their pockets. I don't know if they made the Capt. open the safe before they shot him, or if it was open, but anyway that's what they were doing. We knew he had the money to pay us at the end of the trip, and also the payment for the load of coal we dropped off in Savannah. Capt. also bragged that he kept his life savings in the ship's safe, as he didn't trust banks.

I told the other fellows that the weight of the coins would just weigh them down and make it harder to float or swim which we would have to do if we had any chance to survive. They agreed with me, and we came up with the idea to empty the two whisky barrels and put the coins in them and the paper money in our pockets. We worked fast and got that done and the barrels up to the deck. By then we had to jump as the ship was in three pieces and going down fast.

After we hit the water, me and Thomas grabbed one barrel and the three other guys grabbed the other one, but I never saw Jacob after he jumped. I guessed he still had a heavy weight of coins in his pockets. After just a minute or two the other barrel began to sink. Either they put too much money in it, or maybe it was damaged when it hit the water and sprung a leak. Me and Thomas had been pushed quite a ways, but I'll never forget the screams from those guys as the barrel sank and one by one they were covered up by the waves and disappeared.

Thomas wasn't in too good shape, he'd become desperately ill during the day, but we kicked as long as we could and rode the waves through the night, just hanging on and praying. Just after dawn a boat from the Life Saving Service appeared out of nowhere and picked us up. I begged them to get the barrel too, and they did. They rowed us through the still raging storm to the beach.

I learned later they were from the Little Kinnakeet lifesaving station, and that's where they took us. They gave us food, water, dry clothes, and a bunk to sleep in. Unfortunately, Thomas's fever got a lot worse, and he died that night, making me the only survivor of the Amelia Pearl.

Because everybody was so nice to me over the next few days I decided to stay here. I sent a message to my mother to let her know I survived and would see her soon. One of the lifesaving crew gave me a room at his house. The brother of another one gave me a job at the sawmill. I kept the barrel in my room, and just told everyone it saved my life, and I had a sentimental attachment to it. They understood.

I liked the job at the sawmill. They even had some of the lumber there that washed ashore from the ship over the next few days. I walked by it every day and said a little prayer of thanks when I did.

I thought a lot about what to do with the money. I only had about $80 dollars in paper money, but the barrel had quite a bit of coin in it. I decided I wanted to use some of the money to build a house. This house. But I needed a story about how I came into the money. I didn't want people to know I took it off the ship.

I came up with a story about getting a wire that I got an inheritance from my uncle who just passed. I had to go to Rhode Island to claim the money. So, I took time off and took the train north. I certainly wasn't going to go by ship! I visited with my mother for a couple days, then came back here. I deposited some of the money in the bank, so I could pay for things with checks. I was able to buy this piece of land, which I think is just about where the lifesaving boat brought me ashore. With the help of the guys at the sawmill I began building this house.

I bought the safe on my way back from Rhode Island and built the little room around it on a couple days that I worked here alone. The guys asked me about it when they came back to work on the house. I told them I just made a stupid mistake but wanted to leave it since it was built with wood from the ship I was on. And that's true.

After I moved into the house, I kept working but tried to spend a little of the money here and there to help others in this kind community. I bought food and clothing for both Little Kinnakeet and Big Kinnakeet to have for others they'd rescue. I met several they saved over the next few years, and we swapped stories. I also gave a little to help rebuild the fire station and donated money every time someone lost a home to a storm. The guys from the sawmill always helped with the rebuilding.

I tried to do good with the money and hope maybe you will too if you can. I also said a prayer of thanks every morning with my hands on the barrel. Maybe you will think of me once in a while when you look at that beautiful barrel that saved my life.

So, that's it. I wish you good luck and a long life. Goodbye.   Benjamin Pugh

Jenny wiped the tears from her eyes on her sleeve. She had no doubt she would think of Benjamin Pugh every time she noticed the barrel protruding from the living room wall or thought about what to do with the gold coins.

After a couple minutes thought, she decided she wanted the coins upstairs with her. After the many years they had been safely hidden in the secret room, and locked away in the safe, she hoped they would be equally secure under her bed. At least until she could decide what to do with them.

Ten minutes later, the bags were in their new secure place, except for six of the coins she deposited on the desk in her office. The letter rested beside them.

Over the next couple hours, she learned from the internet that the current price of gold was just under $1,800.00 an ounce. She also learned that the $20 "Double Eagle" gold coins had just under an ounce of gold in them, while the $10 "Eagle" coins had just under a half ounce.

On various coin merchant sites, she learned that the $10 coins were selling for anywhere from $1200.00 to $1600.00 each, and the $20 coins were worth $1900.00 to $2700.00. The price variation depended on the condition of the coin, the number that were minted that year, and the number known to still exist.

Her mind simply boggled at the riches stashed under her bed. She decided they would need a safer place. Soon. Perhaps locked away back in the safe with the room door closed and latched. Or perhaps in a bank safe deposit box.

She slept well that night after an hour of thinking about what to do with the money. After she decided she could take several days, weeks, or even longer to make that decision, she drifted off to sleep.

The next morning, she took a quick detour to her office to eyeball the coins and letter on the desk before getting her coffee. A smile lit her face upon seeing the coins. She picked one up, held it in her hand, and admired the gleam of gold from Lady Liberty's face. She felt reassured it had not all been a dream.

She fixed eggs, bacon, and toast and was enjoying breakfast on the deck when she saw a ship moving slowly north in the far distance. She was saying a little thank-you to Benjamin Pugh when the idea hit her like a lightening bolt. She left the dishes on the chairside table and rushed to her office. While the computer powered up, she studied the gold coins, then began typing.

What was to become a long, tragic night, and the turning point of young Benjamin's life, began with the routine loading a day earlier of a shipment of lumber on the schooner, Amelia Pearl, in the port of Savannah.

Perfect

It was "Perfect." The song playing over the speaker system at the Food Lion.

Wes strolled down the aisle humming the song. He'd always liked the tune. As he approached the clerk kneeling to fill the shelf in the frozen pizza section, he heard the lyrics being sung at a low volume. It could only be her. There was no one else near in the aisle at the moment.

"So, you like this song too," he said, after stopping behind her and listening for a few moments.

She turned in surprise and stopped mid-verse. "Oh ... Yeah I do." Then turned away and added, "Sorry."

"Oh, no. Please continue. I was enjoying listening to you," Wes said. "You have a beautiful voice."

She shook her head and stared into the boxes of pizza in front of her. "No, not really. But thanks for the compliment."

"Well then, you must dance with me," Wes announced. "This is a great song for a dance right here in the frozen food aisle."

That got her attention. She turned and looked at him like he'd just asked her to fly to the moon with him. "Really? You've got to be kidding! I can't do that. I'm working."

"Sure you can," Wes said. Then to the four people making their way down the aisle pushing carts in front of them, "She should dance with me, shouldn't she?"

One at a time they all chimed in. "Sure." "Yes!" "Of course." "I'd love to see that!"

"We've got about half the song left," Wes put out his hand. "It'll only take a couple minutes." He paused to watch her brown eyes melt from no to maybe. "Please."

She shook her head, but slowly rose to her feet and turned to face him. "You must be crazy," she said. A nervous smile gave him all the permission he needed. He put his arms out. She hesitantly did the same.

He took her right hand in his left, then put her left arm around his waist. He encircled her waist, resting his hand lightly just above where her Food Lion shirt tucked into her khaki slacks. In a second, they had picked up the rhythm of the song.

He led her gliding down the aisle until they were a couple feet from where carts were hurriedly being pushed to the side to allow them passage. They paused for a moment, then continued to the end of the aisle. They made a graceful turn and waltzed back to the other end, to the accompaniment of polite applause and words of encouragement from the nine shoppers now enjoying the unexpected entertainment.

Her steps following his lead were effortless. She was a natural.

Wes encouraged her to sing while they moved up the aisle, but she shook her head. She did, however, slightly tighten her grip on his waist as they made their second turn. Wes did the same.

As the song, and their moment, approached its final stanza, he moved them back to her stocking cart and accompanied Ed Sheeran with an inspired, "You look perfect tonight." She shook her head in response. As he released her, he saw the hint of moisture in her eyes.

The audience, which now packed each end of the aisle, rewarded them with a round of applause. Wes offered a quick nod and wave, his partner only the briefest of smiles.

"I'm Wes, by the way," he said.

"I'm Rose." She turned away, then quickly back. "And... thank you. That was nice. I haven't danced in a long time." Her lips offered a timid smile.

He returned her smile with an appreciative one of his own. "Neither have I." He reached to touch her shoulder before she could turn away again. "What time do you get off work?"

Her smile quickly faded. "I can't ... I don't ..."

Wes jumped into the chasm. "I just want to go for a walk with you. A walk on the beach. Just to talk. You can do that. Nothing more. I promise."

She studied him. Her thoughts jangled. Her lips pressed together. But after a few moments her resistance broke. She thought he looked like a nice guy. About six-foot tall, short hair, brown summer slacks, blue striped shirt. Not that she was that familiar with the type. The boys who used to be interested in her were of the tattered shorts, copious tattoos, and unkept hair variety. "I'm ... I get off at 6:30."

"Great. I'll meet you here, in front, in the parking lot then."

"No. I can't. I've got to go home first. Maybe ... 7:30. But don't ..."

"Okay. Seven-thirty. Just a walk."

The sun was still fully above the Pamlico Sound when she pulled into the parking lot at 7:35. But the sky over the ocean had begun to turn. Wes was pleasantly surprised and greeted her warmly. He'd prepared for disappointment. She'd changed from her work clothes into blue jean shorts and a Taylor Swift tee. Not dressed up, nor down. Just more suitable for a walk in the August heat.

He wanted to take her hand, but instead gestured to the street and walked in silence on her right as they crossed Route 12 and walked down the short street to Ocean View. Then south a ways and up and over the dune to the beach. They took off their shoes and left them by the walkway. He rolled up his pantlegs almost to his knees. At the edge of the water, he steered them north, then broke the silence.

"Tell me why you like that song."

"You mean "Perfect"?"

"Yeah, that one."

Rose knew the answer but walked a few yards while she debated. She decided she'd come this far. Might as well keep going.

"It's kind of ... I guess wishful thinking. I wish someone felt that way about me. But no one ever has. Not even close. It's kind of escapism. A way to make myself feel better when I get down. I've never felt attractive, like anyone could think I was perfect. Or anywhere close to it. I've never had boys, the good ones, interested in me. But I can listen to that song and sing it to myself. I can pretend someone wrote it just for me. It's my song." She hesitated for a moment, looked past him to the breaking waves, then added, "The psychologists call it a coping mechanism." She really thought it was just delusional.

"Oh no!" Wes complained, stopping in his tracks. "That can't be true. You're ... beautiful. You obviously are a nice person. You have a lovely smile. You sing. And ... you're a dancer!"

Rose stopped and stepped back to his side. She shook her head, but her face eased into a weak smile. "Yeah, maybe some of that. But you don't really know me. If you did ..." Her voice faded and she jumped a couple steps up the sand, away from a wave.

Wes was quickly by her side again. "So, tell me. What are you like, Rose? And start with your last name."

She headed up the beach again. Wes caught up in a moment. "It's Morales. And to start off, I'm not beautiful. I've got this black hair, and these days every guy wants a blond. Or at least a girl with light brown hair colored or streaked blond. Girls like me don't get a second look. And hair this dark doesn't look good dyed."

"Doesn't matter," Wes said. "Beauty isn't in the hair color."

"Okay, but have you noticed my skin color? My mother's side of the family is from Mexico. My father's is from Spain. There's been some intermarriage with Anglos, but I have enough Hispanic blood in me to look like I could have snuck across the border from Mexico yesterday. Not exactly a popular look in this country these days. Especially here at the beach where 98 percent of the population is as white as you."

"Also doesn't matter," Wes said. "Your skin is another beautiful part of you. And those stunning eyes were the first thing that caught my attention when you turned to look at me in the store."

"That's nice of you to say, but I don't feel that way. My life experiences haven't exactly made me feel beautiful."

"That's too bad."

"You know, the song that really tells the story of my life is "Fast Car" by Tracy Chapman. Do you know that one?"

"Yeah, I do. That's a pretty sad one."

"Right, so ..."

"Tell me."

Rose shook her head and stared at her footprints in the wet sand as she walked. Yet, some part of her wanted to tell him. No one else had ever shown any interest. She'd always just been the different one. She'd kept her family life, her hopes, her dreams to herself. Not even the sort-of girlfriends she'd had in school had known much about her. And the couple of boyfriends along the way, well, they weren't interested in that part of her.

But there was something about walking on the beach. With a man who had asked her to dance. Who had revived that little spark inside her.

"Okay, you asked for it. So ... My family moved here when I was six. My dad got a job with one of the landscape companies. My mother worked in one of the restaurants. We got by. Then my dad got injured on the job. His back. The workers' comp company fought for a year against paying his medical bills and his pay. That made it really tough. Even after they gave in, what he was getting was a lot less than when he was working so ... Anyway, he began drinking and things went downhill from there."

She stopped. Picked up a shell fragment and threw it thirty yards into the crest of a wave.

"Please, go on," Wes said. "Tell me the rest."

It took another minute and two more shells into the surf, but she continued.

"My parents fought all the time. My mother became real mean after his injury. Everything fell on her. And I was caught in the middle. I always wondered if she was so nasty because of his drinking, or if he was drinking because she was so mean to him. But, anyway, she left when I was 14. She just couldn't take it anymore. Didn't ask if I wanted to go with her or anything. By that point, my dad was a real mess— drinking, in pain all the time, depressed. So, my aunt, his sister, came to live with us. To take care of him and me. She was the one who taught me to dance."

"Ah ha," Wes said. "I knew there was some history of dance lessons in the way you moved. What did she teach you?"

"Well, since the family was from Spain, she thought I should know the Flamenco. She taught me the basics of that, then moved on to other kinds of ballroom dancing. She used to be a dance instructor. She was my only partner. My dad wasn't interested and even though she tried to find someone, there just wasn't anyone else available or interested in dancing with me."

"I bet you enjoyed the dancing."

"Yeah, I did. When I was dancing was the only time I felt ... Well, maybe the only time I felt anything."

"You were fortunate she came into your life."

"Yes, I was. But she was only there for a little while. She left when I was 16. She developed some serious health problems and there aren't many medical specialists out here on the island. So, she moved back to Florida. Taking care of my dad became my job."

"That's too young to take on that job," Wes said. He grabbed her by the shoulder and turned her to look at him. "So, what did you do?"

"I went to work at Food Lion. Continued in school and worked part-time. After I graduated and a few months of working full-time I started college, on-line. I've been taking classes ever since."

"That's great. What are you majoring in?"

"I started as a psychology major. Imagine that! Trying to figure everything out. Then I decided I needed to be more practical, so I switched to a business major. But I still like the psychology classes. I'll graduate in another semester."

"And you continued to work all that time?"

"Yes, full-time. I do a little bit of everything. They say I'm next in line to be an assistant manager, but who knows? Between what I make, and my dad's workers' comp, we get by. I've been at Food Lion so long I get a little bit of a discount on what I buy there. So that helps."

"So, after you get your degree, what then?"

"I don't know. I'm pretty much stuck here." Rose marched into a wave and stood in the surf with water half-way to her knees. She studied the peach-colored clouds above the horizon for a full minute.

When she turned back to Wes, she said, "That's enough about me. Your turn. Tell me about you. You're obviously not from here."

They resumed their walk but shortly did a 180 back toward the pier.

"I'll do that," Wes said. "But before I do, how old are you?"

"I'm 22," Rose said.

"Wow," Wes said. "I'm 33. I've always had a thing about double numbers. Ever since I was a kid. Do you remember what aisle we were dancing in at the store?"

"Yeah, let's see. It was the first frozen food aisle, so that makes it ... 11."

"Yes!" Wes exclaimed. "You see, that's magical. Sort of poetic. Our meeting has a touch of fate to it."

Wes caught Rose's eye roll as he stepped away from a wave.

"So, your story?" Rose said. "And start with your last name."

"Yes. Last name is Gardner. And ... let's see. You're right, I'm not from here. Just kind of passing through. I'm a lawyer. I came here to interview a client who lives here. I got here late yesterday, did the interview this morning, and I'm leaving tomorrow. Headed back to Charlotte where I was born and raised. My father is the head of the law firm. We have a real nice thing going. My father has made the firm into a family friendly one. We try to limit everyone to about a 40-hour work week. We do lots of family dinners and outings for the whole firm—secretaries and paralegals included. So, we've become a pretty popular place to work."

He shrugged and added, "That's about it. Nothing special."

Seems pretty special to me, was Rose's immediate thought, but instead she said, "Married?"

"Nope. Never been. Haven't met the right woman yet. Been waiting for someone special. Maybe a dancer."

Rose gave him another eye roll. This one accompanied by a "Ha!" and a shake of her head.

"And where did you learn to dance?"

"That was my mother's doing. She insisted I take dance lessons. She thought it was part of the education of a 'gentleman'. So, I did when I was 15. Not really into it, but I guess I got something out of it. At least enough to fake it."

"I see," Rose nodded. "And where are you staying while you're here?"

"I've got a little two-room suite in a nice B&B here in Kinnakeet. An older house they did a good job converting."

"That's nice," Rose said.

They walked for a couple minutes, each aware of the sky darkening and the temperature dropping a bit. About a hundred yards from the pier, they stopped for a moment to watch a fisherman make a long cast into the surf. They continued their stroll once the bait and weights hit the water.

"You know," Wes said after another minute, "I have that song, "Perfect" on a playlist on my phone. Do me a favor. How about we do a proper dance to it right here?"

Rose stopped and stared at him. "Really?"

"Sure. Why not?"

She didn't have an answer for that.

Wes took the phone out of his pocket. He pulled up the playlist and touched the screen. When "Perfect" began playing he maxed the volume and tucked the phone in the chest pocket of his shirt.

The dance this time was slower. And closer.

Rose closed her eyes after the first few seconds and drifted along in his arms. She was lost in her own world.

Wes studied her hair, the side of her face that wasn't pressed against his chest, and ran his hand up and down her back, gently caressing the curve he found at her lower back.

When the song ended, he pulled her tight for a moment, kissed the top of her head, then released her.

He muttered a soft, "Thank you" when she opened her eyes.

Rose returned the "Thank you" as she stepped away from his arms. She spun and sprinted a few steps down the beach before turning back to him.

"Now, I want you to do me a favor," she said.

"Sure," Wes said, catching up to her. "Anything."

"I want you to take me to your room and make love to me."

Wordlessly, Wes took her hand, and they walked back to the parking lot. Rose followed him in her car to his B&B.

Afterward, as he held her in his arms, Wes asked, "When you said earlier that you were stuck here in Kinnakeet, what did you mean?"

Rose rolled to face him. "My father."

"Oh. I thought maybe that was it."

"Yes. He's pretty helpless at this point. He's taking medication for his pain, his heart, and for depression. None of those seem to be doing much. He goes from the bed to the couch, and that's about it. That's why I had to go home after work. I had to get him his meds and try to get him to eat something. There's no one else to take care of him, and there's no money to get him in a nursing home, which is where he belongs. With his workers' comp he doesn't qualify for Medicaid. We've had that discussion, about a nursing home, and he refuses to even consider it anyway."

Wes wasn't sure what to say. Finally, he said, "That's a real mess. I see how you feel trapped. But you're a good person for taking care of him."

Rose was silent for a minute. Then, "In the first psychology class I took the instructor said that a person's success and happiness in life are determined by the choices they make. He said your life a year, a month, a day from now, depend on the decisions you make today. That's always stuck with me. I've tried hard to make good decisions about my life ever since I heard that. But this situation, my father, is the one place in my life where I feel like I don't have control. There are no decisions to be made. I have to take care of him. And that keeps me right where I am. Now, and after I finish my degree."

"I see that," Wes said. He wished it were otherwise. His arms tightened around her.

For a few seconds, Rose let her mind drift. Then, she jerked herself back into reality, abruptly terminating the fantasy. "So ... I guess I should get going," she said. "I'm sure he's wondering where I am." She pulled away and sat on the edge of the bed. Then she gathered her clothes and dressed.

Wes watched her. He wanted to do something but couldn't think of what. He dressed, and before he walked her to the car, they exchanged phone numbers.

Beside the car they hugged and clung to each other for a last few precious moments.

After Rose pulled away, Wes returned to his room, pulled up "Perfect" on his phone, and hugged the pillow where her head had been minutes earlier and where her scent lingered.

Six days later Rose's father died in his sleep. The second call she made, after her aunt, was to Wes.

57

On The Bench

The first time he noticed her on the bench she was wearing a gray winter jacket against the easy spring morning breeze. He walked from the wet to the dry sand to get a little closer. "Good morning."

It took a couple seconds, but she looked up and returned a sliver of a smile. "Good morning."

"Nice day, isn't it?" he said, almost in front of her now on the narrow beach of the sound.

"I guess it is. Or going to be." She tugged slightly on her pink wool beanie, pulling it down over the top of her ears. Strands of wavy gray hair poked out around the edges.

"Yes, it is," he said, taking another step toward her. "My name's Sy. Seymore actually, but everybody calls me Sy."

"Julie," she said, hesitantly.

While he'd never been good at guessing people's ages, he would have guessed she was a little older than he was. It wasn't the wrinkles on her face—they were fewer and shallower than his. She'd probably taken better care of her skin over the years. Maybe it was the way she was sitting—her shoulders hunched forward. Her sunglasses looked prescription, though his were as well.

"You certainly have a nice spot here for a morning sit. Do you live in this house?" He nodded to the waterfront style house with multiple decks a few yards behind her.

"Heavens no," she proclaimed, showing a little life for the first time. "They just told me it was okay for me to sit here in the mornings. My daughter and son-in-law know these people. I live with them back down the road a ways."

"Well, enjoy your morning," he said. "Hope to see you again."

She nodded as he tipped his cap and continued his morning walk.

As brief and superficial as it was, Sy thought there was a danger that would be the highlight of his day.

The next morning, she was there again. This time wearing a cardigan sweater, brown slacks, and sneakers. Same beanie. He was walking in sweatpants and a Radio Hatteras tee-shirt on this warmer morning.

"Good morning, Julie. Nice to see you again." Sy veered in her direction. She had been watching him for several seconds.

"And good morning to you," she said.

"Two mornings in a row. Are you here every morning?"

"No ... well, I just started coming here. I like to get out in the mornings and it's not a far walk. I like to watch the activity out there on the sound."

He took the couple steps to stand just to the side of her and peer out to the water. "I like that too. That's why I walk over here every morning. The boats going by, and the kiteboarders on the windy days." He paused for a second to consider. Then turned to her. "I could use a little break. Mind if I sit with you for a minute?"

She seemed surprised but slid to her right. "Oh, no. Have a seat."

Sy took his spot on the bench, careful not to crowd her. "I live with my son. His 24-year-old stepson lives with him now, too. He's supposed to be working but says he can't find a job. Shoot, there's jobs everywhere. He worked at a restaurant last summer when everybody was crying for help, and says he'll work this summer. But for now, he's just 'hanging with his friends.'" His air quotes were flippant.

Sy took a moment to glance at Julie. She was staring straight ahead, but he thought she was listening, so he continued. "He likes to smoke pot. I guess they call it weed now. He asked if I wanted to try it. I turned it down. Afraid I might like it too much, like back in the day." He saw her nod of recognition and not-quite-suppressed smile out of the corner of his eye. "You ever try it?"

She offered up a little bigger grin this time. "Oh, yes. But only a couple times. I guess most of us did. My parents would have killed me if they knew."

It was his turn to smile and nod. "Yeah, I did it a few times, then stopped. Kind of interfered with other things." He slapped his legs with both hands. "Well, I'm going to get going. Thanks for the nice break. Hope to see you again tomorrow, Julie." He used the left arm of the bench to push himself to his feet.

"Yes," Julie said. Then, "What did you say your name was?"

"I'm Sy," he said as he bathed her with an encouraging grin. He paused for a moment to catch the smile that crept across her face before heading off toward home.

The next day as he approached, Julie was sitting tight to the right side of the bench. She had on cotton pants, a navy-blue cardigan sweater, and a multi-colored scarf tied loosely around her neck against the gentle wind. She beat him to the smile and greeting.

"Good morning, Sy."

He thought she seemed proud of remembering his name. "Good morning to you, Julie. You look nice this morning."

"Thank you. So do you." She closed her eyes and looked to her lap for a moment. Then returned to his eyes. "Do you need a little rest?" she asked, as she patted the bench beside her.

"Indeed, I do," he said. He sat and endured a few seconds of silence while they both watched the gentle movement of the water in the sound. Then he turned to her. "You said you live with your daughter and son-in-law. How long have you lived with them?"

She thought for a minute. "I'm not sure. It's been a while. Ever since my husband, Sid, went into the nursing home. He's up in Nags Head. They take me there to visit him every now and then." She drifted for a few seconds. "Sometimes I forget I'm married."

Before Sy could figure out how to respond she added, "Once I forgot when I was a lot younger, too." She smiled sheepishly. "But I don't talk about that." She turned to monitor a seagull as it coasted by.

Sy's face brightened with amusement. He liked that surprising flash of openness. He glanced down at her hands. "You're not wearing a wedding ring."

"Yes," she said as she stole a look, then turned back to him. "I lost it a while back. I took it off because of the arthritis. I think it's somewhere in my daughter's house."

"I know about arthritis," Sy said. "It's the prize you get for living so long." He hesitated a moment to enjoy her smile. "I've got it a lot of places. Elbows, shoulders, knees. A little in my neck. Fortunately, I'm able to still get around. I try to walk a couple miles a day. It's easier on the wet sand than this soft stuff." He kicked the fluff at his feet.

"I don't walk so much anymore," Julie said. "Tracy and Randy are afraid I'll get lost if I go out for a walk by myself. A couple times I did get just a little lost. But I didn't tell them that. I can walk down here because it's just a straight shot down the road from their house."

"Do you like living with them?" Sy asked.

Julie seemed to study the water and the few yards of sand in front of her. Sy waited patiently. He thought about how he'd answer that question if she asked him. It wasn't a simple answer.

She leaned toward him just a bit. "They get up early and get started. Then Tracy comes and wakes me up. Sometimes I haven't slept much, but I get up. She fixes breakfast. I try to eat. Then they leave for the day. I go out for a little walk, down here now. Then back to the house and take a nap. I may eat a little lunch if I'm hungry. I try to find something to do for the afternoon until they get home. There's nothing on TV anymore."

She hadn't answered his question, but Sy got the drift. "I don't watch TV much anymore either. Just some sports and maybe a movie."

"I wish they still had a movie theater here in Kinnakeet," Julie said. "Not that there's many movies made these days for people our age. Seems like they're all horror ... or, what do they call it ... when it's all that far out stuff?"

"Maybe sci fi or ... fantasy?"

"Yes, that's it. There haven't been any good movies for us older folks since *The Bucket List*."

"That was a good one." Sy kicked sand for a moment. "Do you remember *Driving Miss Daisy*?"

Julie's face warmed. "Yes, I do. That was a good one too. I can relate to that one more now than when I first saw it. I was still a ... relatively, young woman then. Wish it would come up on reruns." She thought for a moment. "But it seems like it ended kind of sad. I'm not sure."

Sy nodded. He remembered the ending. "Think I better get going. Got about another mile to go back home."

"Oh! ... Well, yes." Julie fumbled with the top button on her sweater.

Sy noticed the slight tremor in her hand. He realized she'd kept her hands tightly clinched in her lap until now. He pushed himself to his feet. But before he could leave Julie grabbed his arm.

"Are you married?" she asked.

"No. Widowed," Sy said after he recovered from his momentary surprise. "My wife died two years ago."

"Oh. Okay," Julie said. "Well, have a nice day."

"You too." He stumbled as he headed back to the firm sand.

The next day the bench was empty.

It couldn't be the weather, Sy thought. While it could be cold here on the sound in the mornings with a mild wind, there wasn't even a slight breeze. And the temperature was probably a degree or two warmer today. He thought back to their interaction yesterday, searching for something he might have said to offend her. Nothing. He didn't think his response to her question that he was widowed would bother her, but he didn't know.

A few steps past the bench it occurred to him that it was Saturday. Hard to keep track of the days of the week. Maybe her daughter and son-in-law were home on the weekends. Maybe her schedule those days was different. His wasn't.

When the bench was empty the next day, he chalked it up to the combined factors of the weekend and a cold front moving through. A couple of kiteboarders were out in their wetsuits today, but he encountered few others on his walk out on the road or back on the sand.

Monday morning it was still a bit chilly, but certainly warmer than the first day they met. Yet there was no one on the bench when he passed by. He thought if he knew where she lived, he would walk up and knock on the door to check on her, but that wasn't possible. He wondered why he cared so much. They'd barely spent 15 minutes together.

Her absence was more profound than it should have been. She had, indeed, become the high point of his day. He cared about her. He hoped she cared about him. At least a little. The nice man who walked on the beach every day. At least she could give him that.

The next day Julie was waiting for him. She greeted him with a smile and a little wave. He returned both from ten steps away.

"I've missed you," Sy said as he slid into the empty side of the bench. He left it at that. He didn't want to push. He thought it would be easy to push her away.

She smiled but hesitated a moment. "I ... missed you too."

The look in her eyes made him change his mind. "I was concerned when you weren't here. I thought maybe I'd said something to upset you. Or you were ill."

"No, neither of those things." It took a few seconds for her to continue. "My daughter and her husband are home on the weekend, and I don't usually walk then. They'd have asked a million questions. Yesterday ... I wanted to come, but my daughter was home. She works from home Mondays and sometimes Fridays. She wanted to know why I wanted to go for a walk. Then she offered to walk with me. I didn't want to bring her ... tell her about you. She would have wanted to come here ... to meet you."

Sy nodded. He understood. He hadn't said anything at home about Julie. "I'm glad you're here," he said as he leaned over to bump shoulders with her.

After a shared moment watching a boat speed by in the sound he said, "I'm curious. Did you work outside the home as a younger woman?" His wife had taught him years ago how to ask that question properly.

Julie perked up. "Yes, I did. I played the violin. Once upon a time I was ... well, let's say I played a lot."

"Oh really! How good were you?"

"Well, pretty good, I guess. I played in a junior orchestra in high school and played all through my years at the music conservatory. Then I played with three orchestras over the course of the next thirty years. One of them was quite famous."

"And what orchestra was that?"

"The Boston Symphony Orchestra."

"Really?"

"Yes. I played with them for 14 years. I was first chair the last three."

"Then you were exceptionally good, not just pretty good. I bet you enjoyed it."

"Yes, I did. My one claim to fame was that I played in Leonard Bernstein's last concert. He died just a couple months later." Julie's hands tented for a momentary prayer. "We played Beethoven's Seventh Symphony."

"That's amazing."

"Yes. I quit shortly after that."

"Why?"

"The arthritis was catching up with me. And ... I just got old. Couldn't keep up with the kids."

"Do you still play?"

"Oh, heavens no! These hands won't let me do anything like that." She held them in front of her for just a moment, then returned them to her lap. "Now I play dominoes with Tracy and Randy. And the grandchildren when they come and feel like doing something nice for Granny."

"That's wonderful. How many grandchildren?"

"Four. And two greats. No ... three."

"You're lucky," Sy said.

"In that sense I guess I am."

They sat and watched the water for a few seconds.

"How about you?" Julie said. "What did you do when you were younger?"

"Ah! I had a few different careers, but as a very young man I was a baseball player. Played in the major league too." Sy paused to register Julie's look of appreciation. Then he added, "For two weeks."

A frown etched into the side of Julie's face. Then a hint of a smile brushed her lips.

"Yep, kicked around in the minor leagues for three years, then got called up for the last two weeks of the season to see if I had what it took to be a major league player. I guess my 'claim to fame' as you put it, was that I was playing third base, in Yankee Stadium, when Micky Mantle hit his last home run. As he came into third, I said, 'Nice swat, Mick.' He said, 'Thanks, kid.' I'm sure he had no idea what my name was."

"That's really great," Julie said. She reached over to touch his shoulder.

"Yeah. Thanks. I played two more games, then played in the minors one more season before my manager politely informed me I would probably never make it back to the show. I wasn't surprised, so I quit and moved on."

"What'd you do then?"

"I married Cindy, then moved to Florida and became a cop. I lasted about five years doing that, then worked a few years in security at Dis ... uh, Disney World. Hated that, so I went to work for Cindy's father in the advertising business. Pretty boring, but I made good money. So, I stayed with it until I retired."

"That's quite a life," Julie said.

"Yes, I guess. It's not quite over, yet. But you know your days are numbered when your son takes a CPR class and pushes you to update your will and write down your wishes for your funeral when you come to live with him."

"Oh my!" Julie's hand flew to cover her own heart. "Do you have a heart problem?"

"I did. Well, I guess I still do. I had a heart attack a couple years ago while I was driving. The doctors said I shouldn't drive anymore and informed the DAV ... I mean the DMV. The driver's license people. They suspended my license. The doctors told me I needed to start walking and lose weight. So, I did. I'm walking two miles every day now and I've lost 35 pounds."

"That's wonderful. And you look great."

"Thanks. I feel pretty good. But apparently, I still can't get my license back. At my age, once it's gone, it's gone."

"That's too bad. I can't drive either. My daughter took my keys, then sold my car when I moved in with them."

Sy shook his head and put his hand on hers. It was shaking. "They probably think they're looking out for you. But I know it doesn't feel that way." He let his hand stay for a couple seconds then removed it.

"Well, time for me to head back home." He stood, then said, "Could I walk you back to your house before I take off?"

"Oh, no! Think I'll sit a while longer."

Sy debated for a second. "Do you have a cell phone? Can I have your number?"

"Well ... I don't have one of those. I did for a while, but I could never seem to keep it charged. And now I don't have anyone to call. All my friends have ... well ... you know. So, they just put it away somewhere."

Sy nodded. He did know. Most of his friends were gone too. "Okay. Enjoy your day. It's been nice talking with you. See you tomorrow?"

"I hope so."

It was at least 75 degrees the next morning when Sy approached Julie on the bench. The beanie was gone, replaced by a wide brimmed straw hat. He'd spotted the long sleeve, multi-colored, tie dye shirt with a psychedelic pinwheel on it from 50 yards away. As he got close, he threw his hand in front of his eyes as if to shade them from the glare.

"Don't you look nice!" he said, nodding at the top. "All decked out in your 70s finest." He got a radiant smile in return as he sat.

"This old thing?" She teased him with her eyes. After stroking the sleeve for a moment, she confessed. "My daughter bought this for me at some music fair they took me to several years ago. There was a booth selling these and I told her I used to have one like this more than a half-century ago. She insisted on buying it for me. I wore it the next day to please her, then put it away. Haven't worn it since."

"Well, I appreciate your wearing it today. I had one kind of like that once upon a time. It brings back some good memories."

"It does for me too." She closed her eyes for a few seconds and her face clouded. "Isn't it funny how I can remember some things from way back when I was in school, but lots of times I can't remember what I had for breakfast?"

"Me too," Sy said immediately. He suspected this was true more so for her than for him. "I get words mixed up sometimes and can't remember the names of things. My son is always correcting me. I get tired of that. I can't wait until he's my age and sees what it's like."

Julie nodded her agreement.

Sy became aware of tightness in his chest and stopped for a couple deep breaths, as he'd learned to do. It helped. "Of course, I won't be around to see that. He's still in his 50s. But maybe I'll be looking down on him from somewhere up above." He glanced to the heavens and grinned. "But then, probably not."

"Oh, I bet you will be," Julie said with an encouraging smile while she patted his arm.

"Well," Sy said, shrugging his shoulders, "I read somewhere that you learn about getting old by watching people around you get old. I'm not sure he's learning anything."

Julie nodded her agreement. "This getting old thing is no fun, is it?"

"No, it isn't. But it keeps the doctors in business. I see one here for general stuff, and two specialists in Kill Devil Hills. One for my heart and one for my kidneys. The one here gives me medicine for the arthritis."

"I've got to go up there to see a couple doctors too," Julie said as she dropped her lower lip in a pout. "One of them is treating me for some kind of neuro ... Oh, I don't know what they call it. It's got a long name. It affects my walking and my ... muscles, I guess. She gives me something for my memory too. I don't think it helps any. At least not that I can tell. I get my arthritis pills from the doctor here, too."

"Yeah. I don't like getting older, but I don't think I would like the alternative either."

Julie frowned. "What do you mean?" Sy was figuring out how to delicately explain when she said, "Oh. I see." The frown was replaced by a smile. "I guess you're right."

Sy glanced at his watch. The new one that tracked his movement, monitored his exercise and heartrate, and warned him of any irregular heart rhythms. He didn't care for it, but his son insisted. "Well, I better get going." He pushed his way to his feet. "Can I walk you to your house?"

"Oh, no. I'm fine. I'll just stay here a bit longer and enjoy the warmth."

"Okay. See you tomorrow?"

"Yes. I expect I'll be here."

The next morning was again a warm one, but clouds and a breeze warned of changes on the way.

Julie had been waiting for Sy for 25 minutes when he arrived.

After an initial warm greeting she abruptly said, "Will you do me a favor?"

Sy was surprised, but just took a moment. "I ... well, sure. If I can."

"I want to go for a ride. Will you take me for a car ride? My daughter left her car at home today, so we can swipe it for a few minutes. Please?" She reached to touch his shoulder, then rubbed it for a moment.

Sy almost said yes before he even thought about it. Then reality set in. He had no driver's license and hadn't driven a car for over two years. His coordination wasn't as good as it was two years ago. But then, it's not like driving a car is something you forget how to do. And driving on Hatteras Island was easy. Only one main road, and usually, except in tourist season, not a lot of traffic. He decided it sounded like an adventure. He hadn't had many of those lately.

"Okay. I'm game. Where do you want to go?"

"Walk me to my house and let's get the keys, then I'll tell you."

Julie had Sy wait outside while she went inside. It took her a couple minutes to get herself ready and find the keys, even though they were right where Tracy usually left them. When she came out, she had a white sweater draped over one arm. She handed Sy the keys and he unlocked the Honda CRV, then helped her into the passenger side seat. He got in behind the wheel, and after a minute to get himself oriented to the controls, Sy announced himself ready to go. A minute later they were headed south on Route 12 per Julie's directions. Sy felt, almost, like a young man again. He was behind the wheel with a smiling, excited woman beside him.

"Where we heading?" he asked while pushing buttons trying to find a classic rock station on the radio.

"There's this ice cream shop in Hatteras I always liked. I don't remember the name of it, but I think I'll remember it when I see it."

Sy responded with a nod. Once they passed the village limits and hit the National Seashore, he was careful to keep his speed at 55.

"Can we stop at the lighthouse?" Julie asked. "I haven't seen it in years and would like to just see it up close again."

"Sure thing," Sy said. "I'd like to see it again, too."

He pulled into the uncrowded lighthouse parking lot, found a spot close to the walkway, and helped Julie out of the car. They walked to the visitor center and stood for a moment. Shading her eyes from the sun perched just to the side of the lighthouse, Julie staggered as she looked up, though Sy caught her before she could fall.

"I ... thank you," she said after Sy released her once he was sure she was stable again. "I forgot that my balance isn't what it once was." She grabbed on to his arm and held on.

"Mine isn't either," Sy said, though he knew it had gotten better with the weight loss and daily walking. He was happy to have her leaning on him. "Another fun part of getting older."

In short order they were headed back down Route 12. Creeping through Hatteras Village, Julie spotted the ice cream shop on the left side of the road. It had just opened, and Sy parked in front. After she grabbed her sweater, he helped her out of the car and up the short flight of steps.

Once inside, it took Julie several minutes to decide what she wanted. She had no trouble reading the menu on the large blackboard but was distracted by the wall of candies and other merchandise. She eventually decided, "You only live once, and I don't know if I'll ever get back here, so I'm having the banana split." Sy knew he was having the "Brownie Bomb" from the moment his eyes spotted it on the menu board.

There had been no discussion of who was paying for the treat. Sy assumed he was and was happy to do so since he always had his wallet, with at least a couple $20.00 bills, with him whenever he went out the door. To his surprise, Julie pulled a $10.00 bill out of her pants pocket and offered to pay. That wouldn't have covered the bill, and barely her half. He waved her offer away. "A gentleman always pays," he insisted. Julie graciously accepted his kindness and put her money away.

They sat on the covered porch to enjoy their treat. After putting her sweater on, Julie stated this would be her lunch. Sy agreed that he would need nothing else to eat until dinner time.

Talk of favorite foods and comments on how they couldn't eat as much as they used to led to a discussion of various realities of aging. Some positive, but mostly negative.

"I never thought much when I was younger about what life would be like at this age," Sy announced upon concluding his assessment of his three generational living arrangement. "I guess when I did, I just thought I'd be with my wife, and we'd take care of each other as we got older. I always figured I'd die first, probably of a heart attack, since women usually live longer than men." Sy chomped on a bite of brownie. "My father died of a heart attack five years before my mother died."

"I think you said your wife died a while back. If you don't mind my asking, how did she die?" Julie snatched a napkin and touched her lips.

Sy took a moment to consider his response. "She died from lung cancer. I was driving home from visiting her grave for the first time after the funeral when I had that accident and had to give up driving ... until today." He grabbed an imaginary steering wheel and navigated an effortless turn. "Easy peesy."

"Well, you did just fine," Julie said. She reached across the table to stroke his hand. "And I'm sorry about your wife," she added a moment later.

"Thanks," Sy said. "I guess it's just one of those things life throws at you. Lots of times you don't have much choice about accepting them."

Fifteen minutes later they'd each eaten little more than half of their sundaes, and declared they'd had all they could eat. They stepped back inside the shop for a few minutes to consider some candy to take home. Sy purchased saltwater taffy for both of them. They shared a laugh that they'd have to hide their goodies from their children or answer a million questions.

When they stepped out the door there was a Dare County Sheriff's Department car parked directly behind the CRV. After they'd negotiated the steps, a deputy stepped out of the car and approached them.

"Are you Julie Erwin?" the officer asked.

It took Julie a moment before she could answer. "Yes."

Sy took a half step forward and asked, "What's the problem, Officer?"

"Just a moment, Sir," the deputy said. He introduced himself as Deputy Frank Call and directed Sy to go back inside the shop so he could speak with Julie for a minute. Sy reluctantly did so but kept his eye on the exchange outside. He left the door open an inch, hoping he could hear the conversation, but Deputy Call moved Julie to the rear of his car.

He informed her there had been a report from her daughter that she was missing and that her daughter's car, the Honda CRV, was missing as well. Julie's expression of horror changed to one of amusement as the deputy's words sank in. She informed the officer that her friend, Sy, had taken her for a ride. She apologized for not informing her daughter, but added, "She'd of had a fit if I told her, so I just didn't."

Deputy Call asked Julie if she felt safe in the company of her companion. She assured him she did and added, "We've had just a delightful time!" He asked for her identification, but when she informed him she didn't have any with her he accepted her response but did ask who'd driven the car. She told him. He asked for Sy's last name and acted a bit concerned when she admitted she didn't know.

The deputy asked Julie to wait by the car then motioned for Sy to join them. He met Sy at the front of the car and asked him for his report of the couple's morning together. When it matched Julie's he asked for Sy's last name, then his driver's license. Sy replied, "I don't have one," then quickly added, "with me." When Deputy Call looked at him skeptically, he admitted the truth.

When the deputy brought the couple together, he informed them he was going to ask dispatch to notify Julie's daughter that Julie and the car were safe. He added he was going to ask another deputy, who was responding to the call from Salvo, to stop in Kinnakeet and pick up the daughter. He'd ask her to come drive the car and her mother home. He looked at Julie and added with a grin, "I'll let you explain this situation, and your companion, to her."

He then looked at Sy and said, "Since I didn't see you drive the car, I'm not going to cite you for operating a vehicle without a license. However," he added with piercing eyes and a shake of his head, "I'd strongly advise you not to do this again." Sy's nod clearly expressed his understanding.

When Tracy arrived 35 minutes later Sy and Julie were laughing over glasses of iced tea on the porch. Deputy Call had left 20 minutes earlier after getting a call from the other deputy that he was in route with the daughter.

Sy and Julie were coming down the steps when Tracy exited the patrol vehicle. Before the obviously upset Tracy could begin with her questions, Julie put her hand out and touched her daughter on the shoulder. "Now Sweetheart, before you get too worked up, let me introduce you to Sy. He's a wonderful friend and has been taking good care of me this morning. And," she added with a hopeful smile, "this was all my idea."

Tracy's hard-set jaw loosened just a bit. Her first response was, "I hope you can imagine my upset when I got home and found both you and the car missing." After Julie's appreciative nod, and heartfelt apology, she added, with a stare at Sy, "You could have told me about him."

And so, Julie did. By the time they were back in Kinnakeet, Julie had given Tracy the story of her meeting Sy and their time together on the bench. Sy added a few pieces to the story and a bit of his own circumstances.

When they pulled into the driveway in front of the house, Tracy invited Sy inside, then asked him to join them for lunch. Both Julie and Sy declined the lunch offer, but Julie did offer her daughter a piece of cherry saltwater taffy as a peace offering.

The Surf Lesson

After hours of internal debate, Linda decided to tell him. She wanted to maintain her status as the honest one in the relationship.

"I've signed up for a surfing lesson tomorrow while you're fishing."

Zack's head spun from the baseball game on the television. "You've what?"

"I said, I've—"

"I heard what you said," Zack roared over the call of a base hit. "I just don't understand why you'd do something silly like that."

"Because I want to. And I think it would be interesting to see if I can actually get up on the board."

"You've got to be kidding. Right? That's a ridiculous waste of money."

"I don't think so. I think it would be fun, challenging, and just ... a new experience. Something to try."

Ryan's head was pivoting back and forth. He shot her a look of total distain, then turned back to the ball game. "I think that's silly. It's not like it's something you can continue with or do once we get home. It would make more sense to take a painting lesson or learn how to make pottery. Something you might actually be able to do and follow up with at some point. Trying to learn how to stand up on a surfboard on tiny little surf like they have here is just stupid." He glanced her way again. "Not to mention a big waste of money."

"Actually, you've mentioned the money issue twice now," Linda said, then paused for a deep breath. This felt like round 37 of the same issue, the same argument. She'd gotten better at keeping her control. But playing it out was still important.

"But I'd bet it's not even half of what you're spending on your fishing outing tomorrow. Going out for the entire day on that charter boat can't be cheap. And I haven't said a word about that. I'm actually glad you're going."

"It isn't that much," Zack countered, still focused on the game. "And at least I'll bring home some fish for us to eat the rest of the week." He got up and headed to the refrigerator. "I say no. It's a waste."

Linda felt the heat flushing through her body. She took several breaths and closed her eyes for a moment. That helped. Then she studied him and wondered if he really thought she was asking permission. That bothered her. A lot.

"Why don't you just rent a bicycle for the day? Get some exercise," Zack said as he passed her on his way back to the sofa with his beer in one hand. With his other he patted her bottom while he raised his eyebrows. "Nice."

How does he expect me to react to that? Linda thought as she headed for the bedroom. *Am I supposed to take that as a compliment and give everything he just said a pass? As long as he thinks I'm pretty am I supposed to be happy and nothing else about my life really matters? I'm supposed to just always take care of him and put my wants and needs aside?*

It only took a second for Linda to answer that. *Well, yeah. That's pretty much the way it's been. For a year and a half now, I've put up with that. And I don't know why! I don't need him. Stupid me!*

She began to make her list. It was easy. She'd made it a few times before. *I make almost as much money as he does. I can pay my own bills. I've got a support system—friends and the people at work. I've been without a man before and been happy. I'm not ready for children. I've got interests and hobbies I can get back to and enjoy.*

She stared out the bedroom window at the increasing darkness over the sound. It was a clear night, and she could see a few dim lights on the other side, miles away. *I'm pretty sure this isn't the way love is supposed to be. It felt nice, in a way, at first, but ...* What came to her mind then, after a moment of contemplation, was, *But not in quite a while.*

After another couple minutes, Linda decided she couldn't let Zack think the issue was resolved. She wasn't going to be able to sleep and didn't want to seem to be waiting for him to come to bed. Thank goodness Keisha and Michael weren't back yet. Keisha knew her plan and was supportive. She and Michael were off to Ocracoke on the first ferry in the morning. She'd planned to go with them until she saw the surfing lesson sign by the pier. After a few moments to get her thoughts in order she went back to the living room.

"I understand you don't want me to do the surfing lesson," she said when Zack finally looked in her direction. "But I'm going to do it anyway. I've already signed up and paid for it."

"So, you're just going to throw that money away and possibly get yourself hurt in the process?" Linda felt the contempt accompanying every word. "You know, people get hurt surfing all the time. That's a totally new experience for you and you'll probably have some teenaged boy as your instructor." He made air quotes for that last word.

"You'll be falling off the board about 25 times. And ... there's no emergency room here in Kinnakeet. Even a serious cut from the board flying through the air or a badly sprained ankle gets you a trip to the hospital up in Nags Head. And who's going to take you? Michael and Keisha will be gone all day, and I will too with the car."

Linda had only briefly considered the chance of an injury when she read and signed the consent and release from liability forms on her iPad. Having Zack bring it up to try to stop her made her worry about it even less. "I'll take that chance," she said. "I'm sure I can find someone to take me if that happens. But it won't."

"Well, I hope not," Zack said a couple seconds later when the center fielder caught a fly ball for the last out of the game. He glanced her way for just a second. "Hey Babe, you know I'm just trying to look out for you."

Linda didn't believe that for a moment. However, she'd made her point, taken her stand, and no longer cared what Zack thought.

"I'm ready for bed," Zack said as he hit the remote and pushed himself off the sofa. "Maybe you can think about it some more in the morning and see if you can get your money back."

"You go ahead," she said. *And don't expect me anytime soon,* she thought but didn't say.

The instructor that greeted her at eight fifty-five in the morning beside the "Surf Lessons" sign was not a teenager, but probably in his late 40s or early 50s. He introduced himself as "Doug." Every part of him not covered by the black wetsuit was a firm golden bronze, except for the gray hair that topped his head. Linda wore a modest blue one-piece swimsuit that freed her from worry about what might happen as she was tossed in the surf, as she knew she would be. She was also well coated in sunscreen to greet the already 78-degree heat.

Doug welcomed her with an engaging smile that, along with his age, put her at ease. After some initial small talk about where she was from and whether she had ever surfed before, he led her to the board she would be using and began explaining the steps they would follow to get her riding the waves like a seasoned pro. He seemed genuinely excited that the surf was larger than it had been for several days. He assured her she would get some great rides before the lesson was over.

With the board in the sand, they started out getting Linda comfortable laying on the board and learning the proper technique to rise to her knees. Then she learned how to smoothly rise, or as Doug called it, "pop" to a standing position and establish her balance. After a couple minutes practicing this, he pronounced her ready to start surfing. He had her attach the leash from the board to her ankle and led her into the waves. When they were a little more than waist high in the water, he established their position in the surf.

He explained that with her lying on the board he would give her a forward push when the timing was right for her to catch the wave coming from behind them. She would then "paddle like crazy" and rise to her knees. She would pop up as she had practiced when she felt the wave take the board. He assured her she would quickly learn to balance, but when she felt herself falling to slip as gracefully as possible into the water and never try to dive off the board.

Linda's attempts on the first two waves were not pretty. However, Doug took responsibility for that, stating that it was his fault for mistiming the waves. Linda knew better. On the third wave she almost got it, falling with both arms flailing wildly moments after she got to her feet.

On the fourth wave Linda stood for three seconds. On the fifth she was up for seven. Her "dismounts" from the board (not "falls" Doug had insisted) were not as painful nor scary as she had expected. She rode the next wave until it nearly dissolved. As she gathered her board and headed back into the surf, she shot Doug a huge smile and pumped her fist in the air.

When she got back beside him, she said, "That was great!" and they exchanged high fives. She declared herself ready for a rest. She mounted the board and propped herself up on her elbows.

Doug held on to the board and asked, "So, did you think it would be that easy?"

"Absolutely not," she said, "You're a great instructor."

"Thanks," Doug replied, then added, "You're a natural. You must be a good athlete."

"Not really," Linda said. "But I did do some swimming in college, and I run a little now."

"Not surprised," Doug said as he rocked the board back and forth, then turned to keep an eye on approaching waves.

"How long have you been doing this?" Linda asked.

"I've been at this for four years now. Started shortly after I moved to the beach, but I've been surfing since I was a kid. Of course, doing this is only for about four months of the year. And when the storms come through there's a few days off."

"You can't make a living just teaching surfing for four months," Linda said. "What else do you do?"

"That's a bit complicated," Doug said. He looked quickly behind him. "Why don't you catch this wave first. It's a good one."

Linda nodded and Doug pushed her forward, reminding her to "Paddle, paddle, paddle!" Five seconds later she was up on the largest wave so far and rode it out.

"Having fun yet?" Doug asked with a huge grin when she got back beside him.

"You know I am!" Linda said, saluting him with another high five. "Most fun I've had in a long time."

"Yeah, most people who are able to ride a few waves see what the attraction is and why some people spend their whole lives doing this."

"Well, I don't think I'm going to do that, but I do get it." Linda pulled herself up on the board but gestured to Doug to hold on. "Speaking of which, what else do you do beside the surfing lessons?"

"A couple things, actually," Doug said. "During the off-season I do some painting. Interiors mostly. Murals, seascape scenes, things like that. Sometimes scenes on ceilings, usually a bedroom. People like to lie in bed and look up at star patterns. Some of the wealthier homeowners want things like that to set their homes apart from the others, whether they live in them or rent them. It keeps me busy."

"That's amazing," Linda said. "You must be really talented."

"I don't know about that," Doug said. "But it helps me pay the rent. I also cook at one of the restaurants three nights a week for about six months of the year." He turned away to study an incoming wave. After a couple seconds he turned back to Linda. "How about this one?" She nodded her agreement, and he pushed the board. She was standing seconds later and looked back at him and waved.

After she rode out that wave, Doug suggested they move down the beach a ways where the waves looked a little bigger. Once they were established there Linda caught three straight waves, striking a pose on the last two—knees bent, arms straight out at her sides, head up, trying to mimic what she thought a real surfer might look like. Doug greeted her each time with an appreciative smile and laugh when she got back to him.

Ready for another rest, Linda asked Doug what he'd done for a living before moving to the beach.

"I was a lawyer, actually."

"Really?" Linda grabbed his arm for a moment and frowned. "I'm a lawyer. What kind of law did you practice?"

"Criminal defense. For almost 20 years."

"Why'd you leave?" Linda asked.

"Burned out," Doug said. He began pushing her board forward and pulling it back. "So was everybody else in the firm. Started out thinking I was joining the noble profession of law to help people and make sure the justice system worked the way it was supposed to. Over time that just changed. Too many horrible clients, over-zealous prosecutors wanting to lock everybody in prison and throw away the keys, and the occasional innocent person whose life and bank account were ruined to prove their innocence. Lots and lots of negativity. Finally decided I didn't want to live my life surrounded by that every day."

"Yeah, I've seen a lot of that," Linda said. "Felt a lot of that too."

Doug nodded. "You do criminal defense, too?"

"Yes, for four years now."

"Well, good luck. Hope your experience with it is different than mine was. But I've got to tell you, once I got away from that, and started thinking about some other options, I became a much better, and happier, person."

Linda simply nodded. She couldn't speak.

"Enough of that," Doug said with a grin, and turned away. After a minute of studying the waves, he said, "Here comes a good one. Let's get this." Linda grabbed the board with both hands, Doug pushed, Linda paddled, then rode the wave all the way in. The best of the day.

When she dismounted the board in knee deep water, she waved to Doug to come in. As he reached her side Linda announced, "I'm ready to stop. I've had a wonderful time and I've gotten what I wanted from the lesson." Then she mumbled something Doug couldn't hear.

He assured her they had a few minutes left if she wanted a couple more rides. Linda declined. She released the Velcro of the ankle leash, then gave Doug a hug.

When Zack arrived at 5:45 Linda was sitting on the deck with lemonade in hand. She'd heard the car pull up but waited for him to find her.

After the surf lesson she'd walked back to the house, showered, and dressed for a bike ride. She rented a bike and rode to Hatteras. She had a leisurely lunch then rode back. The rest of the afternoon, after a second shower, she'd relaxed on the deck and got her ducks in a row. She thought a lot about negativity. She made one phone call.

"Hey, honey, I'm home. Be right with you," Zack shouted toward the screen door as he headed for the kitchen. Five minutes later he took the chair beside her. He guzzled a beer and put a second one on the deck beside his chair. No kiss was offered by either.

"I had a very interesting day," he began.

Linda interrupted. "Before you tell me about your day, I've got some things to tell you."

"Well, I ..."

"No," Linda said, her eyes squinting. "You listen to me for a change. You always go first, when you feel like talking at all. Today it's my turn."

Zack pursed his lips and sat back in the chair. Linda set her lemonade down.

"I did the surfing lesson this morning and it was great. I was able to stand up after just a few falls and rode a lot of nice waves. I had a great time. And as you can see, no injuries or trips to the hospital."

"I know," Zack said. Then, as Linda held up her hand to stop him, he quickly added, "I was there."

Linda stared at him with pinched eyebrows. "What do you mean you were there?"

"I was there, on the beach. I was watching you practically the whole time. You were fantastic."

Linda shook her head. "I'm not sure I believe you."

"I can prove it," Zack said. "I took pictures."

Linda skewered him with a look of disbelief. After a gratuitous smile in return, he reached in his pocket and pulled out his phone. A few seconds later he passed it to her.

While the figure on the surfboard in the picture was small and distant, the blue swimsuit and body posture looked a lot like her. The next few pictures confirmed he was there.

"Believe me now?" Zack said, grabbing the phone from Linda's hand.

"I guess so. But ... why?" Linda rubbed her forehead with one hand and reached for the lemonade with the other. "You were going fishing."

"I was," Zack said. "But on the way, just after the jug handle bridge, there was an accident. A pretty serious one. Looked head-on. That kind of stirred me up. Got me thinking. What if that was you? What if you were seriously hurt? Surfing, or otherwise. I'd want to be there for you. I wouldn't want some hunky surf instructor or someone to have to pick you up and take you to the hospital."

Linda sat back in her chair. While she was surprised, she heard all kinds of messages in his statement. That he realized how much he loved her and wanted to show his support for her was, unfortunately, not what popped into her head. Her first thought was that the road was closed, and he was going to miss the departure time of the boat, so he came back to keep an eye on her. That made more sense.

She'd had enough experience with him to know that the reality was perhaps not quite as bad as that cynical assessment, but probably closer to that than he was there out of love and caring for her. He still thought he could B.S. her. And why not? His comment about the surf instructor told her he'd seen them hug.

"So, what else did you do?" Zack asked while Linda was still sorting through her emotions.

Based on their history, she figured he probably knew. "It doesn't matter," she finally said. "What matters is ..." She took a breath and stared him down. "I'm leaving." She took another breath. "Tomorrow morning. I'll pack my things tonight. Keisha's taking me home. You and Michael can come home when you're ready. But I hope you'll give me a couple days so I can be gone when you get home."

Zack looked at her like she'd suddenly grown a pair of horns.

His voice was carefully measured when he said, "No. You're not leaving. I don't know what's gotten into you ..."

"Nothing's gotten into me." Linda tried to keep her voice as controlled as his. "Except the realization that I don't love you anymore. This ... us ... isn't any fun. It hasn't been for a long time. I've just put up with it. And I'm done."

Zack pulled forward to the edge of his chair. He looked ready to pounce.

"Linda, we're back!" Keisha announced from the top of the stairs. She rushed to the screen door. Ryan edged back into his chair. "How about you and I go out for a seafood dinner? We'll let the guys fend for themselves. What do you say?"

"Sounds great," Linda said. She got up and stepped around Zack without even a glance in his direction. "I'll be ready in one minute."

96

98

That Old House

The house had been empty every time he'd walked past it before. This time a woman, maybe 40ish, making her at least 20 years younger than him, was unloading a small box from the back of an SUV. He waited for her to come out the back door for her next trip.

"Can I help?"

She turned and greeted him with a weak, and brief, smile. "No, thanks. I've got it." She reached for her next load and disappeared into the house.

The next afternoon was cool and blustery, but when he walked by, he decided he wanted to meet her. He had a history with the house and was curious. He hadn't seen a "For Sale" sign in the lawn, and a Tuesday on the second week of November was an unusual time for a renter or seasonal guest to be coming in.

Just before he knocked on the front door a disquieting odor hit him. The SUV was next to the house, so when there was no reply to his patient third knock, he decided she wasn't ready for visitors. But curiosity got the best of him, and he knelt by the window next to the door and peeked in.

Through the blinds he could see a body lying in the floor of the living room next to the fireplace. Then it hit him. The odor, now more prominent through a crack in the window, was gas. Propane gas.

He grabbed the front doorknob and found it locked. He reached in the pocket of his jacket for the gloves he knew were there and quickly punched a jagged hole through the small window beside the door. He knocked some shards out of the way, then reached through, and at full extension, turned the doorknob and pulled the door open.

The gas smell literally knocked him backward. He shook his head, took another step retreating into the fresh air, turned away and took a deep breath, then charged into the house.

His eyes began to sting, but he quickly made his way toward the brown-haired figure lying face down on the floor wearing a sweatshirt and sweatpants, no shoes. He knew immediately it was her. He stepped over the papers lying in a semi-circle around her and turned her over. Her head bobbed side-to-side, her face was impossibly white and blue, drool dripped from her mouth. But she was breathing.

He grabbed her by both armpits and dragged her out the door. Once they cleared the doorway, he exhaled and took a deep breath in. He continued to pull her another 10 feet into the weedy front lawn before lowering her upper body carefully to the ground. He grabbed a few breaths, then once he assured himself again that she was breathing, he hustled to the side of the house and found the propane tank. He lifted the lid and turned the knob to close down the flow to the fireplace in the house.

When he returned to the front lawn, the woman had her eyes open and was rocking slowly side-to-side. He knelt beside her and held her in his arms to quiet her.

"You're going to be okay," he said. Her face was a slightly more normal color. "Just try to stay calm and breathe."

"No," she whispered, then closed her eyes.

Just then, a car stopped 30-feet away on the road and a man got out and rushed toward them. "Need some help?" he asked.

"No, well ... yes. I think so." He struggled with what and how much to tell the stranger. He wanted to keep it simple rather than tell him what he suspected. "I just found her and think she's going to be okay, but I want to get her to my house so I can keep an eye on her for a bit. She's here alone. I'm an EMT and I was out for a walk and came across her. She doesn't need the hospital. Can you take us to my house in your car? It's a little less than a mile away."

The man's puzzled expression seemed appropriate. "Well ... I guess so. But what's your name?"

"I'm Rod. What's yours?"

"It's Dontae. I live just down here on North End Road about another quarter mile." They nodded their greeting. "What's her name?"

Rod looked at the lady still in his arms who seemed to be trying to follow their conversation. "What's your name, Ma'am?"

"Name ... is ... Kate," she mumbled, with her eyes open only long enough to get the words out.

"Okay, Kate," Rod said. "This nice man is going to take us to my house. I'll monitor you there for a little while, then get you back here when you're feeling better." He didn't give her a chance to respond before motioning to Dontae who helped lift her to her feet. They carried her to his car and Rod got in the back seat with her head in his lap.

Five minutes later they had her on the bed in the spare bedroom at Rod's house. She closed her eyes and seemed to drift off as Rod put a quilt over her. Dontae insisted on exchanging phone numbers at the front door before he left. Rod saw him pause to write down the house address into his phone before getting into his car. *Good idea,* he thought. *I'd do the same thing.*

He grabbed his laptop on the way back to the bedroom. When he slipped into the room Kate was asleep. He settled in the bedside chair and woke the computer. He Googled "propane gas inhalation." He quickly learned the gas was not toxic, but its harmful effects came from filling the lungs and keeping oxygen from getting in. The typical effects of short-term inhalation were just what he'd witnessed. As he'd suspected, hospitalization was not necessary if the person responded well to a renewed oxygen supply. However, the effects could linger for hours.

As he closed the computer and looked at Kate, it struck him that he'd left the front door wide open at her house. Probably a good thing, but that and a broken window were an invitation that some people might not be able to resist. Even in Kinnakeet. Not to mention the critters that would be on the prowl as soon as dusk approached. He decided to make a quick trip to secure the door and tape up the window until he had a chance to repair it.

As he rose from the chair Kate stirred. After a moment of confusion her eyes focused on him. He noticed for the first time they were a fascinating shade of brown. Actually hazel.

"Who are ... you?" she mumbled.

"I'm Rod."

"Okay," she said as her eyes drifted around the room.

"Do you remember what happened?" Rod asked.

She seemed to be probing her memory banks. "No," she finally said.

"You inhaled a dangerous amount of propane gas at your house. I found you and brought you here. You're going to be okay. In a while."

She seemed to understand but closed her eyes again.

"How are you feeling?"

It was a full minute before she responded. "My head is ... splitting. And I feel just ... exhausted."

"That sounds pretty normal, under the circumstances," Rod said. "It'll get better. I was just thinking I want to go back to your house and secure it. I think I left the front door open. It will just take me a few minutes. Can I trust you to be right here when I get back?"

Kate almost grinned. "I'm not going anywhere ... feeling like this."

Rod took a quick look around the room for any potentially dangerous objects. Seeing none, he promised her he'd be back shortly. He grabbed his toolbox, threw a couple pieces of wood in the bed of his truck, and was at her house two minutes later.

The gas smell was much weaker, and he felt comfortable going through the open door after filling his lungs outside, but he wouldn't want to stay long. At the place he'd found her next to the fireplace there were still about 15 pieces of paper scattered around. He knelt and picked up several of them, then turned them over. They were photographs. Of smiling people—a baby, a young boy, probably the same boy as a teenager, and several of a man. There were two of what looked like her and the man together. Then one of an older couple. The other papers he examined as he picked them up were similar, except one which was a brief handwritten note. He read it once, then put it with the photographs on a table.

Satisfied for the moment, he went to work on the window with a small plywood board and a roll of duct tape. Once he had done what he could, and picked up the broken glass, he did a quick walk around the first floor, noticing the sparse belongings and almost non-existent furniture among the general disrepair of the house. On his way out the door he noticed her purse on a table by the door and took that with him. He rushed back to his house and breathed a sigh of relief when he peeked in the bedroom and found Kate exactly where he'd left her. He got some water and Tylenol from the kitchen and returned. She turned toward him as he walked in.

"How are you feeling now?" he asked. Her color was continuing to improve.

"Same."

"Time for some water and Tylenol," he said sitting gently on the bed beside her. He slid his arm around her and helped her slide up to a sitting position. She took two sips along with the pills without protest. She grinned her thanks and slid back down. Rod pulled the quilt back over her and decided to let her rest. He needed to rest as well and settled in the living room.

An hour later she appeared, leaning unsteadily against the hallway. "Where's the bathroom?" she said.

Rod jumped to his feet and pointed to the door to her right. When she reappeared five minutes later, she looked like she'd washed her face and run her fingers through her hair. When she walked into the living room, he motioned her to the sofa and retook his seat in the recliner.

She looked at him, then shifted her gaze around the room for a few seconds. "Thank you," she said when she looked back to him. "I don't know what happened. A gas leak ... I guess."

Rod grabbed her eyes with his. "I saw the photos." He waited. When she didn't respond he added, "And the note."

"Oh." She looked at the rug between her feet and rubbed her thighs with both hands.

"Want to talk about it?"

"No."

"Okay." Too soon.

"I don't suppose you're going to let me go home?"

"Right. I'm an emergency medical technician, or at least I was once upon a time. And you're not ready to be alone. You're going to stay here, or the hospital. Your choice. You're safe here. Besides, your house isn't ready for you yet. It's going to take a while to air out. I can start that tomorrow."

She looked like she wanted to argue but didn't.

"Do you feel like eating something?" Rod asked. "It's dinner time."

She shook her head.

"Would you like to call someone? Or I can call for you."

"No. There's ..." A look of panic crossed her face. "My phone, my purse ..."

"Your purse is on the kitchen counter. I didn't look in it."

She nodded. Her face relaxed. Then a quiet, "Thank you." She pushed herself to her feet and walked slowly back to the bedroom after a quick detour to the kitchen for her purse.

Rod decided to let well enough alone. He fixed himself a couple hot dogs, added some potato chips, and called it dinner. Afterwards, he checked on his guest and found her asleep under the covers of the bed. He brought her a glass of water and an apple and put them on the bedside table. He figured even if she was planning to sneak out during the night she wouldn't be going far without shoes or a jacket.

The next morning, she met him in the kitchen. "Care for some toast and eggs?" he asked.

"Yes, please," she said as she pulled out a chair and sat at the table. Her color looked normal, and she had obviously brushed her hair. Other than the wrinkled sweats, she looked like she probably did on any other morning—an attractive, sturdily built, middle-aged woman preparing for a day of work or a relaxing morning at home.

He sat a mug of coffee in front of her and three minutes later scrambled eggs, wheat toast, and grape jelly. She ate hungrily, but silently. After she cleaned her plate, she smiled at him and asked, "Can I go home now?"

Rod took a minute to clear her dishes then sat at the table across from her. "I was planning to go there and take a look at the place. Probably start airing it out and do a couple quick things. You're welcome to go with me, but I don't think you should stay. I was thinking maybe you could grab a few things and come back here with me."

"It's my house," she said defiantly.

"Good to know. I didn't want to think you were squatting there." He smiled and ignored her aggravated expression.

He gave her some tennis shoes to wear and a light jacket, both of which were just slightly big for her. As soon as they got to the house, he made her wait beside the front door while he stepped inside and took a breath. The smell of propane was still there, but not nearly what it was on his last visit. He motioned her inside, then left the door open behind her.

She disappeared upstairs and came back 25 minutes later in fresh jeans, blue wool sweater, and her own sneakers. Her hair was wet. Meanwhile, Rod had been doing an inspection of the first-floor rooms of the house, making notes on his phone of work that needed to be done. He was looking over the list when she approached.

"What are you doing?" she asked, with obvious annoyance.

"You've got a lot of work that needs to be done here. Some of it pretty urgent. I'd say even before you come back to live here."

"That's good to know, but that's my business. Like I said, I own this house."

"For how long?" he asked. He was curious but also wanted to distract her from a debate.

"I ... my husband and I have owned this house for about 13 years."

Rod nodded. "Don't remember you, but I remember your husband. Chris, or something like that. I lived here for a few years. Left about four years ago. Wrote rent checks to Chris somebody."

"That would be Chris Wingate, my husband. He handled this property. I had nothing to do with it."

Sounded like a tough divorce. She probably got the part of the assets that were run down, he didn't want, and she knew nothing about.

"I did a few small fix-up jobs when I lived here. I was working as a handyman back then." He looked at his list, then at the water stain on the ceiling, from a leak in an upstairs bathroom. "The place has really run down since then. You've got obvious leaks from the roof, dripping faucets, holes in a couple walls, missing calking around windows, not to mention that window by the door that I broke to get in here yesterday. And I'd be willing to bet your electrical is in trouble, and maybe dangerous. And, I haven't even seen the upstairs." He didn't mention the mouse turds he found in several rooms, including the kitchen. He decided to hold that in reserve in case she insisted on spending the night there.

She didn't seem to be as concerned as he thought she should be. But on the other hand, she wasn't ordering him out. "When was the last time someone lived here?"

"I don't know. Maybe a year or two."

"Looks like it." He debated for a moment, then decided to go there. "I'm guessing you weren't really planning to live here." *Just die here.*

She stared at him, then turned and walked away.

He chased her with his words. "Ready to talk about it?"

"No!"

"Okay. Then I'm going to get to work after I go outside for a couple minutes to get some fresh air and grab my toolbox. I suggest you spend a little while outside for some air, too."

He started by working on the leaking faucets, upstairs and down. He was able to fix about half of them, the others needed replacement. He got two toilets to stop running. Three of the electrical outlets he checked were dead. He opened windows in each room as he went.

When he got to the master bedroom upstairs, he found Kate lying on the bed. She looked tired but okay. He stepped to the end of the bed and, with some effort, opened the window. He and Claire had painted this room and the other upstairs bedroom when they lived here. They were probably the only rooms in the house that weren't desperately in need of paint.

"I'm going to make a trip to the hardware store," he announced. "You be okay for a while?"

She raised her head to look at him. "You don't have to—"

"I know. But I'm going to."

Just after Rod got in the truck, Dontae stopped his car in the road, rolled the window down, and asked how Kate was doing. Rod gave him the positive update and thanked him again for his help.

Forty-five minutes later, after a quick stop by his house for a ladder, Rod was back and found Kate sitting with a glass of water at the small kitchen table. He acknowledged her with a smile and a wave as he walked through. She shook her head slightly in response.

He worked until a bit after one o'clock and was pleased with his progress. Faucets and toilet fixed. He had the front windowpane replaced and decided to work on caulking after a lunch break. He didn't figure she had any food in the house, so he told her they were going to Subway. She grudgingly grabbed her purse and went along.

She insisted on paying, then over chicken salad subs he asked her where she was from. It took her two bites to answer, but then she said, "Charlotte." After another bite she said, "What about you?"

He figured he'd model openness. "Lived most of my life in California. Born and raised. Came here to Kinnakeet a few years ago. My wife had family here and wanted to be close. Been here since."

That didn't accomplish much. The rest of the meal was consumed in silence except for Rod's reciting his plans for afternoon repairs. Kate shook her head after each item on his list.

The window work took the rest of the afternoon, interrupted only by a short walk. A brief examination of the roof revealed several weak spots and two obvious sources for leaks where shingles were missing or broken. In his younger years he would have tackled that job. But with a phone call, he got a roofer buddy to agree to do the patch work a couple days hence, with a promise he'd get to the roof replacement job when he could fit it in.

Kate put up no resistance when Rod announced he was done for the day and asked her to gather things she wanted to take with her. The last things he did, after he got Kate to the truck, was close windows and set eight baited mouse traps he'd gotten from the hardware store.

Over a dinner of burgers and fries, Rod tried again to get Kate to talk about anything, but she either shook her head or simply said, "No." As he got up to clear the plates, she jumped to her feet and nudged him aside. She insisted, "I've got this," and Rod sat while she washed the dishes. *Progress* he thought. He dried and put the things away.

"You know, I'm going to pay you for all the work you're doing," she said once they finished. "Be sure to keep all the receipts for everything. What's your hourly rate?"

Rod smiled at her and said nothing. He figured a dose of her own medicine might be good for her.

After a full minute of silence, she grinned at him and said, "Well, thanks. We'll talk about it later, but I am going to pay you. I'm going to bed now."

Rod was more than ready to do the same. It had been the longest and most draining day he'd had in a long time.

The next morning, he fixed frozen waffles in the toaster topped with real maple syrup. She ate two to his one and had two cups of coffee. When he asked how she was feeling she said, "Fine. One hundred percent."

He laid out his plan for work at the house, and she said, "Thank you. You know you don't have to do that. You must have other things to do." He assured her he didn't and was happy to do it.

After clearing out four dead mice, Rod opened windows again and spent most of the morning working on the electrical system. He did what he could replacing outlets to bring them up to code, then got an electrician friend to come out in the late afternoon to check his work and do some wiring work in the breaker box that he wasn't comfortable doing. Kate got the cleaning supplies he brought from home and together they worked on the kitchen. He cleaned cabinets, counters, and the floor, she tackled the oven and refrigerator. Shortly after 1:00 she got pizza for the two of them from Nino's.

As he worked his way through the house, Rod added significantly to the list of work that needed to be done. He replaced light bulbs and changed air filters but decided to call his HVAC contact to check out the furnace which seemed spotty. He'd originally thought the house was cool from the open windows, but now with them all closed there was little heat to warm the house from the 50-degree temperature outside.

In the middle of the afternoon, Rod sat for a while, then took his walk. When he got back, he asked Kate if she knew who they'd used for pest control or to clean the carpets.

"I don't know any of that," she said. "Chris had a property management company arrange those kind of things for several years, probably during the time you were here. But then when Chris started to let things slide the company ended their contract with us. I think Chris rented it one more year, but I doubt any kind of upkeep got done."

Sounded about right. Then the house set empty for a year, or more. But somebody must have been at least looking in on it. Someone was paying the water and electrical bills. Doubtful Kate would know who.

Rod was exhausted by four o'clock and called it quits after he reset the mouse traps. When they got back to his house, he looked up the names of the local pest control and carpet cleaning companies he used. To his surprise, she wrote down the phone numbers and said she'd make the calls. He also wanted the propane company to look at the gas fireplace and do a safety check before that got fired up again. He'd make that call in the morning.

Over the dinner of salad and leftover pizza, Rod filled Kate in on his considered opinions about various things Kinnakeet. Mostly the differences between the summer "tourist mania" and the "cool" off-season. He also suggested they should visit a couple of the local sights but got no encouragement. When the meal was finished, he asked if she was ready to talk about "things."

She considered the question for a moment, then said, "Not yet. Maybe soon." Then she turned the table. "How about you tell me why you're doing all this."

Rod mimicked her pause for consideration, then said, "I asked you first."

Kate smiled. Then, "Can you at least give me a hint?"

Rod thought for a minute. "I'm just an old guy with a big debt to pay."

Kate seemed to process that cryptic comment for a few seconds then said, "I'm headed to bed. Good night."

Rod collapsed into his own bed minutes later.

The next four days followed a similar pattern of breakfast, various work projects at Kate's house, then lunch. They were finishing up a bit earlier each day and there was more conversation. One day Rod took her for a walk on the pier before heading to his house. Another day he took her to the Hatteras lighthouse, and shared pirate and shipwreck stories. They made a trip to Manteo for her to buy some furniture.

Dinners at his place got a little more appealing, not to mention nutritious, after a joint trip to the Food Lion and once Kate started helping with meal preparation. She took some time out to do some shopping each day, giving Rod time to rest, and for his walk.

By Saturday, his concern about her safety dissipated. She was even smiling now and then.

With all major systems working at the house, bathrooms cleaned, the roof patched, and some furniture delivered, Rod wondered when Kate would stop spending the night at his house. She'd started talking a little every day about the possibility of living in Kinnakeet, but not about the obvious elephant that stood in the room between them.

When she insisted before leaving her house Monday afternoon that she was taking him out to dinner, Rod suspected she might be ready to talk. She cleaned up and changed out of work clothes before she drove her car to his place. Rod did the same once he got home. She told him to pick the place. He chose the Mad Crabber, and they were seated at a corner table at six-fifteen.

After they placed their orders she reached across the table, took his hand, and leaned in. Her eyes seized his. "I can't thank you enough for all you've done," she said as she squeezed his hand. "Not the least of which was saving my life. You've more than earned that explanation."

Rod nodded and returned his most encouraging smile. She waited until their iced tea arrived.

"I've never been particularly good at talking about feelings, as you've no doubt noticed. One of my many faults. But it's time. I'm going to try." She let go of his hand and pulled a small pack of tissues from her purse. She pulled one from the pack and gripped it tight. Her eyes returned to his.

"My son, my precious Tommy, committed suicide just over two years ago. He was only 16 years old." She broke eye contact and put the tissue to work. After a full minute she continued. "That's the most horrible thing a person can face, especially a mother." Her voice broke and she stopped again to fight the tears.

Rod felt his own tears coming and dug the handkerchief from his pocket.

"I knew this was going to be hard," Kate said. With a last wipe she started again. "My husband took it as hard as I did. We both blamed ourselves. There were signs ..." Another break to soak up tears. "The damage that did to our marriage was just awful. Neither of us could deal with ... the guilt. We just didn't have anything left to help each other, even though we tried."

Rod's eyes were closed but the tears seeped out anyway. He took a deep breath, reached across the table for her hand, and said, "You don't have to do this." His face was contorted in pain.

"Thanks," Kate said squeezing his hand, "but I do." She squeezed again, pulled the hand away, settled it near the tissues, and continued. "Chris made it a year. He committed suicide on the anniversary of Tommy's death. He shot himself lying in Tommy's bed. And that ... is the second worse thing any person, any wife, could have to endure."

The tears rolled down Kate's cheeks. And a second later, Rod's. It took a minute or two for them to face each other again.

Their concerned waitress appeared and asked gently if they were okay or needed anything. Rod told her they were okay, then asked Kate if maybe they should step outside for a minute. She nodded her agreement. After Rod told the waitress they'd be back in a couple minutes she said she'd hold their dinner until they returned. They put their jackets back on and found a private spot to stand on the corner of the porch. The brisk evening air seemed to help both of them regain some degree of control.

"My friends were really concerned about me, for good reason," Kate said, staring out into the darkness of Route 12. "They were very helpful and supportive. I promised them I was okay and wasn't going to hurt myself. What I didn't tell them was that my promise was only good for a year. If I was still hurting that much after a year the promise was null and void. And ... I was. That year was twice as bad, twice the guilt, as the year after Tommy died. So ... on the anniversary of Chris's death I packed a few things and took off for that old house in Kinnakeet to get my courage up. The condition of the house itself was pretty depressing. And ... that's where you came in. Literally."

Rod stepped forward and took Kate in his arms. They sobbed, pressed tightly together, for several minutes.

When they made it back inside, they apologized to the waitress, and the few other diners, as they made their way back to their table. At Kate's urging, they focused on enjoying the dinner and kept the conversation on lighter topics. Rod was able to eat little of his meal.

Once they were back at Rod's place, they settled into the living room and Kate said it was now his turn. "Why were you ... why did you do all you did for me? Why did you rescue me, put up with all my rudeness, and with your kindness and compassion, give me a reason to live?"

Rod was afraid this was coming, and after the emotions of hearing Kate's story he wasn't sure he could do it. But Kate insisted.

"I don't know about that giving you a reason to live thing, but I did what anybody else would do when I saw you lying on the floor in the living room. The rest of it, working on your house, just gave me something to do. I haven't done much of anything the last year or so."

"Why?" Kate asked with a troubled look, not letting him off the hook.

"Well, that's because ... my wife, Linda, died 17 months ago. She's ... she's buried just down the road from your house in that little family cemetery on North End Road. That's her family's cemetery."

"Oh, I'm so sorry," Kate said.

"Thanks." Rod debated telling the rest of the story, then decided to go ahead, since Kate had shared her pain so bravely.

"She died because of me. I was driving the car. I got some minor injuries and she ... died." That was enough. The rest didn't matter. That the accident wasn't his fault was something he could never accept.

"Oh, no!" Kate jumped from the sofa and landed on her knees beside the recliner. She immediately took Rod in her arms. He leaned forward into the embrace, and after a moment let go to wipe a tear on his sleeve. Kate was crying as well.

"Guess we're both pretty raw," Kate said as she got to her feet and made her way back to the sofa. Rod simply nodded and used his handkerchief.

After a couple minutes of awkward silence, Kate said, "This may not be the best time to tell you this, but I've got to." She waited until his eyes came up to meet hers. "I'm going to go back to Charlotte for a little while. Tomorrow. I left a pretty big mess there. A lot of friends who are worried about me, and a lot of financial things to sort through. Also, there's a house to put on the market. But ... you, Kinnakeet, and what that old house is becoming, have won me over. I'll be back here before Christmas."

Though he was surprised, Rod managed to say, "That's fine. I might do a little of that painting we talked about in the house while you're gone, if you'd like."

"That'd be fine. But only if you want to. I'll leave you the key. And that brings up what I owe you." She reached for her purse on the floor beside her. "Can you give me a number?"

"How about zero?" Rod said with a twinkle in his eye.

"Not acceptable," Kate countered with a vigorous shake of her head. "If you don't give me a number, I'm going to write you a check right now for $20,000.00. Of course, you might want to hold it for a couple days until I get home and get some money moved around at the bank."

When Rod couldn't dissuade her, she wrote the check and put it on the kitchen table. She gathered her jacket and gave him a huge hug. She whispered, "Thank you, thank you, thank you," then made a hurried exit out the door, fighting tears again.

When she got back to Kinnakeet on December 22nd, Kate made a brief stop at her house to unload, then drove directly to Rod's. His truck was there, but there was no response to her repeated knocks. As she stepped back from the door a neighbor lady she'd seen a couple times approached.

"Are you looking for Rod?" she asked.

"Yes, I am," Kate said.

"Well then, you must be Kate," the lady said.

"I am. Is Rod here?"

"Well, he's not. But he told me if you came looking for him, I should tell you where he is."

"And where's that?" Kate said, growing a little impatient, and a bit worried.

"Well, he's in the hospital in Nags Head. That cancer he's been dealing with flared up, big time. He said you could come see him. If you wanted to."

Kate made the one-hour drive to the hospital in 50 minutes. She was at his bedside four minutes later.

"You came back," he said when he opened his eyes, and she was there. His tired smile greeted her.

Kate reached for his hand. "Of course. I told you I would."

"I'm sorry I didn't get to much of that painting," Rod said, rolling to his side to face her. I'll ... get it done when I get out of here."

"No, you won't," she declared. "You've already done so much for me. Too much. Besides, you didn't cash that check."

"Didn't need it." He caught his breath. "And you've done a lot more for me than I've done for you."

Kate looked shocked. "There's no way. I haven't done anything for you."

"Yes, you have," Rod said. "You're the one who gave me a reason to keep on living."

Kate's expression now registered disbelief. "What do you mean? It was the other way around."

"No." Rod grabbed a tissue from the box on the bedside table. "You see, this cancer had about got the best of me. With Linda gone and what the cancer was doing to me, I'd pretty well given up. I'd stopped the medicine because I didn't think it was doing any good. I stopped eating what I was supposed to and ate what I wanted. About all I could do in a day was walk down to the cemetery and talk with Linda." He paused to catch his breath. "That day I found you I was going to tell her about stopping the medication and that I didn't know how much longer I'd be able to come talk to her, but that I hoped I'd see her again soon."

"I didn't know about the cancer and where you were going on your walks," Kate said with a tight-lipped frown. "You should've told me."

"No need for you to know. But, you see, when I started going back inside that old house it brought back a lot of memories, good memories, from the time Linda and I lived there. Those were good years. Great years. You see, we were a couple of newly-weds. We'd only been married six months when we moved there. Kind of a late-life marriage for me." With a spicy grin he added, "Married a younger woman."

Kate smiled. "That's wonderful."

"Yeah. Like, that living room. Linda and I had an old rug laying in front of that fireplace. We made love on that rug, in front of a fire in the winter, quite a few times. And the kitchen ..." He paused for a breath. "Linda liked to watch those cooking shows on TV, and when I'd walk in the door from work the smell from the kitchen of whatever new dish she was making for dinner would just hit me. And I'll tell you, it was a lot better than the smell of that propane!"

"I'm sure," Kate said with a bemused smile.

"And then the bedroom. The master bedroom. We painted that one the light blue color it is now. But right after we decided to paint it, we started writing things on it in markers and colored pencils. Things like love letters to each other, drawings of each other, cartoons, even poems. We had them all over the walls. It was a good couple months before we painted over all that. Then, we started doing the same thing on the walls of that other bedroom up there. We just kept doing it until the month before we moved. Then we painted it. Made love in that room, too. Lots of great memories in those two rooms."

"That's wonderful!" Kate said again.

"Sure is." Rod's pensive smile lit his face. "There were lots of delightful memories in that old house. And once I was back in there again, all those came back to me. And then ... when I went to the cemetery, I started sharing those with Linda. Every day I was in the house new memories came back. It kind of, I don't know ... picked me up. I had more energy than I'd had in months."

"That's so nice!"

"Yep. So, you see, you, and that old house, gave me a reason to keep going, to keep living. I was doing a lot better until I had this little flare-up. But now ... they've got me on some experimental medicine that seems to be helping. The doctor says I could be out of here in another day or two."

"In time for Christmas," Kate said with a cheer in her voice. "And we can have Christmas at my house!"

"Oh, I don't know ..."

"Of course, we will." Kate thought for a moment. "There are a couple things I need to do, but you call me when you're going to be released, and I'll come get you. You can stay at my house until you get your strength back, then you can start on painting those rooms."

When Rod frowned his reluctance, Kate proclaimed, "Turnabout is fair play."

Rod did have Christmas at Kate's house. However, he never got the painting done.

The medication stopped working shortly after the new year. But with the assistance of the local hospice organization, he was able to stay in the first-floor bedroom Kate set up for him until he died on January 24th.

By the time of his death, the walls of that bedroom were covered with poems, love letters, and drawings of his beloved Linda. On a daily basis, Kate had helped him stand by the wall for a couple minutes or helped him into a wheelchair then pushed it to his chosen spot. There were also notes of appreciation to Kate and sketches of some local landmarks.

Four days later, Kate stood in the chilly wind at the little cemetery on North End Road and watched Rod's coffin interred beside Linda's. With tears in her eyes, she promised him, again, that she would never, ever, paint that beautiful bedroom.

KINNAKEET
COMMUNITY
CEMETERIES

Adrift

The sea was calm, almost unnaturally so, as the sun began its descent toward the horizon. Off Cape Hatteras, where the Atlantic and its notorious graveyard of the Atlantic swallowed hundreds of vessels over the centuries, the Coast Guard cutter *Morris* plowed steadily through the waters. Its crew of ten had been dispatched to investigate a report from a passing cargo ship. A fishing boat had been spotted adrift, its lights flickering like a weak signal in the growing twilight. No one had responded to radio hails and there was no sign of activity on the deck.

"Anything yet?" Lieutenant Commander Grace Holloway asked as she entered the bridge. Her voice was calm but laced with the authority born of experience.

"No ma'am," replied Ensign Peter Garcia, hunched over the radar screen. "Still no response. If she's out there, she's likely dead in the water. AIS isn't picking up any ID."

Holloway frowned. Fishing boats off Hatteras Island were common, but they were rarely unresponsive to radio calls, and even the most battered trawler typically broadcast its location. "Could be a mechanical issue," she said, more to herself than anyone else. Fishing boats broke down all the time. "Or something worse."

"Or nothing at all," chimed in Chief Bosun's Mate Victor Pierce. "Could just be a ghost story waiting to happen. You know how these waters are."

Garcia glanced at Pierce with a raised eyebrow but said nothing. The young ensign had grown up in landlocked Kansas and was still adjusting to the superstition-laden lore of mariners. Halloway didn't share Pierce's taste for tall tales of all sizes and shapes, but even she had to admit there was something eerie about the waters off Hatteras Island. The area's history of shipwrecks and disappearances had earned it a reputation few dared to dismiss entirely. The waters here often didn't give second chances.

She'd grown up there, in Kinnakeet. As a child she'd memorized all the pirate and ghost ship stories. They'd given her a fascination with, and healthy respect for, the ocean and its immense power. She knew all about the Life Saving Service, the precursor to the Coast Guard, and their stations along the island. It had taken her 24 years in the Guard to earn her rank, and the assignment to the Coast Guard Station at Oregon Inlet.

"Bridge to engine room, slow to one-third," Holloway ordered. "Let's not spook anybody if they're out there."

The *Morris* eased forward, her twin screws churning the water and her searchlights slicing through the dimming light. The fishing boat came into view minutes later, its silhouette a dark smudge against the rippling sea. Holloway raised a pair of binoculars.

The vessel was a small, weathered trawler, the kind that dotted harbors up and down the East Coast. Its name, *Persephone*, was painted on the hull, but barely legible due to years of salt, sun, and peeling paint. The boat bobbed gently; its nets trailing limp and tangled off the stern. A metal bucket rolled lazily back and forth on the deck. No signs of life.

"Bridge to deck crew," Holloway called through the intercom. "Prepare to board. Let's see what's going on there."

"Aye, ma'am," came the reply.

Pierce, Garcia, and Petty Officer Susan Tran suited up in foul-weather gear and climbed into the cutter's small inflatable boat. The sound of the motor was the only noise as they bounced over the waves and closed the gap to the *Persephone*. Tran cast a quick glance at the trawler, her eyes narrowing.

"Something doesn't feel right," she murmured.

"Agreed," Pierce said, his earlier bravado muted now.

Garcia said nothing, gripping the side of the inflatable as they bumped against the trawler. Tran secured the line, and the three climbed aboard. Their boots thudding against the slick deck.

The silence was immediate and oppressive. No hum of machinery, no creak of footsteps from below deck. Nothing. Garcia wrinkled his nose at the faint but distinct smell of fish mingling with the metallic tang of saltwater.

"Ahoy!" Tran called, her voice ringing out. "U.S. Coast Guard. Is anyone aboard?"

No answer.

They moved cautiously across the deck, their flashlights illuminating scuffed wood and coils of rope. A bucket of bait set forgotten near the stern; its contents now rotted. A tackle box lay open, its content scattered as if dropped in haste.

"Looks like they left in a hurry," Pierce said. He opened the wheelhouse door and peered inside. "Power still on, but everything's dead. Radio and ... compass ... nothing's working."

Garcia joined him, running his hand over the controls. "Battery's drained. That shouldn't happen this fast unless somebody deliberately disabled it."

Tran stood at the edge of the deck, staring out at the open sea. "Where would they go?" she asked softly. "There's no life raft. No signs of a struggle."

Pierce emerged from the wheelhouse, his flashlight sweeping over the deck. It stopped on a scuffed life preserver tangled in netting at the stern. "Maybe they jumped ship? Tried to swim to shore?" Tran and Garcia looked at him with skepticism. He nodded.

Holloway's voice crackled over the radio. "Report."

"No signs of the crew, ma'am," Tran replied. "Boat's powered down. No signs of a struggle. No clue where the crew went."

"Roger that. Secure the vessel for towing and return to the cutter," Halloway instructed.

Pierce began tying the tow line while Garcia and Tran continued their search. The trawler was small, and it didn't take long to confirm there was no one aboard. As they prepared to leave, Garcia noticed something wedged between the slats of the deck. He crouched and pulled it free. A waterlogged notebook.

"What's that?" Tran asked, stepping closer.

"Not sure." Garcia flipped through the pages, careful not to tear the damp paper. The writing was smeared, but a few words were still legible: strange lights... engine failure... something watching us.

He felt a chill creep up his spine. "I think it's the captain's log."

"Let me see." Tran leaned over his shoulder, her brow furrowing as she read.

"July 12," she murmured, deciphering the scrawled handwriting. "Saw lights on the horizon. Not a ship. Too big, too fast. Something's watching us. Crew uneasy."

She looked up. "This doesn't sound like a storm." She reached over his shoulder to turn the page, squinting at the next entry. "July 13. Lights came closer last night. Power cut out, then came back on. Twice. Something's wrong. No idea what's out there."

Pierce leaned over Garcia's shoulder to glance at the book. "Lights on the horizon? Maybe they saw a cargo ship. Or a flare."

"Or a pirate ship," Tran said, almost under her breath.

"Let me guess," Pierce said... "No entry for July 14?"

Tran shook her head. "Nothing after that."

Pierce's jaw tightened. "Well, that not ominous at all."

They returned to the *Morris*, leaving the *Persephone* to trail behind them on the towline, her nets dragging like the limbs of a drowned corpse. Back on the cutter, Holloway examined the notebook, her expression unreadable.

"We'll send a copy of this to HQ," she ordered. "I want them to run a search on this vessel. Let's find out who owns her."

The *Persephone* was brought into the Oregon Inlet station and impounded for further investigation, but the mystery deepened. Records indicated the boat belonged to a Captain Willis B. Wormell, a seasoned fisherman with over thirty years of experience. Wormell and his crew of three had departed from Hatteras five days earlier and hadn't been seen since. Nor was there any radio contact. While it was unusual for them to be gone that long, it wasn't unheard of. No alarm had been sent up yet.

Interviews with family members and locals yielded no leads. Wormell, who hailed from a Hatteras family of boat owners and captains, was described as reliable, not prone to risky behavior. His crew, too, were experienced. Two of them were well known by locals and had family devastated by their loss. The third, Bill Brice, was a loner and described by some as "odd," but also as, "a decent enough guy." No one had any explanation for why the *Persephone* had been abandoned. Or what the "strange lights" mentioned in the log might have been.

The Coast Guard investigation panel's initial theory was speculative. That the crew had encountered trouble—perhaps a mechanical failure or sudden storm—and had abandoned ship. But they acknowledged no distress call had been sent, and extensive search efforts failed to locate any sign of the missing men. There was no damage to the boat as would be expected from a bad storm.

As days turned into weeks, the story of the *Persephone* spread. Some blamed pirates, though there was no evidence of a struggle on the ship, and no reports of other pirate activity in the area. Others whispered about Bermuda Triangle-like phenomena, even though the trawler had been far from that region. The more superstitious pointed to the logbook's mention of lights, claiming it as evidence of something otherworldly. Old maritime tales of ships disappearing off the Outer Banks resurfaced and made the rounds.

For Halloway, the case was a puzzle she couldn't let go of. The *Morris* had been assigned other missions, but every spare moment she had, she spent poring over the details. She read the logbook so many times she could recite the entries by heart. She studied weather patterns, shipping lanes, even local folklore. But no matter how many angles she considered, the pieces refused to fit together.

Like all Coast Guard officers on the Outer Banks, Halloway was aware of the mystery of the *Carroll A Deering*. In fact, she'd written a paper on it in college summarizing the theories and known facts about it.

The ship appeared one stormy night in 1921 off Diamond Shoals. The five-masted schooner, on its way from Argentina to Norfolk, Virginia, was found on a sandy shoal in a rough sea empty of all crew members. When crews from four lifesaving stations got to her, there were no lifeboats on board and a ladder was hanging over the side of the ship.

The three theories of what had happened to her boiled down to; mutiny against the captain, piracy, and abandonment by the crew in a panic during an intense storm. Of course, there were also those who blamed the disappearance of the men on alien abduction. The mystery remained unsolved despite many years of research and speculation.

It wasn't until nearly a month later that the next clue to the current mystery emerged.

It was a stormy evening when the report came in. A cargo ship had spotted a body floating 15 miles south of Cape Hatteras, tangled in a mass of seaweed. The Coast Guard retrieved it the following morning—a man, bloated and unrecognizable, wearing a life jacket with the name *Persephone* stenciled on it.

The autopsy confirmed it was Willis Wormell. The coroner ruled drowning as the cause of death but noted unusual abrasions on the body, as if Wormell had been dragged through rough coral or wreckage of some kind. There were also long, parallel gouges, almost like claws. No one could explain how his body had ended up miles from where the *Persephone* had been found or why the other crew members were still missing.

The discovery reignited speculation. Halloway felt the weight of unanswered questions pressing down on her. She was only the third female to captain a Coast Guard cutter. And while it was not her job to solve this mystery, she knew many eyes were on her and how she handled this case. She spent long nights in her quarters, staring at charts and photos, replaying the events of that night aboard the *Morris* and the reports from her crew who first boarded the *Persephone*.

One detail nagged at her—the lights. Whatever Wormell had seen clearly disturbed him enough to record it. But what were they? A natural phenomenon? A rogue vessel with ill intent? Or something else entirely?

Halloway wasn't a believer in the supernatural, but as she delved deeper into the history of the area, she found unsettling patterns. Tales of strange lights off Hatteras Island went back centuries, from pirate lore to modern-day UFO sightings. Many people connected these to ships disappearing and crews vanishing without a trace—too many stories to dismiss as mere coincidence.

One night, unable to sleep, she found herself staring at the logbook again. She flipped to the final entry and froze. There, scrawled faintly in the margin, visible now under the intense light of her reading lamp, was a word she hadn't noticed before: *maelstrom.*

Her pulse quickened. Was Wormell describing a whirlpool? A vortex? She searched for references, finding accounts of sailors claiming to have seen such phenomena in the area. Most were dismissed as hallucinations or exaggerations, but a few described details eerily similar to what Wormell had written.

The next morning, she requested permission to lead a new search near the site where the *Persephone* had been found. She didn't tell her crew about the logbook entry, knowing it would only fuel their nerves. Instead, she framed it as a routine follow-up.

The *Morris* returned to the ocean off Cape Hatteras, cutting through the gray, choppy waters. The air was thick with tension as it arrived at the coordinates. Halloway stood on the bridge, scanning the sea as the sun slipped below the horizon.

"Anything on radar?" she asked.

"Negative," Garcia replied. "Just open water."

She frowned. "Keep an eye out. If anyone sees anything—"

Before she could finish, Tran's voice crackled over the intercom. "Ma'am, you need to see this."

Halloway rushed to the deck, where Tran was pointing to the water. At first, Halloway saw nothing unusual. But then, faintly, she spotted it—a flicker of light beneath the surface, shifting and swirling like fireflies in the deep.

"What the hell is that?" Pierce muttered.

The lights grew brighter, closer, their movements hypnotic. The water around the *Morris* began to churn, the calm surface gave way to roiling, then violent, waves. The power on the cutter went off. Then back on.

"Bridge, full reverse!" Halloway shouted. "Get us out of here!"

The engines roared to life, but the cutter barely moved. The lights circled faster, the water formed a spiraling vortex. Halloway gripped the railing as the *Morris* pitched violently.

And then, as suddenly as it began, it stopped. The lights vanished. The sea returned, in a matter of a couple minutes, to a state of unnatural calm.

The crew stood in stunned silence, their faces pale.

"Ma'am," Garcia said quietly, "what just happened?"

Halloway didn't answer. She didn't know. She looked out at the empty horizon, her gut churning with disquiet. As the *Morris* turned back toward shore, she couldn't shake the feeling that whatever had claimed the *Persephone* and her crew, it wasn't natural—and it wasn't finished.

It was only as the *Morris* docked back at Oregon Inlet, and her nerves settled somewhat, that Halloway recalled that the captain of the *Persephone* had the same name as the captain of the *Carroll A. Deering*. Willis B. Wormell.

At The Church

The gust of wind nearly blew them off the bikes.

"I think we're going to be drenched in about two minutes," Ryan shouted. "We need to find a place to get off the road and under cover."

Angie was quick to agree. "That looks like a church just up there on the right. Let's try that."

They pulled off the two-lane road into the parking lot in front of the church and leaned the bikes against the brick wall in front of the building. The sign said Kinnakeet United Presbyterian Church—All Are Welcome.

"No need to lock them," Angie said, "Let's just hope the church is open."

Ryan climbed the steps and tried the door. He looked back at her with relief. "It is. Let's get in."

Angie grabbed the rain covers from her saddlebag and slipped them over the bike seats just as the first drops fell. The rain turned to a deluge in a matter of seconds. A blast of thunder accompanied a lightning strike no more than a quarter mile away. She rushed up the steps and Ryan pulled the door open.

Once inside, they dropped their helmets by the door and took in the 20 or so old wooden benches separated by a central aisle in the sanctuary. The walls were adorned by large and small paintings, as well as hand-carved wooden sculptures, many of crosses or Christ figures. The appearance was of a church well-loved and treasured by a, probably small, congregation.

Just a couple minutes after they began strolling around the edges of the sanctuary to examine the works of art more closely, a figure appeared from behind the chancel. He was wearing old-style sailcloth pants, a black dress shirt, and a bright white clerical collar. His face was rugged, defying an accurate estimate of his age.

"Welcome to our church," he said as he spread his arms, his face set in a cordial smile. "I'm Pastor Gordon. I'm so glad you're here." He took a couple steps toward them and rested a hand on the front bench. "Please, feel free to rest here and take shelter from the storm. It sounds like a big one out there."

"Thank you," Ryan and Angie said in near unison. Angie continued, "We're on a bike ride and this is a very welcome break for us. We were about to get soaked."

"Yes," Ryan added, "and we were just looking at these wonderful paintings and carvings. They're really beautiful."

"Thank you," Pastor Gordon said. "They were all done by our parishioners. An exceptionally talented bunch. May I show you a few?"

"Yes, please," Angie said.

Pastor Gordon stepped to the wall just to his right. Ryan and Angie joined him.

"This one," he said, pointing to a large painting just above his eye level, "was painted by Carl Estop. He was a member of the lifesaving service at Big Kinnakeet and a long-time member here."

The painting was an oil on board of a sinking frigate ship. A smaller boat was manned by several men wearing yellow storm jackets. A couple were struggling with long oars, while others were throwing red and white flotation rings to several men in the churning ocean struggling to keep their heads above the crashing waves. A heavenly figure peered down on the scene through the storm clouds above. The expression on his face was ... difficult to interpret.

"Yes," Pastor Gordon said, watching their faces. "I love to ask people what they think God is thinking at that moment. It leads to some interesting discussions and, I think, an interesting sermon or two."

"I'm sure," Angie said. "I'd say he caused the storm, the damage to the ship, and the trauma and maybe death to some of the people. Now he's allowing some of them to be rescued. But they'll probably be scarred by this the rest of their lives."

"Indeed," Pastor Gordon nodded. "And the most interesting discussions are why he'd do that. Why would some people, presumably good men, just doing their job on a ship, have to die? Did they do something to deserve death? Or do people sometimes die ... well, just because of being in the wrong place at the wrong time? We know many men have died just this way right off the beach here before the lifesaving service could get to them."

"I guess that's why people come to church," Ryan said looking at Angie. "To get answers to those kinds of questions."

Pastor Gordon gave a nod of agreement. "We try our best."

Ryan turned to a large cross resting against a corner of the chancel. "Can you tell us about that?"

The building lit up for a few seconds as a bolt of lightning struck near-by. A loud clap of thunder a moment later caused them all to flinch.

"This storm is really a good one," Pastor Gordon said. Then he stepped to the seven-foot tall cross and rested a hand on it. "This was assembled by Henry Peterson. He put it together from timbers washed ashore by a storm, probably a lot like this one. Presumably, they were once part of a ship that met an unfortunate fate out there a few years before. These timbers likely rested on the bottom of the ocean until one storm after another pushed them our way and they finally washed up here in Kinnakeet."

There was no doubt the timbers, probably four-by-fours, were very old. They were pitted, stained a multitude of dark colors, and it was easy to imagine they once had barnacles and other forms of sea life growing on them.

"And over here," Pastor Gordon said, pointing to a much smaller cross perched in front of a stained-glass window, "is a cross made entirely from flotsam and jetsam found on the beach. As you can tell, there are many different objects bound together by wire and glue. Some of these no doubt came from ships, others are just God's natural creations."

He walked to the window and admired the cross, then paused for a moment while a gust of wind shook the building. "And this one," he continued his walk down the aisle to the next window, "was made from seashells."

"Those are really ..." Angie wanted to say beautiful, but couldn't quite get it out. "Unique."

"Yes, many in our congregation are quite good at making things out of what they have at hand. Most of them come from a long line of people who had to learn to make do with what they had. Many of the things that people feel are necessities, or take for granted, are hard to come by here on the island."

Ryan and Angie looked at each other for a moment. Before they could say anything, Pastor Gordon continued.

"These people are a hardy stock. Almost all of them were born here and choose to stay here, even when they could have left the island for ... I guess they say 'greener pastures' elsewhere. They know that life is precious, especially places like this, and they come to the Lord's house to give thanks to God for all his blessings. And," he paused and looked to the heavens as another deafening blast shook the building, "they know not when their time here will end."

"That's certainly true for all of us," Ryan said, nodding. Angie tipped her head in agreement.

"Well folks, feel free to wait out the storm here," Pastor Gordon said, as he stepped through the line of benches to the center aisle. "Stay as long as you want. I've got to go get my dog. He took off with that first blast of thunder. He's a good dog but really scared of loud noises."

"Oh, before you go," Ryan said, looking first at the pastor, then Angie, "could one of us take a picture of you? Maybe next to one of these beautiful crosses?" Angie reached into the pocket of her biking pants.

"Well, of course. Happy to. Do you have a camera with you?"

"Yes, of course," Angie said, waving her cell phone.

Pastor Gordon looked momentarily confused. "Well, I ..."

"Angie will take it," Ryan said. "Maybe step over here with me in front of this one." Ryan led the way to the seashell cross. Pastor Gordon followed. They placed themselves on each side of the window and turned to Angie. She had the picture a moment later.

"Thank you," Angie said, shoving the phone back in her pocket.

"Well, I must go now," Pastor Gordon said as he walked toward the front door. "But before I do, let me say a quick blessing for the two of you and your union."

While Ryan and Angie studied each other with quizzical expressions, Pastor Gordon closed his eyes, silently mouthed a few words, then opened his eyes, and looked toward the heavens.

"Now I must go," he said. He walked to the front door and pushed it open against the wind and stepped outside. A gust slammed the door behind him.

Ryan was the first to speak. He looked a bit beguiled. "That was something. I've never had a union blessed before."

"Yeah. I'd call it a bit bizarre," Angie said, a mischievous look on her face. "We're not even a couple. We've known each other exactly three days. And three days of staring at each other's butts while riding bikes for six or eight hours a day hardly makes us candidates for a union."

"Oh, I don't know ..." Ryan said with a boyish grin.

Angie shook her head but said nothing.

"So, let me take a look out the door and see how much longer this storm is going to last," Ryan said. "It shouldn't be much longer."

A minute later Ryan was back with good news. "I see blue sky just to the west and the wind is starting to die down. We can get back on the bikes in a few minutes."

After ten minutes wandering inside the church looking at the paintings and other religious artifacts, Ryan peeked outside again and gave the all clear. They grabbed their helmets and were back on the bikes and ready to take off a minute later when Angie said, "I could use a drink. My water bottle's been empty since shortly after our lunch stop. Think we could find a place to get a soda or some kind of energy drink?"

"Sure," Ryan said as he pushed off. "We'll find something before we get out of town."

What they found was the Sea Foam Grill. As they took their seats at the bar, the bartender introduced himself as Jeremy. He commented on their biking outfits and Ryan told him that they were part of an eight-person biking group on a five-day ride. The rest of the riders saw the forecast for storms and decided it was a good day to visit the Wright Brothers Memorial and do a little shopping in Kitty Hawk where they'd spent the night. They would ride the support van down to Hatteras where they'd all meet up and spend the night in a B&B.

"A bunch of wimps," Angie added with a chuckle.

After a quick wipe of the bar with a rag, Jeremy asked if they had managed to stay out of the storm. Angie told him they'd just made it to the church at the other end of town and waited it out there. Jeremy grinned, then took their orders. A Coke for Angie and a glass of iced tea for Ryan. As he headed for the fountain, the only other patron, a bearded old man seated at the end of the bar away from the door, turned to look at them. After a moment he moved a few seats closer.

"So," he said as he raised his beer mug and motioned toward them, "did you happen to meet Pastor Gordon?"

"Yes, yes we did," Angie said. "He was very nice and chatted with us for a few minutes and told us to stay safe in the church until the storm ended."

Jeremy arrived with their drinks and paused for a moment after putting them on napkins in front of them. The old man continued.

"And did he say anything by chance about needing to go find his dog who ran away when the thunderstorm started?"

"Yes, as a matter of fact he did," Angie said. She shot a confused look at Ryan, then at the old man. "But ... how would you know that? We didn't see you in there. We thought we were alone."

"Oh, you were alone all right," the old man said. He tipped his mug to them again. After a quick grin at Jeremy he said, "Pastor Gordon is a ghost."

After startled looks at each other, Ryan and Angie turned to Jeremy who nodded at them. "Yep, that's right," he said. "Wanna hear the story?"

Ryan's excited, "Yes!" beat Angie to the punch by a half-second.

"Well, let's see," Jeremy began, as he pulled up a stool and took a seat behind the bar. "Pastor Gordon was the minister at that church for just a couple years, about ..." He pondered the ceiling for a few seconds. "About 90-some years ago now. He was just getting to know the community and the members when, one afternoon, a big thunderstorm pounded our little village. Lots of lightening and thunder, trees getting hit, pretty much like today."

"Yep, just like today," the old man chipped in. He contemplated his almost empty mug for a couple seconds. "Or so they said."

"Anyway," Jeremy continued, after sliding his stool closer to the bar. "There were a handful of parishioners in the building at the time taking shelter.

Then, Pastor Gordon came in from the back and said he couldn't find his dog and thought he'd run away when the thunder started. He said he had to go find him. Several of the parishioners tried to stop him, but he dashed out the front door into the storm. He only made it about 15 feet, right outside the door, when he was struck by lightning. He died on the spot as the people inside the church watched in horror."

"That's awful," Angie said, her voice just a whisper.

"Yep, sure was," Jeremy continued. "And there was a tree just a few feet from him that wasn't hit, but over the next few months it died too. Over the next year or two all the upper limbs fell off, but the trunk stayed the same, just like it is now. Did you happen to notice that tree trunk?"

Ryan glanced at Angie, "We did. It was almost shaped like a person. We thought it was unusual."

"Just like a person," the old man said, nodding.

"Yeah, well, starting the following spring, every now and then, when a bad thunderstorm came up, usually when there was only one or two people in the building, Pastor Gordon would show up. He always greeted the people and welcomed them to the church. Usually, he talked to them about the church or some of the religious art works and things in the building. Then he told them he had to go out and find his dog. Nowadays that happens about once a year when we get the bad storms, like today."

"That's really something," Angie said, with a sideways glance at Ryan.

"Yeah, he seemed so real," Ryan said. When both Jeremy and the old man grinned at him, he added, "He was real."

"Okay," Jeremy said as he turned to walk toward the kitchen. "Not the first time people have thought that. I'm sure it won't be the last."

"Yep," the old man said. "He's a real bon-e-fide ghost. Even had one of those ghost hunting TV shows here once that said that."

Angie shook her head and looked at Ryan. He didn't look at her, but his expression said he was as unconvinced as she was.

The old man got up from his seat. "You all have a good day," he said and moved back to his original seat. Ryan and Angie quickly finished their drinks. Ryan paid the tab and left a generous tip.

As they saddled back up, before they put their helmets on, Ryan said, "Do you suppose everyone here in Kinnakeet likes to tell that tall tale to visitors? Is it like, part of their ... I don't know ... trying to create some special mystical aura or something about this place, or the church?"

Angie nodded her agreement. "Yeah, but probably only to people who are passing through, like us. Or people who took refuge in the church during a storm. That can't be very many people. Other people, who are staying here for a vacation week or something, could always go back to the church when it's not storming and visit with Pastor Gordon again."

"Sounds about right," Ryan said. "I wonder how many people fall for that crap?" He scratched his head for a moment then added, "On the other hand, he was a little odd."

Angie was quick to disagree. "Not that odd, considering he was a man of the cloth. A lot of them are a little strange, in my experience."

Ryan's experience was different, but he liked Angie too much to want to go there. He put his helmet on. Angie put hers on and they pushed off.

A mile down the road Angie abruptly pulled off to the shoulder. She turned to Ryan when he stopped beside her.

"Wait! The picture." she said. "I took that picture of the two of you." She reached into her pocket and pulled out the phone. "We should have showed that to those couple of wise guys." Seconds later she had the photo app open and the picture she took in the church was on the screen. She used her fingers to enlarge the central part.

In the photo, Ryan was smiling brightly next to the seashell cross. There was no one on the other side of the window. Nothing but blank wall. She enlarged it further. Nothing. She looked up at Ryan and passed the phone to him.

As he looked at the photo the smile on his face disappeared. Then he took a second look. He said nothing, then passed the phone back to Angie.

They rode on to Hatteras in silence, each struggling to keep their focus on the road. They easily found the B&B and at the check-in told the group leader, and two other members of their party who were in the adjacent living room, about their ride. They explained they had taken refuge in a church in Kinnakeet when the storm hit. Pastor Gordon was not mentioned. They got their keys and went to their rooms to shower and prepare for dinner.

That evening, sitting in white rocking chairs alone on the front porch of the house, Ryan turned to Angie. "You know, I was really hoping there was something in that blessing of our union. Do you think it could mean something special, coming from a ghost? Maybe he knows something."

Angie turned slowly. She graced him with a cryptic grin. After a moment she said, "Maybe so."

Bernie Lewis

150

152

The Portrait

"I want you to know your job is an impossible one and I'm not happy at all about this."

Kent took a half-step back on the porch and a full breath. "Well, nice to meet you too, Ms. Merk. And now that the pressure is completely off me, may I come in and talk with you for a bit?"

When she pushed the screen door open Kent stepped in. The living room was bright and cheery. Ms. Merk remained the opposite.

She stood directly in front of him and glared. "I told them several times I didn't want to do this. But finally, since everyone insisted I had to, here you are. And here I am. I'm not ready to do this but you can have a seat." She took a breath. "And call me Carol."

After a quick look around, he settled in an old wooden rocking chair with an oak leaf cushion on the seat. Carol continued to stand and stare at him. Her dislike of the situation, and probably of him, was evident from the indignant expression that covered her heavily wrinkled face.

She looked like she'd spent most of her life in the harsh sun without sunscreen, and had the lines and creases to prove that, along with numerous scars and pockmarks left over from years of battling an unfortunate case of adolescent, and probably adult, acne. She was going to be a real challenge.

"Thank you, Carol. And please call me Kent. I'm sure you know I'm here to do a photo portrait for the book."

"I do. And I'm sure you know by now since you've had a chance to look at me that taking a picture of me that will in any way enhance the back cover of the book or encourage sales is impossible. There has never been a good photograph of me, and I seriously doubt you're going to be able to take one today. I asked them to just use a photo of my husband and leave me out, but the powers that be convinced our agent that I had to do this."

Kent both genuinely felt and tried to look empathetic. "I understand how you feel. If I was in your situation, I'm sure I wouldn't be happy about this either." He nodded and offered her a tepid smile. "But, I think I'm up to the task. Sometimes the camera, with just a little help from the software program, can do wonders. And ... I always make it a policy to show the images to my client as we go along so they can see how they look in the camera's eye and work with me to get something we're both happy with. After all, I may take two or three hundred images today and we're looking for only one that you like, I like, and ultimately, the publisher likes."

She shook her head. Her expression softened a touch, but her voice didn't. "I'm still not at all sure that's possible. And by the way, how were you chosen as the lucky one for this assignment?"

Kent took that question as a step in the right direction. "I think several things went into that. First, I've worked a few times before with the publisher and I think they liked my work. The last few shoots they've trusted me to select the image that I think is the best one. Secondly, I live about three hours from here, in the Tidewater area, so I'm fairly local. And thirdly, I was available on short notice. I just got the call two days ago. I think they're in a bit of a hurry to get this done."

"Yeah, I'm sure they are," she muttered. Then a bit louder she said, "Two days ago is when I finally gave in. They've been after me for three weeks. They essentially said now or never. Meaning, I think, if I didn't agree to do the picture the book publishing deal was off. That's very unreasonable, but that's the way they run things. So, here we are." Her hands were firmly planted on her hips and her eyes were cold and hard.

"Yes, here we are," Kent acknowledged. "And I'm sure we can make this work. By the end of the day, I think you'll feel good about what we've done." She gave no acknowledgement. Kent figured a shift in direction was called for.

"Maybe it would be helpful if you could tell me a little about the book. The director of photography at the publisher told me nothing about it. That might give us both some sense of direction about what kind of photos we should be thinking about."

She looked at him with a pained expression, but he knew she was considering his suggestion. She looked out the window for a full thirty seconds then quickly wiped her eyes. "I guess we should do that, but you'll have to give me a minute."

Without looking at him, she hurried down the hallway toward the back of the house. In the bathroom she threw two hands full of water in her face, then looked at herself in the mirror.

"Pull yourself together," she demanded before grabbing a towel and drying off. She stared at her reflection for another few seconds before she shook her head, shrugged her shoulders, and headed back down the hall. When she got to the living room, she took a seat in the upholstered wingback across from her guest. It looked to Kent like she tried to smile but couldn't quite get there.

"Okay," she said, leaning slightly forward. "First, let me say I'm sorry. I've been going through a difficult time. You didn't deserve that anger and that's not the usual me. Let's start over."

Kent rocked forward and smiled. "Great. Apology accepted. No problem. Are you ready to talk about the book, or ..."

"I'm ready," she said. "I hope this isn't going to take all day, for both of our sakes, so let's get on with it."

He nodded and planted his hands on his legs. "So, what kind of book is it?"

She looked over his shoulder out the window again. "It's a book designed to help people get a grip on their lives. To find a way to a simpler, more satisfying life. A life with more enjoyment and appreciation of the little things, the many things around us that we should be taking time to notice and enjoy instead of killing ourselves with the rat race." She focused on him for a moment. "Not exactly the kind of book you expected from the crazy lady you met a few minutes ago, I'm sure."

He shrugged his shoulders. "No, I really didn't know what to expect. I'm ... It sounds great."

"Well," she said, looking away from him again, "it's a book my husband, Harvey, and I have worked on for the last five years. It's been a world of work, and we've put our heart and soul into it."

"That's great," Kent said. "But now I'm curious. Is there some reason I'm not making a portrait of your husband too?"

She looked at the wall to her left where the image of a smiling, gray-haired man greeted them from the frame. "Harvey died just two months ago. It's been very difficult for me since then. He was the love of my life and the driving force behind this book. He was also the one who dealt with the agent and the publisher a lot more than I did."

"Oh, I'm so sorry," Kent said. "I can see why this is such a difficult time for you."

"Yeah, well, I tried to convince them to just make Harvey the sole author, or at least just use a picture of him, but they've refused. Getting this thing published at this point is kind of a tribute to him. I feel like I've got to do it. The only thing they agreed to was that I didn't have to do a studio portrait. I could do something more casual, since they're going to have to use that one up on the wall as the picture of him." She turned to study the photograph of her husband sitting on the steps of their back porch.

Kent got out of his chair and examined the photo for several seconds before returning to his seat. "Great, we can certainly do something that will go well alongside that one. I like casual portraits much better than studio ones anyway. That's probably another reason I was asked to do this."

"Well, I still think you've got your work cut out for you. This face does not photograph well. Trust me, after all these years I should know."

Kent took a moment to study her face. Other than the skin, it was a good one. He'd done many portraits over the last 17 years and thought the basic structure of her face, the high cheekbones, the jaw line, the lips, the nose, and especially the bright blue eyes, were the kind that photographed well. The short white hair provided a lovely frame for her face. The skin, on the other hand, was most unfortunate.

"Challenge accepted," he said. He looked around the room, then out the window for a moment. "Can we talk a bit about where to take the photo?"

"Okay. I guess."

"Great. Since the photo of your husband was taken outdoors, I think we should be thinking outdoors as well. There are some great backgrounds in this room, but I'd really like to work outside. From what I saw as I drove in, I bet there are lots of good spots right around here we could use."

"That's fine with me. I'd prefer something with a good bit of background in it rather than a closeup of my face. I'm sure the publisher would too if they want to sell any books."

"We can do that. It probably should have about the same proportions as the photo of your husband. And since he's dressed casually, you probably should be too."

"Good. I did give a little bit of thought to that. Should I go change now?"

"Sure, that would be fine. We might try a couple of different outfits as we go along, maybe a change at the mid-way point, but start with whatever you like best. I'll step outside for a moment and take a look around while you're doing that."

She rose from her chair. He rocked forward then pushed himself out of his.

"You go right ahead. Just about everything you can see from the back porch to the sound is our property. So anyplace you like will be fine."

"We'll probably shoot at several spots, but I'll take a look."

She disappeared down the hallway as he let himself out the front door. After walking around the house, Kent identified several locations that looked good to him—the pier sticking out to the water, the grove of old oak trees down the path a ways, and the rocking chair on the front porch.

He was getting his equipment out of the trunk of his car when she appeared on the porch. It struck him that her brown jeans, blue cotton button-up shirt, and hiking boots were probably her daily wear here, but they looked clean, and the shirt was recently ironed.

He gathered his gear and met her on the porch. She'd brushed her hair, but it didn't look like she'd applied any make-up. He guessed she'd probably given up on that long ago, but it might have helped some. He directed her to the white wooden rocking chair and began setting up.

"Why don't you tell me a little more about the book while I'm getting ready," he said. "Like, exactly what kinds of things do you recommend for people?"

She settled into the chair and turned at a slight angle to face him. A perfect pose to start off with. "Okay ... A lot of the book is aimed at convincing people to slow down and improve the quality of their lives, not the speed. So many people are rushing, rushing to do more, accumulate more, see more, and not enjoying life as it speeds by. We would like to help people adopt the attitude that the goal of life is not to acquire, but to become."

"Sounds good to me," Kent said. He had the light stanchion in place and was attaching the camera to the tripod. "But, to become what?"

"Basically, to become at peace with the world around you. At peace with your family members. And first and foremost, at peace with yourself. The others are kind of dependent on that."

"Probably a tall order for a lot of people," Kent said, as he adjusted the tripod so the camera was at her eye level.

"Yes, and they should all buy this book," Carol said, with the first almost-smile he'd seen. The smile was not necessarily a good look for her. It seemed to increase the number and depth of wrinkles, especially around her mouth and eyes.

Kent adjusted the light to the best angle for the chair she was in. Balancing the flash and the natural sunlight was going to be his biggest challenge, besides getting her to relax and look comfortable. He set the camera to silent shooting mode then asked her to close her eyes, imagine herself in a peaceful, idyllic scene, and when she felt at peace to open her eyes. It took almost five minutes.

The tension in her face made her look far from being at peace with herself, but he shot a few dozen images over the next several minutes, directing her to small adjustments in the angle of her face and where she settled her eyes. It was immediately clear that looking straight into the lens was not going to work. She was one of those people for whom looking into the lens of a camera was like looking into the barrel of a gun.

After getting all that he could from this spot on the porch he knew there was unlikely to be an image that would please her, or him. He decided they needed to move. He asked her to walk with him to the back of the house. On the way he asked, "So, how are people supposed to get to a place of being at peace with themselves?"

Her response came slowly. "That's a little bit individualized ... I mean, it depends a lot on their individual situation. But, slowing down, letting go of conflict, and taking a serious look at priorities are the kind of things we talk about in the book. There's a chapter on each of those in there. Most people just don't know how to be happy in their lives. Even those on a good track are usually trying to *pursue* happiness instead of just slowing themselves down and *experiencing* happiness."

"That's probably difficult for people in high pressure jobs and with big families to support."

"It certainly is. But one of the things we talk about is the importance of finding pleasure in your job, whether that's in Wall Street high finance or taking care of a home and children. If you're willing to work at it, and truly want to be healthy and happy, there will be a way. Thousands and even millions of people have done it—gone from depression and living every day in anger and frustration to making a happy life for themselves. We cite quite a few examples in the book of people who've made amazing transformations."

Kent let that settle in as they walked in silence across the lawn and a short distance to the sound. There were a few clouds in the sky and the light was good. Kent positioned her initially several feet away from the pier and set the camera to an f-stop of 4.0 to let the background blur. He thought the clouds in the sky would look nice framing her blue shirt and help her blue eyes pop. He set up the light then talked her through several poses.

He looked at a couple of the images on the back of the camera, then had her walk to the pier for several more. She was getting more comfortable, but not much. He moved her to the end of the pier. He decided to try to get her to express several different emotions; a favorite technique that usually resulted in good images. "Look happy ... now look pensive ... now try excited ... now let me see relieved ... now proud."

He snapped away at each look. He was getting some variety, but what he was seeing on the viewer on the back of the camera didn't thrill him. He helped her to a sitting position on the pier, had her brush her hair back a bit, and took a dozen more shots. He called for a break and looked at his watch. It was already a little after noon.

"How about we take a break for lunch then try for a few more after? I'll make a quick run into Kinnakeet and grab a bite then meet you back here."

"Nonsense," she said. "I'll fix us some lunch at the house." She turned and walked away.

It was a 10-minute drive to town, and he figured a little extra time talking with her might help her get more comfortable for the afternoon shoot, so he gathered his gear and followed her back to the house. He left the light and tripod on the porch but carried the camera inside.

She directed him to a seat at the kitchen table and poured them both a glass of water. While she fixed ham sandwiches, he scanned the images on the screen of his camera. He deleted about 90 percent of them after an initial look. She made a couple passes behind him to peek over his shoulder and see what he was doing.

"See what I mean?" she said after the second look. "I told you it was impossible."

He glanced briefly at her then back at the screen. "Not at all. This is what I always do. I'm narrowing the possibilities down to the best ones. No use uploading ones into the computer I'm not going to consider and looking at them again. This is a great time saver." He spent a couple more minutes on his task while she got the sandwiches ready and brought them to the table. She added a bag of potato chips and a bowl of apple sauce for each of them.

"The apple sauce is from our little orchard at the house we owned in upstate New York," Carol said as she took her seat. "When we sold the house, the new owners agreed to let us pick a couple of bushels every year. We made a trip back there, picked the apples, and made apple sauce every August." She slowly shook her head and looked at the bowl. "Guess we won't be doing that this year."

Kent seized on the opportunity to keep her talking. "Can you tell me a little more about your husband?" The sandwich was exceptional—some kind of different mustard on it. Maybe maple.

Carol took her first bite and a swallow of water before she answered. "We were married 51 years. He was in the corporate world for the first 30. A financial planner in New York City. Handled a lot of high-net-worth clients. He reached a point where he couldn't stand it anymore. So he quit, and we started working on just being happy. We bought this place two years later and started caring for it. We discovered we both loved being at the beach and doing all the work this little place demands. The friends he made over the years at work, and some of my friends, began coming down here to visit. When they saw how we were living, and how happy we were, several of them wanted to do the same. He started helping them work through the tough decisions they needed to make to break free and start the process of being happy, and that led to his small consulting business. Eventually that led to the book."

"You had a really good thing going here."

"Yes, we did." Her eyes glistened. "There's something about living by the ocean, especially here in Kinnakeet, that helps people get to that calm, almost spiritual place."

They ate in silence for a couple minutes.

She ate half her sandwich, didn't touch the chips, but ate all the apple sauce. Kent finished his meal with the apple sauce and thought it was the best he'd ever tasted. He told her so.

"Thank you," she said. "It's made from a very old variety of apple. It's not grown much anymore, and no one replaced the old trees with new ones when they died, except us. Other varieties are easier to care for and are more popular. There were just a few trees left when we took over the orchard, but we managed to keep it going."

She stared out the kitchen window and drifted away for a few seconds. When she came back her eyes were glazed.

"He told me he loved me every day since about a year before we got married," she said. "Actually, it was several times a day. He also told me every day that I was beautiful. Can you believe that? With this face?" She looked into Kent's eyes and her voice faded to a whisper. "He thought I was beautiful."

He saw the moisture in her eyes turn to tears as she pushed her chair back and jumped to her feet. "Excuse me," she muttered as she hurried toward the hall, her hands covering her face. She returned five minutes later.

"Sorry about that," she said as she sat back down. "Obviously it's going to be a while still before I can deal with losing him." She grabbed a napkin from the holder on the table and touched her eyes. "It's just that he always told me he loved me for who I was, and that the total ... package of me was special and beautiful ... And that made my face beautiful, to him, even as it got uglier and more wrinkled over the years." She dabbed again.

Kent just looked at her for a moment. He wanted to tell her she wasn't ugly, but quickly realized a debate on that topic was likely, and was one he had no chance to win. Instead, he said, "Love can make anyone look beautiful."

She half-smiled. "That ... Thank you for that. He was always beautiful to me."

She got up from the table and cleared their dishes. When she finished, he pulled her chair close to his and beckoned her back to the table. "I want to show you some of the images from this morning," he said.

She sat back down, and he placed the camera on the table between them. He worked the buttons on the back. As the images flashed by on the screen, he stopped on four to let her examine them. He explained to her why he thought each one could be usable and how he would soften her skin with the software. Her reaction to each was the same. "Oh no! Not that one. I look so old and ugly."

After she had rejected each of the four, she rose from her chair, walked to the sink, and stared out the window for a few seconds. When she turned back to the room she leaned against the sink.

"I don't think I can do any more today. I know what you have isn't any good, but I don't think you're going to get anything better this afternoon the way I'm feeling. No use putting you through it, and I just can't put any more effort into trying to look presentable for a stupid picture."

He tried for a moment to figure out how to counter her position and get her outside for at least a few more shots. Then he realized that given her mood, anything he could say, or do, was unlikely to make much difference.

"Okay. I understand. I'll tell the publisher that the lighting wasn't any good or that a storm came up or ... well, I'll come up with something. Maybe we can try again in a couple days."

She was shaking her head. "I don't think so. A couple days isn't going to make any difference. Maybe I'll call our agent tomorrow and see if there's any other way. Worst case scenario the book just doesn't get published and I guess that's not the end of the world."

Kent certainly didn't like the idea of failure. He'd never had an assignment end with the client refusing to cooperate. He knew a part of him would feel responsible if the book deal fell apart, and the publisher would probably never use him again. But everything inside him said it was time to grant her wish and bow out gracefully.

Before he could respond, she added, "All I want to do right now is walk over to our special spot and spend some time with him. I've been doing that every day, and it's about the only thing that makes me feel a little better."

He nodded, said, "I understand," and grabbed his camera. They walked together to the door. He held it open for her and followed her out to the porch. As they paused for a moment, he asked, "May I walk with you? I'd like to pay my respects to your husband before I leave."

She turned to stare at him for a moment then said, "I guess. But maybe just stay for a minute or two. I like to be there with him for a while and talk to him. I need to be alone for that."

"Sure. No problem. I can respect that." He looked at the light stand and tripod and decided he'd get them to the car when he came back. He put the camera strap around his neck.

She led the way to the back of the house. Then down a narrow stretch of sand along the edge of the sound for a couple hundred yards. They came to an old grove of live oak trees at the edge of the water. Their twisted trunks and branches stretched every direction. Several touched the ground. They bore many scars from their years of struggle with coastal storms and salt water from the sound. They looked almost like a grove of ancient bonsai trees.

As Carol reached the edge of the grove, she said, "This was our place. We'd walk down here almost every day. Sometimes at sunrise, often at sunset." She took another couple steps and rested her hand against one of the biggest and most scarred trees.

"This was our tree," she said. She stepped carefully around the protruding roots and stood with one arm around the trunk. "We marked it as ours the very first time we came down here. We fell in love with it immediately."

When Kent stepped closer, she showed him the small carving about four feet from the ground. His and her initials embraced by a heart. "We were pretty sure it wouldn't hurt a tree this old and this grand, and obviously it didn't."

Kent stepped back toward the water while Carol gave the tree a kiss. She stood for a moment with one arm around the trunk while she gently stroked the carving with the other.

After a glance to the heavens, she closed her eyes, bowed her head, and appeared to say a brief silent prayer. When she opened her eyes, she looked momentarily at Kent, then settled to her knees. She put both arms around the tree and again closed her eyes. A stratus cloud drifted over the sun.

Kent saw it coming. As he watched, the lines on Carol's face faded and the pockmarks waned. Where there had been tension, there was now calm. Where there was pain, there was now peace. Her face softened more than he would have imagined possible, and the filtered light gave her leathery skin an almost soft, golden glow. For a moment, he could imagine what Harvey probably saw every day they were together.

He remembered the camera hanging from his neck, grabbed it, and brought it up quickly. He fell to his knees, then to his elbows, and put his eye to the viewfinder just as she opened her eyes and looked at him. There was just time for one silent click of the shutter. Her arms were around their tree, her loving eyes were on the camera, and the gnarled tree trunks in the near distance provided the perfect background.

He got to his feet and whispered an unobtrusive goodbye. She acknowledged him with a slight nod as he headed back toward the house. Twenty minutes later he had his equipment in the car and was on his way home.

When he set up in front of his computer that evening, he uploaded the handful of remaining images from the day. He was almost afraid to look at the last one. He was afraid the camera couldn't capture what his eye saw.

But it did.

With only a minor crop he saved it to the hard drive on the computer, then saved it again on a flash drive to be safe.

He sent it via email, with a brief note, to the publisher, then sent it to Carol. At a quarter after nine the next morning he got a message back from the publisher.

"Perfect. We love it."

Ten minutes later he got a message from Carol that meant a lot more.

"You did the impossible. Thank you."

Titanic

"Are you ready to do this?" Lauren asked, stepping into the bedroom that seemingly had not changed in the last eight years. She saw the same curtains, same bedspread, same furniture, but definitely a lot more dust. A different smell that was hard to identify, but not pleasant.

"I think we've got to. Now or later. Might as well hit it now." Greg was a step behind her and stood in the doorway while his eyes and nose adjusted. "This room brings back a ton of memories. Dad, and Mom too. She would have been appalled to see it like this."

"I'm sure. I guess after she died he just didn't care about this room anymore. It was just a place to sleep. Obviously, he didn't entertain any other ladies in this room." She glanced quickly at the unmade bed and wondered how many times it had been made, or the sheets changed, in eight years. "At least I hope not."

Greg chuckled. "Probably not. So, where do you want to start?"

"I guess the closet. I'll bring some of the boxes in and we can just put the shoes and clothes in them then get them to some charity. Other things can go in a trash can. I've got one for paper and one for other stuff. Unless there's something you see that you want."

"Unlikely," Greg said as Lauren left the room. Five minutes later he was on his knees pulling shoes, dust bunnies, and other long-lost items out of the closet floor, tossing them behind him for Lauren to box up or trash.

They had already worked on the kitchen and the living room. Three other bedrooms and the recreation room would take their turn tomorrow. Fortunately, their father had not been too much of a packrat. They had helped him clean a few things out after their mother died.

The sibling relationship had held up well through the stress of the funeral and the start-up work on cleaning out the house, even though this was only the third time they had seen each other in the past five years. They'd only had one brief disagreement—over the photo albums their mother had compiled over the years.

"Here's the safe," Greg said, his head nearing the back left corner.

"Can you pull it out?"

"I think so. It's not that heavy." He got his hands behind it and pulled. It moved six inches. Thirty seconds later it was clear of the closet. "Do you want to open it now or later?" he asked.

Lauren pondered for a moment. She had a pretty good idea what was in it. More so than her brother, she was the one her father confided in about financial issues and the few other confidential matters in his life. "I think later. Let's keep working on this. We just got started. I'll get the combination when we take a break."

Greg nodded his agreement and cleared out a stack of old papers, the rest of the shoes, and dusty coat hangers from the bottom of the closet, then got to his feet and began handing Lauren the pants and shirts. With that completed, he took sweaters and vests from the shelf above, most of them probably unworn and untouched in many years. In the back corner his hand hit something hard. He grabbed it and pulled it out.

"Hey, look at this." He held a pair of old drumsticks secured together with a long piece of masking tape, with two envelopes scotch-taped tightly to them. One of the envelopes said, "Open Me First." The other said, "Open Me Second." He handed them to Lauren. "This is curious. Feel like taking a break?"

"Sure, I'm ready." She examined the sticks and envelopes. "Did Dad play the drums?"

"Not that I know of," Greg said as he stepped around the trashcans and boxes in the floor and sat on the bed. Lauren had him stand, threw the bedspread from the floor over the sheets, then joined him when he sat back down.

"You do the honors," Lauren said, handing the sticks to her brother.

He stripped off the two envelopes and the masking tape, put the drumsticks and envelope number two on the bed between them, then carefully opened the other one. He pulled out several sheets of white paper with small cursive writing stretched across each page. The handwriting was not familiar, and there was no date or salutation like one would expect on a letter. He handed the pages to Lauren. "Here, you can decipher them better than I can. Your eyes still work." She smiled and accepted the papers.

She thumbed quickly through them then looked at the last page. "These are from Grandpa." she said.

"You mean Grandpa Colin, the one that lived with us for a while?"

"Apparently so. I think that's his signature there." She pointed to the bottom of the last page where Colin Stewart was scribbled.

"I think you're right," Greg said after a quick look. "I'm dying to see what this is. Maybe he was the drum player."

Lauren turned back to the first page and began to read out loud.

I got on the Titanic pretty much by accident. The guy who was supposed to play the drums for the band chickened out the day before the launch. I knew one of the violin players, so he asked me if I wanted the job. I was only 16 but I said yes and was ready to go. My mum didn't like the idea, but ships were crossing the Atlantic every week from Southampton and the Titanic was supposedly unsinkable. The next morning, I grabbed my sticks and my bag and snuck down to the dock and got on.

"Did you know that Grandpa was on the Titanic?" Greg asked, his voice exposing his bewilderment.

"No clue," Lauren replied. "The main thing I remember about him was that he was just a grouchy old man during the time he lived with us. Not very nice at all."

"Yeah, that's my memory too. Mom and Dad always said he was really old and we just needed to ignore him but be nice to him. I never heard anything about the Titanic."

"He lived with us about two years before he died. Is that right?"

"I think so. I was nine, so you would have been seven when he came. I'm not sure anybody liked him very much. Not even Dad. I don't remember him talking very much about his father. I think he was out of his life for at least some of his childhood." Greg frowned and shook his head. "The only good memory I have of him is the one time he took me to the beach so I could fish. He lasted only about 20 minutes then we had to come home. He was a weird old man."

Lauren nodded and looked back at the pages. "Yes, he was." She read on.

All of us in the band were put in second class cabins on the middle deck. It was better than steerage which I heard wasn't as bad as on most ships. I shared a room with Jock. He was from Southampton too. Our room was nothing like all those rich people in first class. They said it was like a luxury hotel up there. They even had a gym and swimming pool! We had about 2,200 people all together. After a brief stop in Ireland, we set sail for New York.

White Star had a playbook for the band that had about 200 songs in it. I knew only a couple. I had played with a small band at home, but we played ragtime not waltzes and operas and such. They did have a couple of rags in the book so I could do okay on them but the other stuff I had to learn. The head of the band was one of the violin players and he told me to just play soft. I pretended I could read music, but I was just really trying to follow the rest of the guys, which is kind of hard to do on the drums.

By the evening of the iceberg four days later, I was getting pretty good. We were only playing about 25 of the songs so I was catching on. Some of them I never knew the names of because the leader would say "Number 22" and all the guys would just take off playing. We played every afternoon and evening in the first-class dining room and lounge. Some other places too. We had the mornings off and mostly slept and played cards.

We hit the iceberg late at night. We were finishing up playing in the first-class lounge when we felt something. It took a while for things to really happen and probably an hour or so before the ship really began to lean. That's when we knew we were in trouble. Before that the crew was just trying to keep everyone calm and not saying much about what was happening. We just kept playing for a while, then when everyone left we moved up to the upper deck but stayed together. I left the drums behind of course but took my sticks.

Things were a real mess up there. It was clear that there weren't enough lifeboats. They were letting only women and children on the boats, but a few older men snuck on. Then later some of the first-class men got on. The boats would hold about 40 but some of them were lowered with only 15 or 20 in them. As the ship sank lower in the water the stern began to rise, and people were sliding everywhere. Lots were falling or jumping into the water. The screaming was awful.

We were having trouble standing up, but the band leader told us to play one more song. We played "Nearer My God To Thee." I kept the beat with my sticks on the rail beside us. After that it was every man for himself, and we just tried to find something to hang on to.

At just about the last minute, I jumped into the water. I was wearing a life jacket and holding my sticks. I was scared to death. I never felt anything so cold! I thought my heart would explode. I floated for a few minutes trying to find something to grab on to but then felt like I was dying. All around me people were going down one by one.

The next thing I remember I was on one of the lifeboats and someone was trying to pull the sticks out of my hands. I wouldn't let go. I was crowded on the floor of the boat with a couple other people they had picked up. I remember feet were all around us and on top of us.

It was 2 or 3 hours later when the Carpathia showed up and took us on board. Someone wrapped me in a blanket and tried to take my sticks away. I wouldn't let them. I held on to those sticks like I was holding on to life. To me I guess that's what I was doing because I was really weak and freezing cold. But I warmed up after a while.

We got to New York in 3 days and people there were very nice and helpful. They gave us food and clothes and places to stay at night. There were people trying to interview everyone, but I just kept to myself and didn't talk to no one. I didn't want to go back home. There was no way I was ever getting on a boat again or going out on that ocean!

I stayed in New York for a few weeks with a family that took me in. They were nice and gave me everything I needed. All I wanted to do was forget the Titanic and that horrible night, but I took those sticks everywhere I went. I played with a little ragtime band for a while but that was going nowhere. So, I left New York and just began traveling in the United States. I never let my mum know I survived, so she probably thought I died like most of the men on the ship and all of my bandmates.

Even when I got away from New York I kept running into reminders of the Titanic. There were postcards of the ship everywhere. There kept being articles in the newspapers which I never bought but I saw the headlines. It was like the sinking of the Titanic was the biggest story of the century.

So now I'm quite a few years older and have traveled all over the U.S. I've still got those sticks, and they mean the world to me. I feel like I owe my life to them though it's hard to explain. I still get scared whenever I have to cross a body of water bigger than a river but even the Mississippi made me afraid the two times I crossed it. I just held those sticks tight to my chest until I got all the way across.

I guess that's it
Colin Stewart

"Wow!" Lauren looked at Greg after she flipped the last page over. "That's really something. Who knew there was a survivor of the Titanic living right here in Kinnakeet? I remember reading something about a radio operator somewhere around Kinnakeet picking up a distress signal coming from the Titanic and relaying it on somewhere, but no one paid any attention to it. And our grandfather was out there on that ship! Then he lived the last years of his life right by that ocean! The things you never know about someone."

"And these are the drumsticks," Greg picked them up and studied them. "These were on the Titanic and in the Atlantic Ocean with him. His hands were gripping these the whole time he was in the water and even after he was rescued." He ran his fingers up and down, feeling the rough texture.

Lauren took the sticks, examined them for a few seconds, then played an imaginary drum with them. "I think after that they were like a security blanket to him. Something he always kept with him."

"Apparently, he kept them right up 'till he moved in here with us. And Dad kept them, and this letter, even after he died. I guess he wanted one of us to have them, even though he never told us about them. He figured we'd find them after he died, just like we did."

"You know what surprises me?" Lauren said.

"No. What?"

"That Grandpa never sold these. I think artifacts from the Titanic, even things like jewelry and things that were just on the ship, are pretty valuable. And these were part of the band that played that last song. They feature that in every book and movie about the Titanic."

"I guess that is a surprise," Greg said, taking the sticks back. "I think he was pretty poor when he came to live with us. I got the impression he was coming here because he had no home and nowhere else to go. These sticks must have been more valuable to him than any money they would have brought."

"So ..." Lauren grabbed the sticks again. "The question becomes, who gets them? The will says everything is to be divided equally. There's nothing specific about these."

"I guess that means we could each have one stick. But I don't like that. And that still leaves the letter. But I guess we could make a copy of the letter. Too bad he didn't put a date on it."

"I don't like that either," Lauren said as she passed the sticks back to her brother. "I think you should have them. You're the male lineage after all. Grandpa to Dad, to you, then you can leave them to Gary."

"Are you sure?"

Lauren smiled and nodded. "Yeah, I am. They're yours, big brother. It was just nice to share this discovery with you. Probably the highlight of this whole funeral and house cleaning out weekend."

"Thanks. You always were a good sister." Greg put the sticks back on the bed, on top of the other envelope, and they hugged. "Think we should open envelope number two now?"

"Let's do it," Lauren said. "After the first one, I'm really curious about what's in that one." She grabbed the envelope and carefully opened it. Cautiously, she extracted several typewritten pages then flipped quickly to the last one. "These are from Dad," she announced. Greg nodded and Lauren began to read.

In writing this letter I'm going to assume that Greg and/or Lauren, hopefully both of you, are reading this after my death and after opening and reading the note in the first envelope. This will only make sense that way.

First of all, I love both of you very much. I'm doing this thing with the drumsticks this way in hope you will get a laugh out of it and understand the dynamics between me and my father a little better.

The main thing you need to know is that your grandfather, Colin Stewart, as we knew him, was a con man and a fraud. The note you just read about the drumsticks is all bullshit. The drumsticks themselves are a fraud. He was not on the Titanic. His real name was not Colin Stewart.

Lauren stopped and looked at Greg with just a touch of a smile on her lips. "Well, what do you know?"

"I wouldn't have guessed that. The letter was pretty convincing," Greg said. "But maybe I'm not too surprised. Go on." He pointed to the pages.

My father was born and raised somewhere in the Midwest, according to my mother. His name was Billy Stewart. He was a drifter much of his life and met my mother when he was 22 and she was 18. They spent a few weeks together and I was the result. He left when he found out she was pregnant.

After I was born, he would stop by to see my mother and me when he passed through town, riding the trains. I grew up knowing who my father was but seeing him only once or twice a year, usually for just a few days. My mother let him back into the house, and her bed, whenever he came through. As I got older, I understood he was coming to see her more than me.

I don't know how he was supporting himself during those years, probably a lot of it was illegal, but I remember him talking about working every now and then at menial jobs, like dishwashing or on a farm. He always seemed to have money for alcohol. My guess is that he would work a while and then travel on the train for a while. A real hobo. He talked about that part of the story once in a while.

When I left home after high school, as you know, I went to college at the University of Kentucky and then graduate school at Indiana State. I heard from him once during those years – a phone call. My mother gave him my number. The next time I saw him was at my mother's funeral. I don't know how he heard she died. I didn't talk to him much then. It's possible he was with her or nearby and somehow got word when she died. Your mother went with me to the funeral, but I didn't introduce them. She asked me later who that man was, and I told her.

As I think you can understand, I had little interest in seeing him or talking to him after my mother was gone. Your mom was probably more interested in him, and what was going on in his life, than I was.

Once you two were born, and I got the job in Wilmington, he showed up a couple times. I'd let him stay for a day or two, but that was all I could take.

Your mom put up with him very well, and he was pretty nice to her.

Then, one day, after I got the principal job in Buxton and moved here, he showed up and told me he was down and out, probably dying, and needed a place to stay. I was conflicted about what to do, but your mom, the angel that she was, insisted he had to stay with us. That's when he moved in, and you may have some memories of him from that time. He was drinking regularly then, and it turned out he did have liver cancer.

We got him treatment for the cancer up in Nags Head as much as we could. It was rough, and we tried to keep a lot of that away from you two. Your mom took good care of him, and then we got him in a nursing home when he really started to fade. He died there.

Now to the crux of the story.

One night, shortly after he moved in with us, he got roaring drunk and started talking about how stupid people were. He kept reminding us that P.T. Barnum supposedly said, "There's a sucker born every minute." That led to his staggering to his room and coming back with the drumsticks and note you just read. Then he told us the story.

Somewhere along the line he heard people talking about the Titanic and how everything connected with it was valuable. So, he came up with this story about being on the Titanic and playing the drums in the band. Apparently, as he talked about it with some of his buddies, he worked out the details and had someone write out the note you read. He changed his first name from Billy to Colin because he thought it sounded more British and would fit better with the story he made up. He insisted everyone call him Colin, including me and my mother, because he had grown to like it. He figured he could sell the drumsticks and the note with them as kind of a form of verification.

He found a music store and bought a pair of drumsticks, then dirtied them up really good, soaked them in saltwater for a while, and started looking for his first sucker.

He said before he made the first sale, he realized it didn't have to be a one-time thing, so he made several copies of the letter in case his scheme actually worked. It did. He said he sold the first set of drumsticks with the note for $20.00, a lot of money back in that day. He wasn't sure when that was but guessed it may have been around 1945. He said he came up with a really good story about why he was ready to part with them. He went out as soon as he could to get more drumsticks and started dirtying them up to get them ready. He thought maybe he'd sold 15 or 20 sets of sticks over the years. He got $300.00 for the last set.

I remember seeing a bunch of drumsticks once when he visited my mother and me, and I asked him about them. He said he was learning to play the drums and was thinking about settling down and joining a band. That was one of about a million lies he told me over the years.

After he told us the story about being on the Titanic, I got interested. With the help of the library staff at Hatteras, I read a lot of things over the years about the ship and the sinking. Among the things I learned was that there was no drummer in the band on the Titanic. There were three cellists, three violin players, one bassist, and one piano player. They usually played in groups of five or three. It is questionable whether they played "Nearer My God to Thee" as the last song; that may be more of a myth than a fact.

Also, there was one passenger with the last name Stewart. He was Albert Stewart, 54 years old, and from

America, travelling back home to Ohio. He died and his body was never recovered.

All these tidbits were available to the general public years before your grandfather started his con. Anyone who was seriously interested in buying artifacts from the Titanic certainly would have read any number of the books, each of which discussed the musicians, and a couple of which published a passenger list. Therefore, it is certain the people he was selling to were not serious collectors, but rather people he met in his travels, or "suckers" as he so delightfully referred to them. Thankfully, you are not likely to see any of his drumsticks in museums or hear about them in private collections.

So, there you go. A little family history you need not pass along to anyone else. Just thought you would enjoy the story. Do what you wish with the drumsticks.

Love you both.

Dad

April 12, 1997

Lauren dropped the pages in her lap and turned to Greg, her head shaking. "Oh my God."

Greg nodded, then shook his head. They stared at each other for a few seconds.

"Well, big brother," Lauren finally said, "the drumsticks are yours. What do you want to do with them?"

He sat in silence, thinking. Finally, "We said we'd have a fire in the fireplace tonight to burn some of Dad's old papers and records from years ago. Maybe the sticks can join them. I might want to keep the two letters. At least for now."

"Sounds good to me," Lauren said as she picked up the drumsticks from the bed and tossed them into the paper-filled trash can.

Reunion

"I'll bet you twenty dollars you don't remember me."

She'd been watching him chitchat his way across the front campus yard for twenty minutes. When he finally got to her, she figured that was a better opening line than, "Gee, you've gained a lot of weight," which was her first impression.

"I, uh, ... probably shouldn't take that bet," he muttered after a few seconds of studying her. He thought she was cute, in a decade of success has been good to her sort of way. "But you shouldn't take that too personally, since I don't remember about ninety-five percent of the people here."

"Not surprising," she said with a single nod, careful to hide the touch of disappointment. "I'm Izzy."

"Cal," he said, moving in for a hug which she dodged.

"Yeah, I know." She put her hand out for a fist pump. "We were in a couple classes together our senior year."

"I wish I remembered you." He studied her again. He should have been able to remember the green eyes. He had a thing about women with green eyes. "But I spent most of that year either high or drunk. Actually, I spent all four years that way. It's a miracle I graduated." There was something about her, but he wasn't sure what. After a swig of water, he nodded at her. "You look like you've done well since graduation."

"I have. Put my years here to good use." Unlike you, she thought, from the looks of him. The, 'I don't give a shit' look didn't wear as well now as ten years ago.

"You probably graduated with straight As, then went to law school or grad school, and now have a successful job defending high-power clients or climbing the corporate ladder," he said, toasting her with his water bottle.

"Close," she said. "Actually, I got one B here, then a master's degree, and now work as an environmental engineer."

"That's great. Good for you." So ... smart, good looking, but no wedding ring on her finger. Probably too independent for that. "But I gotta know ... what class did you fall so miserably short in?"

She gritted her teeth and frowned. "I think it was a psychology class. Something about understanding the male ego."

He returned a grin. "Yeah, that's a tough one. A lot of people fail that one."

"And how about you? What are you doing?" she asked.

"I, uh, have a career in retail sales. And have a few other gigs on the side. I do all right." A well-rehearsed bit of exaggeration on all counts. "So, do you still live here in Raleigh?"

Izzy was ready with her prepared response. "Basically, yes. I work for the state, and right now I'm on an assignment in Kinnakeet, over on the coast."

Cal's eyebrows jumped. "Oh really! That's where I live. What are you doing there?"

"I'm helping bring a water and sewer treatment plant up to speed. It's fallen well below the state emission standards for water discharged into the sound, and a new operator has been brought in to get it back in compliance. I'm the state's on-site rep to monitor things and give a little guidance."

"That's great. Sounds important." And boring. "How much longer will you be there?"

"Another few weeks. Depends on how things go. They're making progress, but it's a long haul."

"Well, you know, we should get together," Cal slid a half-step closer. "I bet I know some great restaurants on the island you haven't been to. And now that the tourists are mostly gone you don't have to go super early or late to get in."

Izzy studied him but didn't answer. She'd given a lot of thought to how she would feel, and what she'd do, if he was at the reunion. The emotions were ... so far, so good. But decision time, for where to go from here, came too quickly.

"Give me your email, or better yet, your number," Cal said, taking his phone out of his pocket, "and I'll give you a call next week. You know, I bet you have a business card. Give me one of your cards."

Izzy figured that was his way of getting her last name. She remembered his—Rivers. After a moment of consideration, she decided to go ahead. She would leave the ball in his court. She fished a card out of her wallet. He studied it, then shoved it in the pocket of his jeans along with the phone.

"I'll definitely call you," he said. "Probably Monday." Then he turned and sauntered away toward the lunch buffet tables.

At dinner on Friday, she learned about his career in retail.

"I work at my Aunt Kathy's shop. It's right up on 12, at the north end of town. It's mostly high-end lady's stuff. You know, beachwear, hats, swimsuits, stuff like that. But we also sell some of the usual tourist things—mugs with the lighthouse on them, coasters, and shell jewelry. People love that stuff. She does all right during the season. Now is when things cool off, late September. She keeps it open through Christmas, then closes until April."

Izzy played with her shrimp scampi. It was the dish he'd recommended. "And what do you do then?"

"Oh, there's a lot of painting and remodeling work done on the rental houses here during the off-season. I mostly do that starting about November. I hook up with one of the companies and work real steady during those months. I'm a good painter."

"I always wondered what someone did with an English major after graduation," Izzy said between bites.

Cal pulled back and frowned. "Ouch! That hurts." The frown turned into a smile. "Well, just a little. But, hey, I'm surprised you knew I was an English major." He pointed to the basket in front of her. "Can you pass me a roll?"

"I think I know a lot about you," she said with the pass. "Too bad you don't remember anything about me."

"Yeah, well, sorry about that. But I'm really enjoying getting to know you now." Cal took a moment to butter a roll and take a bite while he watched her watch him. "So, where you living while you're here? I'm surprised you could find a place."

"I'm living with another state employee who lives here. There was an extra bedroom."

"Oh, good. You're lucky." Another bite and swallow of tea. "And is he hitting on you? Having you living right there with him."

Izzy wondered if that was the most sexist thing anyone had ever said to her. Not quite, but maybe in the top ten. "No. He is a she. A widow with two adult children and three grandchildren. I think she's 63."

Cal nodded. "Well, you know, 63-year old's can be ..." He stopped himself and returned to his blackened tuna.

After a momentary scowl, Izzy asked, "And do you live with your aunt?"

"No, I live in a house with a couple other guys. My aunt owns the house, but she lets me live there as part of my compensation for working for her. The other guys pay rent. It's nice. I'll have to show you."

Izzy ignored that. "So, you and the guys party all the time when you're not working?"

"Nah, it's not like that. I don't party all that much anymore. I gave up the beer. I'm sure you noticed what I'm drinking now. Not like the old days."

She had noticed. They were both drinking iced tea. She'd chalked it up to being on his best behavior. He was even dressed a little nicer than at the reunion. Hawaiian shirt, khakis, and sandals. She'd been on the island long enough to realize sandals could be considered formal wear. He'd complemented her pink summer wrap dress when they met in the parking lot.

"I don't get high anymore either. Neither do the other guys."

Cal told Izzy his sobriety story. It involved a late Saturday night kidney stone and hours spent in agony in a hospital bed waiting for his blood alcohol level to drop sufficiently for the anesthesiologist to be willing to put him under for the necessary surgery. He still suspected the doctor had engaged in a form of sadistic punishment for his being so intoxicated. And his less than polite behavior. The surgery was followed up by an exceedingly kind and persuasive hospital social worker, who he dated briefly afterward, convincing him it was time to grow up and stop treating his body like a chemical waste dump. He made it through treatment, had one brief relapse, and had been clean and sober now for over four years.

Izzy offered her sincere congratulations and shared that her brother had battled with substance abuse. This left her with a sincere appreciation for both the pain it could cause, and how hard it could be to maintain sobriety. She asked Cal what he and his housemates did for entertainment since they weren't into partying.

"They both work a lot, too," he said. "We all just enjoy living at the beach. We like to surf a little on our days off when the conditions are right. I read a lot. And I write a little poetry."

"Really?" It was hard for Izzy to imagine the guy she knew in college writing poetry. Or reading poetry. But then, he *was* an English major. He was fond of quoting Shakespeare or Faust, but more often Bart Simpson. Mostly in a show-off kind of way. But, she remembered, there was sometimes a flash of something meaningful, even deep, there. Different than most of the other guys.

"What kind of poetry?" She was curious but getting out of her zone. She knew next to nothing about poetry.

"Haiku, actually."

"Really?" she said, with a slow, disbelieving shake of her head.

A burst of pride ignited Cal's eyes. "Yeah, you know. That old Japanese style that we were taught back in elementary school had five syllables in the first line, seven syllables in the second line, and five in the third. It's more complicated than that. It's evolved greatly and now encompasses a wide range of short poems that make people feel connected to nature or the seasons. I write about both of those. Living here kind of inspires that kind of writing."

Izzy considered the possibility he was bluffing. "Can you share one with me? Do you have a favorite you've written?"

"Uh ... let's see. How about this one ... Wrote this one last week." He bit his lip and glanced toward the ceiling, then returned to her.

"Softly, quietly, now
      The wind drifts the winter sand
           Lines form for a time"

"Wow! Not bad." Izzy stared at him for a moment. She didn't know quite what to think.

Cal jerked his shoulders in a shrug. "Yeah, well. It's a kind of fun and relaxing thing to do."

Izzy tried to put this in context of the person she knew in college. He'd been about 80 percent brassy and show-off, and 10 percent indifferent to the people and world around him. The other 10 percent was hard to define, but definitely what had caught her eye. "I guess people can change," she muttered under her breath. Then she noticed Cal was eyeing the passing waitress and missed her utterance. Some things don't change.

"So, what's the dating life like around here for you and the guys?" Izzy wanted to explore his psyche a little further. See how much change there really was. "You meet a lot of women at the store?"

She thought Cal seemed to study her for a moment. Maybe considering where he wanted to go with that. How revealing he wanted to be.

"Well, yeah. There's lot of women who come in there. Lots of ladies come to the beach for their summer vacation, sometimes in groups of three or four. Like teachers, or sisters, or best friends. Looking for a getaway from their husbands, boyfriends, and stuff. Some of them are unattached. And some of them are open to a little vacation romance."

"Sounds great," Izzy said, with just a touch of sarcasm. She was fairly sure he didn't limit himself to hitting on the unattached ones. "And how do you get their attention? Do you use that, 'I know some great restaurants here that I could take you to' line? Or have you got something better?"

A grin snuck across Cal's face. "It's actually a rather good line. Don't you think?"

She knew what he meant. She was here, wasn't she? She wasn't here because of that line but wasn't ready to tell him that. So, she gave the smile back. "It's not bad."

"Actually, I'm a pretty nice guy," he said. "A guy who looks like me, about 20 pounds overweight ... well, okay, maybe 30, needs to be, if he's going to have any success with the ladies. And I can be quite charming when I want to be. Not like that guy you knew in college."

"Actually, you could be pretty charming at times back then, too." That was a little difficult for Izzy to admit, but it was true. It had to be true.

"Yeah, well ... glad you thought so. I thought I was just pretty much an asshole."

"Yes," Izzy agreed with a nod. "You certainly could be that too. I figured it depended on how much liquor you had on board."

"You're probably right." Cal returned the nod and added a smile. "But now that I've got that under control there's a lot more of the nice guy. As Charles Dickins wrote, 'I have been bent and broken, but—I hope—into a better shape.'"

Izzy smiled again. "That's almost a Haiku."

"Hey, you're right. I could work on that and make it one. Thanks."

"You're welcome."

They ate in silence for a couple minutes. Then Cal put his fork down, washed down his tuna and rice, and said, "You know, that comment you made about me being pretty charming at times back at college was the first nice thing you've said about me. Or to me. Did I do something obnoxious to you? Did I, like, ask you out for some big event, then stand you up?"

Izzy's expression answered his question.

"Okay ... well, look, I'm sorry and ..."

Izzy glanced at the tables full of diners around them. "This isn't the time, or place, to talk about it, but yes you did." She stared into his eyes. "Something ... something a lot bigger than that."

Cal debated for a moment whether continuing to explore a relationship with Izzy was worth getting skewered for the way he used to be. He decided it was. "But obviously you want to talk about it. We need to get it out in the open. And I really want to know so I can try to make up for it. Maybe we could ..."

Izzy seized the moment. "How about we finish our dinner, then go find a place to talk?"

Cal debated again, then, "Okay. Yeah."

They filled the rest of the mealtime with comfortable discourse, as each tried to make the best of the situation. At one point, Izzy asked Cal to give her a verbal lesson about surfing. She asked some questions that reflected her semi-serious interest in the topic, and Cal, at one point, became quite animated in his description. He even jumped up beside the table to ride an imaginary wave to illustrate using his arms to maintain balance on a surfboard.

Cal insisted on paying the bill. "My invite," though Izzy made a serious attempt. They agreed to meet at the Kinnakeet pier, each leaving the restaurant parking lot in their respective vehicles.

In the small pier parking lot, Izzy took a moment to slow her breathing, then pulled on a sweater before putting on a smile as she got out of her car. Cal motioned her ahead of him as they walked up the ramp, through the pier house, then out to the first of the benches. A handful of fishermen were still trying their luck, though the closest was probably 20 yards away. Cal gallantly produced a handkerchief from his pocket and cleaned the day's debris from the wooden strips before they took their seats.

"Okay. I'm ready," Cal said, turning toward her. "Lay it on me. How big of an asshole was I?"

Izzy had pondered a least a hundred times since the reunion, and his subsequent Monday phone call, how she wanted to tell him. And at least 50 times *whether* she wanted to tell him. Now, the moment was here, and the finesse she had planned flew away like a frightened seagull.

"You got me pregnant."

Cal's face turned white against the pink sunset behind him. His eyes squeezed shut, wrinkling his forehead. He turned away. His first thought was to deny her claim, but realized quickly that he had no leg to stand on except a faulty memory. After an exaggerated deep breath, he opened his eyes and turned back to her.

"I didn't see that coming," he muttered. Then, after another breath, "How ...?"

Izzy's heart was suddenly racing. "I think you can figure out how. Maybe you're asking what led up to that momentous occasion."

"Yeah," Cal said. "I'm really sorry. I honestly don't remember anything about even—"

"About even going out with me," Izzy said, through a suddenly parched throat. "I got that. But we did go out. Twice. The pregnancy happened at the second time. And, just so you can rest easy, you didn't force me. This is not about that. And I don't blame you any more than I blame myself. I used you as much as you used me. But in a totally different way."

"Well, I'm relieved to hear that, but I don't ..." Cal's face was slowly regaining its color.

"I know. Let me fill you in." Izzy looked away for a moment. She tried to recall how she'd planned this part. The basics came back to her, so she jumped in.

"I was about as sexually inexperienced as a girl could be who wasn't a virgin. I was just looking for some more ... let's say, education. Some of the girls I knew had been out with you and gone to bed with you. They said you were a 'good time,' but they all said that after you got what you wanted from them you never called them again. Or, if they saw you on campus, you would pretty much ignore them."

Cal was frowning but nodding at the same time. "Probably because I didn't remember. At least some of them."

"Well, maybe. That's what you told a couple of them. But that sounded like a convenient excuse. Anyway, to tell you the truth, that was about what I wanted. I was looking for a one-night thing, without any obligations or complications. The school year was almost over, and I'd missed out on most of those great college experiences you're supposed to have before you graduate. I was too focused on grades and classes."

"But that's not exactly what you got," Cal said. "No complications."

"Right." Izzy took a breath. "So ... I knew you from the classes we'd been in. And you were a pretty nice guy in those classes. Reasonably sober, or at least able to pull that off. You were smart, good looking, and, like I said, you could be charming. I was attracted enough to your personality to decide you might be my one-night guy. But I wasn't attractive enough to be your kind of girl."

"That's hard to believe," Cal said with a grin, trying his best to convey with his expression how he saw her now. He wanted to make that point, but knew the timing wasn't right to interrupt her any further.

"Sure," Izzy was shaking her head, but kept her focus. "I asked you out, for a lunch date. That was a thing back then, among some of us less dating-comfortable girls. To just keep a first date to a lunch to check the guy out before moving any further. We had an enjoyable time, good conversation, and you were pleasant and nice to me. You were about the most interesting guy I'd met. Not that I'd been that into guys, or looking for a boyfriend especially. Actually, quite the opposite. But you were interested enough to ask me out for the next Friday night, which was what I wanted."

"And I'm guessing that went pretty well?"

"It did. It took me a while to get my nerve up, but I was enjoying the time with you. You had just a few beers, and I had a couple. So, when you made your move, back at your apartment, I was ready. I'm not going to go into any details but let's just say no form of birth control is 100 percent effective. I found out I was definitely pregnant the week of graduation."

"Wow. I'm really sorry." Cal reached to put his hand on hers. Izzy let it stay for a moment.

"Yeah, I know. But that's as much on me as it is you. Then, when you didn't ask me out again, and basically ignored me, I was mostly okay with that. I guess a part of me hoped I was good enough, you know, not in bed, but as a person, to warrant at least a little attention afterwards. But I knew better. I really didn't regret the whole thing until I found out I was pregnant. Then the guilt hit like a Mack truck."

"I bet it did," Cal said, staring down at his feet. "So, uh, what happened then? ... Did you ..."

Izzy knew what he was asking. "Well, after the shock wore off, I decided I wasn't going to have the baby. I couldn't imagine having a baby with you. And I was quite sure you wouldn't be interested in being a father. So, then I thought maybe I'd take a year off and have the baby, then give it up for adoption. Of course, that would mean you'd have to agree to the adoption, but I figured you would. I was leaning heavily in that direction. But then, mother nature stepped in and took care of the issue before I had to make any firm decisions."

"So ...?"

"Yep," Izzy grimaced and shook her head. "No baby."

Cal lowered his head and stared into her eyes. "How'd you feel when that happened?"

Cal's sensitivity took Izzy by surprise. She needed a few seconds, so she turned away toward the end of the pier. She studied a sand piper that hopped around on a near-by post, then came back to him.

"I've never felt so torn up inside. Of course, I felt some relief. The decision was taken out of my hands, and I had my year back. But at the same time, there was another bout of guilt for letting the whole thing happen." Her voice turned flat. "And a profound sense of sadness for the life that would never be."

Izzy's eyes misted over, which startled her. She'd talked about all that in therapy, for many months. But talking to Cal was different. "It was a very tough summer before I started graduate school in the fall. I cried a lot."

In a move that surprised even him, Cal immediately slid the two feet that separated them and put his arms around Izzy, pulling her close. To Izzy's surprise, she let him, and settled her head on his shoulder. Her hand rested on his leg. They stayed that way until Izzy pulled away to wipe her eyes.

"Thanks," she said, after a sniffle. "I guess I needed that." Cal fished his handkerchief out of his pocket, then remembered how he'd used it and pushed it back in.

"It's okay," Izzy said with a shaky grin, pulling a tissue from her sweater pocket. After a quick wipe she said, "Let's go. I think that's about enough ... whatever ... for this evening." She pushed herself off the bench. Cal was quick to join her.

They walked in silence through the pier house, then down the ramp to the parking area. When they got to Izzy's car Cal stepped in front of her.

"We can't just leave things like this," he said, lightly resting his hands on her shoulders. "Can't we meet again and talk some more?"

Izzy cast her eyes on the sandy ground. She hadn't expected it to go like this. In none of the scenarios she'd imagined when contemplating this conversation had there been tears and an embrace. Sharp words, denial, storming off had been the primary expectations. She looked up and studied his face for a few seconds. The compassion she saw there melted what confusion remained inside her.

"Okay ..." She found a soft smile deep inside. "Have you got another favorite restaurant?"

Scarlet

"Excuse me! This is private property."

He should have been able to hear her shout from the third-floor deck. But there was a good wind coming off the sound that perhaps had whipped her words away. He hadn't moved from his yoga-like sitting position at the edge of the lawn beside the tree. The way his head was down to his chest he could be asleep. She decided to try again from the ground floor.

After descending the two flights of stairs, she grabbed a coat from the rack beside the stairway, then headed out the back door and took a couple steps into the grass, but not too far from the safety of the house. She cupped her hands around her mouth and reached for maximum volume. "Sir! ... Mister! This is private property. Please leave."

This time he moved, but only to raise his right arm and wave his hand slightly, as if to acknowledge that he heard her. It took another minute for him to rise to a standing position, but still he faced the soft magenta light that painted the sky over the Pamlico sound. After another minute he turned and walked slowly toward her.

He didn't look threatening. At first, he appeared sad, or worried, but then his face relaxed. As he got closer, she could see his angular face was now set in an almost smile. The gray jacket he wore was a bit thin for the late-October briskness. He had to be cold. Wisps of brown hair with bits of gray stuck out from under the faded Durham Bulls baseball cap. He looked a bit like Daniel, her youngest son whose 34th birthday they had just celebrated last week.

"I'm sorry," he said when he stopped and made eye contact from 20 feet away. "I used to live here." His voice was soft, but the breeze carried it effortlessly.

"Oh my!" She took a small step forward, not wanting to shout now. "You mean here, this house, or here at the beach?"

"This house." His brown eyes scanned the building behind her. "It hasn't changed much, at least from the back. Except it was green when we lived here."

"Yes, my husband and I painted it this blue a couple years ago."

"I'm sure it needed it by then." He strode slowly forward. From an arm's length away he said, "I'm Paul." He extended his hand.

"I'm Diane." They shook briefly.

"I'm sorry," Paul said. "I didn't mean to disturb you. It's just that I haven't been back here in ... well, since we sold the house." He turned to the sunset for a moment, then came back to her. "This house, this place, has a lot of memories for me. And I haven't been ..."

"Oh, well then," Diane said, "would you like to come inside? I can show you what we've done to it." He seemed like a nice enough young man.

Paul stared at the sandy turf beneath his sandals. "Um, I don't know if ... I don't want to bother you any more than I have."

"Oh, nonsense. You're not bothering me. Besides, it's getting cold out here with that sun going down. You must be freezing. Come on inside and at least warm up a little bit."

After a moment of hesitation, Paul nodded and followed Diane as she headed for the house. "How long ago did you sell the place?" she asked.

"It's been five years," he said as they stepped through the doorway.

"Oh, that was when Ted and I bought it. We must have bought it from you. I remember the realtor said it was a young couple selling the house. They were moving away. We never got to meet them."

"Yes. That was us. Carrie, my wife ... ex-wife and I."

"Oh, I'm sorry. I know things sometimes just don't work out. My oldest son and his wife are divorced. It's tough on everyone, especially the children." Diane hung her coat on the rack then took Paul's and placed it on the next hook. He put his cap over it.

Diane stepped past him and headed up the stairs. "Let's go on up to the third floor and let you see what we've done up there. Then we can do a brief tour of the second floor. Of course, you know the laundry and storage area are down here. Not much to see. I only wish whoever designed this house would have thought to put the laundry somewhere upstairs. I'm sixty-seven years old, and these stairs get a little steeper every day."

She stopped suddenly and turned. "Oh my! That wasn't you who designed the house, was it?"

"No, ma'am. I think it was built about six years before we bought it."

"Oh, good." Diane continued to lead the way to the top floor. Paul followed but fell a little more behind her with each flight. When she arrived on the third floor, she turned left into the kitchen. Paul walked immediately to the sliding glass door that led from the dining area to the deck and stared at the last vestiges of the sunset. In a matter of seconds, the top edge of the sun slipped into the sound, leaving behind crimson sky and gold rimmed clouds to light the heavens for another few minutes.

"Your husband, will he be coming home soon?" Paul asked as he turned for a look at the furniture arrangement in the great room.

"Oh, no," Diane said, shaking her head, sending the short, gray ponytail flying. "He ... passed away. Almost a year ago now."

"I'm so sorry."

"Well, yes. Thank you. God often gives us the death of a loved one to be faced in life. Especially as we get older. We never want to, but we don't get much choice now, do we?" She turned quickly back to the kitchen, missing Paul's reaction.

Diane called Paul's attention to the new appliances in the kitchen, then the recently replaced flooring in the dining area, and the color change in the great room. She denied him a peak in the master bedroom, which she described as "a mess," by pulling the door closed.

On the second floor she walked him through the largest bedroom, set up with a queen bed as a guest room for any of her three children. The next bedroom had twin beds for the grandchildren, of which there were four. In the third bedroom she noted that the walls were now off-white instead of soft-pink, and the room was set up as an office. After a moment inside the room, she snapped her fingers and said, "Let me show you something."

She grabbed Paul's arm, pulled him into the room, and walked him to the closet door. She pointed to a one-inch strip of the wall at the far side of the door, still a soft pink. There were several ink marks at various heights, along with what appeared to be dates written just beneath them. The marks stopped just over three feet from the floor.

"Our painter pointed these out to us and asked about them. We weren't sure what they were but told him to leave them. Could these be—"

She stopped abruptly when she turned and saw Paul's ashen face. She thought he was going to faint.

Paul stumbled backwards toward the door. He mumbled, "I forgot about those," and grabbed the doorframe to keep from falling. Diane, befuddled for a moment, rushed to his side, and wrapped her arms around him. Between the two of them they managed to keep him vertical.

"Are you all right?" Diane asked, her voice barely a squeak.

Paul steadied himself, now with just one hand on the doorframe. "Yes, I'm going to be. Give me a second." He waited until Diane released him, then stepped out of the room. Diane stayed close. In the hallway she watched him carefully as he took a series of deep breaths.

"Let's go back upstairs," she said as she took his elbow and pulled him gently toward the stairway. She insisted he lead the way this time. She followed a step behind with one arm in front of her, ready to catch him if he stumbled. After the third step it occurred to her that at 105 pounds it was unlikely she could do much to stop a fall except provide a soft body to land on.

After she guided him to one end of the great room sofa facing the back windows, she said, "I'll be right back." She hurried to the kitchen to fetch water for both of them. When she returned, she handed him a glass and perched on the other end of the sofa.

"I don't want to be nosy, but ... perhaps you can talk about it?" She knew perfectly well she was being nosy. But she understood a great deal about that kind of emotional reaction, knew he was hurting, and believed talking would help.

"I really ..."

"Please," she said. She slid a little closer, closing the gap so she could pat the hand that rested on his knee. "You're safe here."

Paul stared into the increasing darkness outside. The wind was blowing the clouds away and a few stars were now visible. Finally, he turned to her.

"I came here because I thought I could handle it. And I can. I did fine outside. That just caught me by surprise." He turned away for a moment. When he turned back there was a single tear edging down his cheek. "That was her room. Emily's."

Diane wanted to wipe the tear but grabbed the pillow between them instead. "Your daughter."

"Yes. Emily. We called her Em."

They sat in silence. Paul studied the sky outside while Diane studied the side of his face. The story was at least partially displayed there, but she wanted to hear it. She thought he needed to tell it. "Please. Tell me about her."

He turned slowly to face her. He was struggling for control, and the firm tenor of his voice said he was winning the battle. "She was two years old. She was the light of our lives." He paused to take a breath, and then another.

"I had gone outside that morning to work in the yard. We had just put down the sod and I was planting some flowers. I'd been outside for over an hour when Carrie shouted at me from inside to come in for lunch and bring Em with me. I told her Em wasn't with me, she was in the house. She said no, Em had come out right after I did. I ... I took a quick look around and didn't see her. I shouted to Carrie to look in the house, then ran in to look myself. It only took us a minute to look through this whole place. She wasn't here."

Paul reached for the glass on the coffee table, then took a drink. After a moment he resumed, his voice now softer, but still steady.

"We ran back outside and searched everywhere, shouting her name. We were frantic. We came together in the driveway out front, and it hit us both at the same time. The sound. We ran to the back and out to the edge of the water. It only took a few seconds to spot her—in the reeds just off the edge of the property. I jumped in and ran to her. The water was only three feet deep there, but ... it was enough."

Paul got up from the sofa and walked the two steps to the window. He stood there for a minute, examining the increasing darkness, and the couple of dim lights on the distant shore across the water. He turned back to Diane after a fast shake of his head and a breath.

"Of course, there's no emergency room on the island, so we called 911 and got the Kinnakeet Fire Department. The EMS people got here quickly, and tried what they could, but ... we knew."

"I'm so very sorry," Diane said. She wanted to jump up and give him a hug, to hold him and let him cry if he wanted to, but hesitated. His eyes were surprisingly dry. She waited for him to go on. It took a minute.

"There was nothing to do. The shock was overwhelming. I could feel Carrie's unspoken accusations from the very beginning. At least she tried to hold them back. Only once, two days later, did the anger and hurt break through and she told me what she really thought—that it was my fault. That I didn't pay attention when Em came outside. That I should have known she'd want to be outside with me. That my carelessness had cost Em her life ... Had taken away from Carrie the most precious thing in her life. And ... that she would never, ever, forgive me." Paul made a quick swipe at his eyes with his hand.

"Oh my God!" Diane said, tears welled in her eyes and her voice cracked into a whisper.

"No," Paul quickly countered. "It's okay. I understand now. It was a struggle, but a lot of therapy over the last five years has helped. I blamed myself for a long time too. Carrie's reaction was normal. She was a great mother ... and that child was her ... life." He turned back to the window. In the reflection Diane could see his tightly closed eyes.

"But ... how did you deal with all that at the time?" Diane said, her voice only slightly recovered. "I mean, losing a child has got to be the worst thing. I can't imagine losing ... one of mine. And a baby!"

Paul found his way back to the sofa and sat beside her. "We didn't cope very well, really. We had her body cremated. We didn't know what to do with the ashes, but eventually decided we wanted some sort of memorial here at the house. Finally, we decided on a tree ..." His eyes shot briefly to the window, and the yard and darkness beyond, then found Diane's again.

"We had a bench down there by the water where Em and I would sit and watch the sunset almost every evening after she turned two. She'd sit beside me, or I would hold her, wrapped in a blanket when it was cold. She'd keep me warm with her smile. I'd tell her a story of some kind. Usually one I'd make up, or one I remember my dad telling me. Then, after the sun went down, it was back to the house and Carrie took over for bath time. Then off to bed and we'd take turns reading her a story.

"Anyway ... we decided to plant a tree where the bench was. I knew ... I could never sit there again. A tree would be something we could care for, nurture, and watch grow into maturity. We mixed some of her ashes in with the dirt we brought in—"

"That tree that's there now?" Diane exclaimed as she sat back and pointed to the window. "You planted it? And her ashes are there?"

"Yes. Some of her ashes are. The tree is a Scarlet Oak. Named for the color the leaves will be in another couple weeks or so. We picked that tree because it does well here along the coast, and when Em got angry her face turned deep red. In fact, we used to call her "Little Miss Scarlet" at those times."

"Oh, my! That tree." Diane's hand briefly covered her mouth. "It's special to us too ... And it's ..." She stopped herself, stood, and headed toward the kitchen. She froze half-way there and turned back to Paul.

"I'd just come from the Food Lion when I saw you outside. I'm going to fix some soup and slice some fresh sourdough bread. You'll stay for dinner." Her tone made it clear that last part was not a question.

Paul stood and walked toward her. "I ... well ... Thank you."

"By the way," Diane said as she began the preparations, "where's your car? I didn't see one in the driveway or in front of the house."

"I parked at the sound access point parking area. I walked over to the sound from there."

Diane nodded and threw herself into her work while Paul stood at the sliding glass door. After a couple minutes he opened the door and stepped out. The chill brought him back inside in a few moments.

"It's still a beautiful view, even in the dark," he said as he watched Diane set the table. "We ate many a meal out there. Em would help Carrie in the kitchen. She'd put her little apron on, stand on her little stool, and help mix things or measure. Then we'd bring everything out to the deck. We had a picnic table. We would watch sunrises or sunsets, or just enjoy the salt air and watch the seagulls." He hesitated for a second, then stepped into the great room to get out of the way. "Do you still have deer wander by?"

"Yes. I see some in the neighborhood almost every day." Diane carried a basket of bread to the table. "Now, go wash up. Dinner will be ready in just a minute. You know where the rest room is."

When Paul returned and took his seat, Diane placed a bowl of tomato bisque in front of him. It smelled heavenly. "Would you like a glass of wine to go with dinner?" she asked.

"No, thank you," Paul said. "I've found it best over the last few years not to have the first one. Water will be fine." Diane nodded, collected his glass from the coffee table, and brought them both water.

"I haven't had someone cook for me in quite a while," Paul said, as he put his napkin in his lap. "It's really nice."

"That's too bad," Diane said as she joined him at the table. "You and your wife have been ... separated or divorced for a while?" Her desire to hear the story overwhelmed her concern about what constituted polite dinner table conversation.

"Yes." Paul dug in the pocket of his jeans for a handkerchief. He touched his eyes with it briefly and laid it in his lap beside the napkin. "We separated about seven months after Em died. We'd been trying to have another child when that happened. Afterwards ... that, or any kind of closeness, just seemed impossible. The pain ... drove us apart."

For a few seconds Paul's eyes glazed and he looked away toward the kitchen. One hand gripped the napkin, the other the handkerchief. He took a breath, then something seemed to settle inside him. He returned his gaze to Diane and his hands to the table.

"We tried not talking about it, then tried talking about it. We went to counseling. We were just both hurting so much that we couldn't help each other. The counselor kept telling us you can't erase the past, no matter how much you want to. But we just ... couldn't get there. So ... after a while ... she left. Went back to her family in Ohio. I stayed here for a while and got the house ready to sell. It was pretty easy to leave the house. But that tree ..." The handkerchief made a quick appearance.

Diane watched the pain flicker on and off his face and heard it in the subtle breaks in his voice. But she wanted to be encouraging. "I'm certainly impressed with how well, or ... uh ... that you can talk about all that. The pain must have been terrible."

"Oh, it was," Paul said. "It was like two shotgun blasts to my soul. One right after the other. My universe just imploded. I had these two beautiful, wonderful ladies to love, and who loved me. Then ..." A quick wipe with the handkerchief again, "I had nothing. Except a boatload of guilt."

"That's ... that's an awful lot to overcome. Are you a religious person? ... Did you have a church to help get you through?"

Paul took a moment for a sip of soup, then put the spoon down. He stared out the window ahead of him. "No. The death of my Em, the most precious thing in my life, then Carrie leaving ... didn't exactly pull me closer to God. I was not particularly feeling a lot of his love." The grimace that lined his face accented his point.

Diane nodded and focused on wiping a piece of bread with butter. She sort of understood. There certainly had been times when her faith had been tested. She considered herself fortunate that she hadn't had to face either of the tragedies that Paul had. It was likely God would have heard some unpleasantries from her. The death of Ted, while expected after a battle with lung cancer, was tough enough.

She gave them both a little time to eat. Then she had to ask. "Well, then. What got you through it? You've obviously come a long way. To want to come back to this house, to be in the house, to be able to talk the way you have about both Emily and ... your wife. Without breaking down. You said you went to counseling, was that it?"

Paul reached for a slice of bread and studied it for a moment, then glanced out the glass doors again. "No, that wasn't it. The therapy helped. No doubt. But ..." He took a bite of the bread, put it down, patted his mouth with the napkin, and caught Diane's eyes. "It was a sunset."

"A sunset!" Diane sat back, tilted her head, and stared at him.

"Yes," Paul said, then closed his eyes for a moment. When he opened them, he looked at her and kindly repeated. "A sunset."

"Please," Diane said, motioning with her hand, insisting he continue.

Paul picked up his spoon, then put it back down. He folded his hands and put them in his lap.

"I was driving along a place called Waterrock outside Waynesville over in the western part of the state. The Smoky Mountains were all around me. I wasn't paying much attention, but when I crested a peak, the sunset in front of me almost caused me to drive off the road. It's like my eyes had been closed, then suddenly, boom! There was this incredible sunset just bursting all over, covering the whole sky in front of me." His hands exploded from his lap and his arms spread in front of him. "Red, orange, pink, gold. It was all there. Fortunately, there was a spot I could pull over right there, so I did. Then I just sat there and stared. I could hardly breathe." As if on cue, Paul drew a couple deep breaths and returned his hands to his lap.

Diane could tolerate only a couple seconds of the ensuing silence. "And then ...?"

Paul sat quietly a bit longer. "Then ... I'm not quite sure how to describe it. But the words that keep coming to me are ... that I melted. Inside." He pondered the soup for a moment. "It's like some hard crust of ice that had frozen up everything inside me just liquefied, then dissolved. The colors, the warmth of that sunset right in front of me, just did that to me."

"You felt all that ... right at that moment?" Diane said.

"Yes. I just sat there. And cried. All the sunsets I'd watched with Em from that bench where the tree is now were all right there in the sky in front of me. All at once. And, somehow, it struck me, how many sunsets I'd missed in the years since. All the beauty, all the joy, that was right out there in front of me had been frozen out. My eyes, and my heart, had been frozen shut. All that came to me ... in a flash."

"Wow!" Diane said, her hand on the side of her face, her head slowly shaking. "Did you ever figure out ... Maybe God ..."

"Not really," Paul said. "I'm not sure I'm ever meant to understand all that. Although ... I will say ... occasionally, I wonder if maybe it was Em looking down, flashing her beautiful smile in that sunset, and saying, 'Daddy, that's enough.'"

His head turned toward the kitchen again, and for a few moments he seemed in a daze. Then his eyes closed, his breathing slowed, and his face set in a smile that melted Diane's heart. She could not believe he could seem so ... peaceful. When he came back, he said, "Sorry," and picked up his spoon.

Diane was wise enough to steer the rest of the dinner conversation away to other topics. The changes on Hatteras Island over the last few years, the constant battle against the encroaching ocean, the new bridge. As they finished their meal, Paul thanked Diane and said he must leave. Diane asked where he was spending the night.

"I'm going to get a room in one of the motels," Paul replied.

Diane shook her head. "I don't think so. Not unless you already have a reservation. One of the big fishing tournaments is this week. I've heard that everything is rented." She paused for just a moment, then grabbed his hand and nodded. "You'll stay here."

Paul protested, weakly, but Diane directed him to get his car, bring it up to the driveway, and bring his things inside.

After he agreed, Diane walked him down the steps to the entryway. When he grabbed his hat and coat before leaving, she wondered for a second if he would return. Had she pushed too hard? Would sleeping in the house again be unbearable? But of course, against the gathering cold and wind, he'd need the hat and coat even for the brief walk to his car.

So, she hurried to the second floor and did a quick check on the guest room. She was certain she had put fresh sheets on the bed and clean towels in the bathroom after Daniel and his family left, but just to be sure. When Paul returned ten minutes later with a small bag, she was reassured, and led him to the guest room.

After he settled in, Paul found Diane in the great room and informed her he'd like to turn in early. It had been a long day. He thanked her profusely for her kindness and generosity. Diane thanked him for sharing the evening and his inspiring story with her.

"I'm going to tell Ted all about you," she said. "I talk to him every night before I go to sleep."

Moments after he settled into bed, Paul heard the faint sound of the back door closing. His curiosity got the best of him, and he rose to peek out the window.

In the light of an almost full moon, and about a million stars, he saw Diane kneeling at the tree in the corner of the back yard.

As he watched, she seemed to talk to the tree. Then, after a few minutes, she kissed her fingers, touched the trunk of the tree, then the sandy soil at its base.

The Book Of Wisdom

I was lost the first time I saw her.

Not in the usual sense. Not physically lost. It's hard to get lost on Hatteras Island with only one main road; the ocean on one side and the sound on the other. I was emotionally lost. Out to sea, in a sense. Much like the island.

She was sitting on the beach. About a hundred yards south of the Kinnakeet pier. She had something in her lap. I couldn't tell if her eyes were open or shut, but she appeared to be looking at the ocean.

I walked slowly in her direction, from under the pier and a little bit behind her. I asked myself why I was drawn to her. I answered myself, "I don't know." When I got within ten yards, I could see her eyes were shut. Perhaps she was mesmerized by the sound of the waves.

"Hello, friend," she said. "I've been waiting for you."

I've been mistaken for someone else before. I'm pretty non-descript in appearance. I took a couple more steps before I said, "I'm not sure who you're waiting for, but I'm not him." She opened her eyes and turned to me.

"Yes, you are."

This was an awkward beginning. But once I saw her face, I felt attracted. Not in the usual physical sense, she wasn't that good looking. But she looked like she was someone I might like to know. I'd had female friends at times in my life and thought they were decent.

"Well then, may I take a seat?" I had nothing else to do at the moment.

She nodded to her side, and I settled into a couple square feet of sand beside her. I studied the sunrise for a few seconds. Then her. I was drawn to the mystery of her calmness.

"I'm Donald," I said, "but my friends call me Don." I put out my hand.

"I'm Angelisa," she said after a brief shake. "But things go a little better if people call me Lisa."

Okay. That's a little weird. "Then I'll call you Lisa," I said. "What's that you got there?" I pointed to the object in her lap.

"This?" she asked turning the thing slightly in my direction. After my nod she continued. "It's a book. Sort of a journal."

It looked old and well worn. "It must be something special," I said.

"It is. It was handed down to me."

"Oh." Enough of that. Nothing special here. It was time to move on. There were better things to do. Although I couldn't think of one now. But I could find one. There were a couple people out on surfboards down the beach. Maybe one of them was a cute chick in a two-piece. I started to get up.

"Keep your seat," she said. After I did, she asked, "What are you doing here on the beach at sunrise?" After staring at me for a moment she added, "I bet you're looking for something."

I wasn't. Unless it was that cute chick. But I kept my seat. "More like just passing some time."

"No. You're looking for something."

The way she said that mystified me. It kind of angered me. But somewhere it struck a chord. "Okaayy ..." I said.

"Why don't you tell me why you're here, really. Why you're at the beach," she said. "Maybe we can figure out together what you're looking for."

The way she said that wasn't confrontational. It wasn't demanding. It was ... almost inviting. I looked at her again. She was staring at the ocean. Not at me. A full minute passed. What the hell.

I told her about losing my job last week. I was unceremoniously let go just short of the end of the one-year probationary period. I was a 29-year-old accountant with my third firm. I knew what I was doing. I rarely made a mistake. Certainly, no more than the other guys. I had a BA in math and an MBA with a specialization in accounting. I had my CPA. About the only thing I was told was that I just didn't seem to fit in with the firm. I had enough money saved for this blowout trip to the beach and then I'd be at the soup kitchen.

She listened for the first five minutes of my rant. Then she asked, "Ever heard anything like they told you before?"

The truth was yes. A couple times. But it took a minute for me to be able to admit it.

"And how'd the girlfriend take the news?"

Her tone made it sound like maybe she knew. Or could figure it out. Wait ... how'd she know I had a girlfriend? Probably just a good guess. She was still studying the ocean.

"Not well," I finally told her. "In fact, she left the same day."

"What'd she say?"

"She said I probably deserved it. She said if she'd been a little stronger she'd have fired me from her life a long time ago. She walked back into the bedroom and started packing. She was gone an hour later."

Lisa finally turned and looked at me. She seemed like she cared. "What do you think the problems were between the two of you?"

I debated for a minute. First, about whether I wanted to get into that with her. This woman I'd met about 10 minutes ago. My track record with women who gave a shit about me wasn't great. But I didn't care what this woman thought of me. She wasn't that good looking.

Then I had to figure out what to say. I probably could have said a thousand things. That was roughly the number of arguments Helene and I had gotten into. I decided to keep it simple.

"She said I was impulsive. That I didn't think things through very well. She also said something about I wasn't very nice to her and wasn't very kind to anybody else." That was part of it. "And she said I always had to have my way."

Lisa nodded. "How'd that feel?"

"Not very good." Who was I kidding? It hurt. A lot. Helene and I had been together nine months. Lived together three.

"So that's why you're here," she said. It was a statement, not a question. "You're trying to heal from the wound, the two wounds, and put yourself back together."

I knew she was right but wasn't ready to admit it. For the first few days I'd leaned heavily on a couple 12-packs of beer. That hadn't helped very much. Last night was the first time I'd eased off on that. Wouldn't have been up this early if I hadn't.

"Have you learned anything?" she asked.

"What do you mean?"

"Well, every experience you have in life is a learning opportunity. Especially the bad experiences and the mistakes."

That was heavy. "What do you mean?" I asked again. I wasn't sure I'd call the job or the girlfriend a mistake. Well, not exactly.

"Every time something goes bad in your life you have the opportunity to look at it and look at yourself. To figure out the why. Ninety-nine percent of the time something you did caused, or at least contributed, to the problem. You made a mistake. Maybe many, or a series of mistakes. And every mistake you make is a gift. Just like everything else in your life is a gift. That job was a gift. Your girlfriend was a gift. From every gift, including every mistake, there's something to be learned. Sometimes several things."

I thought about that for a moment. Maybe she was right. My girlfriend, uh ex-girlfriend, had said something like that. Only not as eloquently. Or as calmly. The words "stupid" and "grow up" might have been in there.

"I guess I haven't figured out what I need to learn from either of those yet. I've just been caught up in ... being angry I guess."

She nodded. "Easy to do. But not very productive. Remember, your mistakes are there to guide you, not define you. From each mistake there is an opportunity to get better. To become a better person."

I tried not to look stupid as I stared at her. Not sure I succeeded. I was also not sure how hard I'd worked at improving myself in the last few years. That hadn't been high on my list of priorities. Or even on the list. So, after a few seconds I shifted to study the ocean.

"Here," she said, "let's see what this says." She nodded to the book she was holding and opened it to a random page. Then she pointed and read out loud.

"Once you've learned everything you can from your mistakes you should go out and make some more."

She turned the book to show me the page. It was right there, written in some kind of fancy calligraphy.

"Okay, I guess I get it," I said. "Always a good idea to not keep repeating the same mistakes over and over again." Easy to say, hadn't been so easy for me to do. Probably because I'd never given it much thought.

I was wondering what that book was when she said, "Here, let's look at another page." She closed the book then ran her finger across the page ends and picked one, apparently at random. She opened the book and read what was printed on the page again.

"Every action you take around others, and every word you speak, should be done with respect."

She showed me the words on the page. Then she closed the book and looked at me. "How do you think you've done with that?"

"What is that book?" I demanded, not willing to answer her question.

"It's something my great-grandmother gave to my grandmother, then she gave it to my mother, who gave it to me. She called it 'Words of Wisdom.'"

"Who wrote that?" I was hoping to distract her.

"Don't know. Doesn't matter. Back to the point. How have you done treating people with respect through your words and actions?"

I thought for a minute about how to answer that. I had a pretty good idea, based on my ex-girlfriend's complaints and a few things I'd been told at the office. "I don't know. I'll have to think about that," I said. Cop out.

"Fine. You do that," she said as she pushed her way off the sand. "I'll see you tomorrow."

With that, Lisa and her fancy book headed down the beach. Eventually she turned and strolled up a walkway through a dune toward the houses.

At first, I was pissed. Who was she to confront me with how I treated others? I hadn't said or done anything inappropriate to her. It took me about five minutes of walking the opposite direction on the beach to accept that I had opened myself up for that by telling her about my current life situation. My bad!

I went on with my day. Drove down to Hatteras. Walked around then ate some lunch. Went to the museum, visited the lighthouse, watched some guys fishing at The Point. But I found myself thinking about our interaction. Eventually that turned into actually thinking about how I'd treated Helene. Then I considered the little bit of feedback I'd been given during my performance reviews. The ones at the office, not the more frequent ones from Helene. Maybe there was something there.

That night at the motel I had just a couple beers. I missed a good bit of sleep thinking about all the stuff from the morning, even though I tried not to. I didn't get far figuring things out.

The next morning at sunrise I was back on the beach. I came down the walkway beside the pier and this time headed north. There she was, about 50 yards away. Sitting with her legs crossed, studying the ocean. I debated turning around, but my curiosity got the better of me. Maybe at some level I wanted to see what she and her mystery book would have to say today.

"There you are Don," she said when I sat down next to her. "I thought you might be back." She gave me a half-smile. The book was in her lap. When I didn't reply she added, "So, what did you learn about yourself as you laid awake last night?"

"Not much," I replied in a flash. "But I don't think I'm as bad of a person as you think I am."

"Oh, I don't think you're a bad person," she said, shaking her head. "We all have our faults and weaknesses. Taken all together, we're probably all about the same on some universal scale of good versus bad. At least until we decide to learn from our mistakes and elevate ourselves into the realm of virtuous people. Then our lives get better as we do better in the way we treat other people."

I sort of heard what she said but lost her while thinking about a scale of good versus bad. I had a thought that I was probably on the low end of that scale. And had been that way since I was a kid. Detention was one of my favorite places.

She snapped her fingers in front of my face. "Let's see what the book has for you today. Shall we?" After I nodded, she handed me the book and said, "Here, you pick the page."

I examined the cover of the book for a second. Just a bunch of fancy shapes and curly-ques. Then I picked my spot and spread the book open.

"When speaking with others, always give that person your full attention. No matter what they're saying, they deserve that from you."

Okay. Now this is getting creepy. And I'm not the one who's usually freaked out by things. I'm the one who laughs at those people who do.

"So?" she said.

"Uh ... I'm not so sure about that one. Let me try again."

She grinned like she knew something.

I closed the book and opened to another page.

"Don't let your pain cause you to treat others cruelly. They probably had nothing to do with it."

I slammed the book shut and shook my head. "This book seems to think I've been cruel to the people around me," I said.

"I don't know that the book thinks anything," Lisa said with an innocent face. "But have you?"

I knew the answer. I'd realized a couple things during my restless hours last night. Helene was a good person. Kind, giving, she let me have my way more than 50 percent of the time. If I was going to be honest, and that's hard for me at this point, probably 90 percent. She deserved a lot better than what I gave her.

It took me a couple minutes, but I told Lisa some of the stuff between me and Helene that I wasn't proud of. I kind of defended it by saying that I was going through a rough time with that job during the whole time we were together. She simply nodded and pointed to the book. With some trepidation I opened it to another random page. I read out loud:

"To be cruel is to choose the easy way out."

"Okay! I get it," I said, perhaps a bit too loud. A seagull that was sneaking up on us took flight. "Enough with the cruel theme."

I tried to hand the book back to Lisa, but she said, "Come on, just one more. There may be a real gem in there for you." I was doubtful but agreed to do one more. I shuffled the pages then opened the book to a page near the end. I read it silently this time.

"Be careful how you treat people. What you do to others has a funny way of coming back to you."

My mind almost exploded. I scared away more than one bird this time. "For Pete's sake, I get it! You made your point you stupid book!"

Lisa gave me a Mona Lisa grin. I thought maybe that should be her nickname. "The book is neither stupid nor smart. It just is. But perhaps you have the opportunity to learn something?"

"Yeah, maybe," I said. Then, "I think that's enough," I handed the book back to her but missed her hand. The book fell open in the sand. When I picked it up, I couldn't help reading.

"Eventually the day will come when you realize turning the page is the best thing you can do. There is so much more to the story of your life than the page you're stuck on now."

I brushed the sand off the book, closed it, and pushed it into her hand. "I've got things to do," I told her. I didn't, but I'd find something.

When I started to walk away, she said, "See you tomorrow."

"I don't think so," I muttered. I don't know if I wanted her to hear me or not.

I spent most of the day on Roanoke Island. I tried to pay attention to the comings and goings around me, but my mind kept returning to that book and how I'd treated the people in my life. As I sat on a bench near the lighthouse in Manteo, a hundred examples came to me of people I could have treated better. *Should* have treated better. It seemed like I'd had a chip on my shoulder since childhood. There was some crap in my early years that wasn't ideal, but it probably wasn't that bad.

While I walked around the harbor at Wanchese I tried to think about my job. Former job. Maybe there too I hadn't been as kind to people as I could have been. There were a few complaints from clients about my being short or impatient with them. When those comments were passed along to me, I blew them off as coming from difficult clients who anybody would have had a tough time with.

That night I laid off the beer and tried to think. I need to treat people more kindly, I need to give my full attention to people when we're talking, and maybe, just maybe, I'm not all that bad of a person. But I sure could be better.

The next morning Lisa was standing in the parking lot of the pier when I pulled in. She had the book in her hand. "Let's go for a walk," she said.

I fell in behind her as she headed out to the road. She turned right and headed north. I was waiting for her to offer up the book, or the next pearl of wisdom, but we walked in silence for several minutes. Eventually we came upon an old man stumbling along the sidewalk ahead of us. He was weighed down by a tattered backpack with a sleeping bag tied to the top. As we got closer, I could smell him from several yards away.

I walked on by, but Lisa stopped and spoke to him. She reached in the pocket of her pants and gave him something, then gave him a hug before she caught back up to me.

"Tell me about that man," she said.

"Well," I began, "I'd say he's homeless and definitely needs a bath or a shower. Just a dip in the ocean would probably help."

"Anything else?"

I shrugged.

Lisa nodded. "So, you don't know if he's a wealthy eccentric or a former accountant down on his luck the last couple of years. You don't know if he's a veteran with PTSD from combat in Afghanistan. Or an alcoholic with three days of sobriety. You don't know if he was horribly physically, sexually, or emotionally abused as a child. You don't know if he suffered a serious head injury saving a child from being hit by a car. You don't know if he had a bad learning disability that kept him from learning in school the way you did. You don't know—"

"Okay, I get it," I said. "You made your point."

She pushed the book at me. Grudgingly I took it and opened it.

"Everyone you meet is a teacher."

I stumbled over the smooth sidewalk. Lisa caught me before I fell. She took the book back. "Want to talk about it?"

I didn't. I shook my head, and we kept walking. The lessons I needed to learn from this man were slapping me in the face. They were about appreciation. And not making assumptions about people, and probably a lot of other things. There were also lessons there about simple acts of kindness that Lisa had just modeled. I had a lot to learn in all these areas.

"Let's go back," I said to Lisa. I wanted time alone to think about these things. I didn't want to be distracted by her or the book.

We turned around and a few minutes later we were back at the pier parking lot. We didn't pass the man on the way back and I wondered where he went. I asked Lisa but she just shook her head and said nothing.

Before we parted, she insisted I take the book again and see what it had to say. I felt like I had enough to work on already but did as she wished. When I opened the book to a new page it punched me again.

"A rich life has nothing to do with money."

I passed the book back to her and got in the car. I didn't want to go anywhere except back to the motel room.

Once I got there, I threw myself on the bed and pulled a pillow over my head. I spent the rest of the morning trying to dig out not only all the things I needed to change about myself, but also how exactly to go about doing that. It seemed pretty simple to say to myself, "You've got to stop doing that," or, "You need to be nicer to people." But that didn't get me very far down the road to actually doing it.

By noon I decided I needed a break, so I went out to a sub shop for a quick bite. While I was eating, and thinking, it occurred to me that it might help if I wrote a few things down. I found a journaling notebook with a seaside scene on the cover at a souvenir shop. I bought it, hurried back to the motel, and settled in for the afternoon.

On the first page of the notebook I wrote, "Words of Wisdom," then I added, "The Path to Change." Seemed about right.

I spent the afternoon contemplating my life—past, present, and future. I laid on the bed a while, sat at the little desk, and paced around the room.

By seven o'clock I had quite a list. It started with "Be kinder to everyone." Next on the list was, "Give everyone respect." Then, "Listen carefully and fully to everyone who is talking to you." It didn't take me long to add, "Learn from your mistakes."

Channeling Helene I wrote, "Slow down and be patient," and, "Be willing to give in 50 percent of the time in a relationship." Then I added, "at least." I made a note to call Helene and apologize. Right after that I made a list of other people I needed to apologize to, starting with my former supervisor at work and a couple of former colleagues.

I added notes to the journal pages about being open to new relationships in my life, even casual ones, and the things people might teach me. Random acts of kindness found a page by itself in the journal. So did, "You don't know anybody's past. So don't judge them." After that I wrote, "Your alcohol use is hurting you and the people around you." Neither the book nor Lisa had mentioned that, but Helene sure had. Then I made a list of things to appreciate and be thankful for. It was a long list. All things considered, I decided I'd had a pretty fortunate life. Even given my current circumstances.

I had something written on about half the journal pages when I decided to try to get some sleep. I didn't even think about having a beer. Before I crawled under the sheets, I heard raindrops beating against the motel roof. I wondered where the man we'd passed on the sidewalk was spending the night.

I got a few hours' sleep but also spent a few thinking about things to add to the journal. I had a lot to work on.

I was awake and dressed a few minutes after sunrise and headed to the beach. Fortunately, I saw Lisa sitting in the sand just a few yards from the pier. I took my place beside her.

"I'm so pumped up," I told her before she could say a word. "I've got a list of things to change and do. I've written them in a journal, so I won't forget them."

"That's wonderful," she said. "And do you have a game plan for when you're going to start on those changes and how you're going to do it?"

"As soon as I get back home, I've got some things I'm going to do right away," I said. "I'm going to work my way through the list. I'll be busy for quite a while."

She grinned and handed me the book. I wasn't afraid of it now, so eagerly picked my page and opened it. Printed boldly on the page I picked was:

"Those who died yesterday had a plan for this morning. Those who died this morning had a plan for tonight."

That was plain and simple. I handed the book back to her. "I'm going to start today," I said, looking her in the eye. "I've done a lot of thinking, and I'll do some more. But there are things I can do today."

Again, Lisa smiled. She pressed the book back into my hand. I opened it and read the words on the page out loud.

"The difference between who you are and who you will become is what you do. It's not what you think, or what you say you're going to do."

"I've got that," I said to her and the book. "I really am anxious to get to work on these changes. But I wanted to see you again this morning and thank you for all you've done for me. I've got to head home tomorrow. I think it would be fair to say that you've changed my life."

"I've done nothing," she said. "I've just shared with you the book and some of the things I've learned on my life's journey." She grabbed me with her eyes. "I was once a lot like you."

I found that hard to believe, but inspiring at the same time. If I could become anything like her, I'd be pleased.

I didn't know quite what else I wanted to say, but I was reluctant to leave. "Is there anything else I need to know?" I asked. "Any other words of wisdom from you or from the book?"

She shrugged her shoulders but handed me the book. I opened it.

"Forgive often and love with a full heart. You never know when you may not have that chance again."

I hadn't thought much about love or being in love again. It only took me a moment to realize I'd probably never really been in love. At least not a healthy, giving more than taking, kind of love. My relationship with Helene wasn't that. It wasn't even close.

I realized I needed to make a lot of changes before I was going to have any kind of chance for a healthy love. And part of that forgiving I needed to do was forgiving myself for the way I'd treated Helene, and a lot of other people in my life. After I made my apologies.

For a moment I felt overwhelmed. I had so much in front of me. So much work to do. So many changes to make. It was going to take a long time, and I needed to keep focused. I wondered how not to fall off the wagon. How to keep myself motivated.

Since I was still holding the book, I thought maybe it could give me some guidance. I closed it, then quickly opened it to another page.

"Simply do the right thing, in the right way, at the right time, in the right place, to the right person, for the right reason, with the right feeling ... The first time."

Well that pretty well nails it. That was something I needed to write in my journal. Heck, I needed to have that written in big bold letters on the walls of my apartment and on the bathroom mirror.

Lisa was watching all this and seemed to be reading my mind. "I know you'll try your best," she said. "It can take time to make these big changes. Lots of times it's a two steps forward and one step backward kind of thing. Besides being kind to yourself and forgiving of yourself, it's a good idea to work on patience. You didn't become the person you've been overnight. It took years. So, you're not going to become the new person you want to be in a few days or weeks."

"I know that," I said. "I'm just a little afraid, knowing myself, that I may slip off track occasionally. Especially with some of the more difficult things." I thought for a moment. "I guess maybe that's one of the biggest learnings I have in front of me. How to keep going forward when it gets tough. When part of me says 'I can't do this,' or 'I don't want to do this.'"

Lisa nodded. "That's tough for everybody." She reached over and tapped the book. "Maybe the book has something to say about that."

I picked the page and opened it up. I read out loud.

"A lesson will repeat itself until you learn it."

I looked at Lisa. Her approving smile filled me with confidence. "Okay, I've got this," I said.

As much as I hated to do it, I figured it was time to get started on my tasks and let Lisa get on with whatever she had to do. I realized I knew nothing about her and her life. Maybe part of my being open to other people included spending time with her, focusing on *her*, and not just my needy self. Maybe there was something I could do for her. Or maybe something she could learn from me, though I doubted that.

"Could we maybe spend some more time together?" I asked. "Just the two of us. Without the book?"

She flashed me an enormous smile but shook her head. "Nice first step, but no." She reached out her hand for the book.

I started to hand it to her, then the thought occurred to me – *I wonder what the last page in the book says.* What was the final piece of wisdom written in this book by who knows who and who knows when. I pulled the book back and turned to the final page. And there it was.

"Just do it."

I grimaced and turned to Lisa. As I handed her the book I said, "The final bit of wisdom is a Nike slogan?"

"You should take your learnings in whatever form they present themselves," she said as she took the book and stood up. "Besides, I think that was written in this book long before any advertising person for Nike came up with it."

She waited while I stood, then put her arms out. We hugged. I felt her warmth, her strength, flowing into me. When we parted, she turned and walked away at the edge of the surf.

I stood, stuck in the sand, watching her as long as I could. As she faded into the distance, she seemed to become one with the waves.

I shook myself out of my trance and headed back toward my car. On the way I spotted a large shell at the surf line and walked over to pick it up. It seemed like it would be a good souvenir of my transformative time at the beach.

As I bent to pick it up, I saw that it had a large piece missing from it. It wasn't whole. It had been injured and battered by the myriad of forces pushing and carrying it along through its existence. But yet it had survived.

Perfect!

Message In A Bottle

"I understand you have a bottle with a message in it you found in the surf."

I'd introduced myself to Betty at her door and explained I was a reporter for the local weekly newspaper and was hopeful of interviewing her for an article. Human interest stories were my specialty.

She invited me in, and I took a seat on an old, upholstered wing chair after she sat on the loveseat. The living room, just like the outside of her house, was small but neat. I would have guessed her age at about 75 or 80. She wore what I always thought of as a "house dress", faded pastel colors, but surely very comfortable.

"Oh that," she said with a shake of her head. When she said nothing else, I asked her if it was true that she'd found an old bottle in the surf many years ago and kept it in her home. When she remained silent, I informed her if she told me it wasn't true, I'd wish her a good day and be on my way. I waited out a coughing spell.

"Well ... I could do that," she finally said, staring down toward the floor. Then after a moment turned her head to look at me and added, "But I wouldn't be telling the truth."

I nodded and said, "Thank you." Then I explained that someone had told me about the bottle, and I thought it would be a great human-interest story for the weekly newspaper. I wanted her to tell me about the bottle, where she'd found it, and what the message inside said. She had apparently told a few people about the bottle, but no one seemed to know the details of the message.

After staring at me for several seconds, during which her face went through several distortions, she said, "I'll have to think about it. Come back another day." Her tone was firm, but not impolite. "I have good days and bad days. Today is a bad one and I don't feel like talking."

I thanked her for her consideration and promised to check in with her in a few days, hopefully catching her at a better time. She suggested I call before coming and gave me her cell number.

Betty lived in the oldest section of Kinnakeet near the harbor, where single story residences like hers still hugged the sandy loam, while near-by homes of the more affluent had been raised above the inevitable storm-driven tide rush from the sound. Ancient live oak trees hung heavy around the lane her house was on. An old family cemetery sat just down the road. As I drove by, I wondered if she could see the headstones from her house and if she planned to be buried there.

Three days later I caught Betty on a better day. I asked permission to take notes, and again explained I hoped to tell the story of the bottle and the message in an article for the paper.

Betty agreed to my note taking, after commenting that my memory had to be much better than hers. However, she would only agree to a published article after she had a chance to review my writing and make her final decision. With this agreement in place, I thought we were ready to begin. However, she had one more request.

"Before I tell you about the bottle you have to listen to a story. I'll try to keep it brief, but it may take a few minutes." I readily agreed. I liked listening to the stories older people tell.

"As a young woman I married a man, Will," she began. "He was a writer and a couple of years older. He had just accepted a job as an instructor at Wheaton College. He'd been working on a novel and planned to continue his writing while teaching. He'd published a novel earlier through a small publishing house, but it went nowhere. He was convinced this one was much better.

"He was frustrated that he had little time for writing with all the academic demands. I worked full-time and provided more of our income than he did. We lived in a small apartment and just managed to get by. But we loved each other and that was all that really mattered."

I was nodding my head and began to realize this story was going to take a while to get out. I wasn't sure how this related to the bottle and note inside, but figured I just had to be patient. She continued.

"One day after we'd been married a couple of years, he came to me and said he'd finished the novel. He asked me to read it, which of course I did." She paused for a moment, then her face lit up. "It was amazing! It touched me on so many levels. I thought it was the best book, the best story, I'd ever read. I told him it was great and pushed him to show it to the agent who'd helped him get the first novel published. He was reluctant. I didn't understand why, but he finally agreed.

"The agent took a while to read it, but when he did, he agreed it was great. He said he would have no trouble selling it. Sure enough, one of the big publishing houses bought it and Will got a nice advance. It took almost a year for it to get published, with a little bit of editing involved, but when it did the publishing house pushed it and it became a best seller. Then it became number one on the New York Times best seller list. It stayed there several weeks. The agent even sold the movie rights to a big Hollywood star.

"Will took the summer off and did all the things that a best-selling author did back in those days. There was a book tour and signing in big cities all around the country. He did NPR and local radio interviews. There was even a TV appearance or two. It was an exciting time for him, and a fun time for us. The money was pouring in."

Betty paused for a moment and seemed to get lost in the memories. "That sounds really great," was all I could think of to say.

"It was," she finally said. "Before long he got a job at Bates College as an assistant professor of English, and we moved to Maine. He basked in the attention, and I worked only part-time, just because I wanted to. Everyone was anxious to see his next book, but he again found little time to write with the increased teaching demands. But after four years the novel was ready. The publisher accepted it, and everyone expected a similar response and big sales. But the reception was lukewarm at best. Many critics outright panned it. Some even called him a one-hit wonder."

Betty looked out the window at the front of the house. She took a sip from the big metal cup on the table beside the love seat. When her eyes came back to me her face had dropped.

"Will became depressed. Finally, he came to me one night and ..." It took her a moment to get through a coughing spell.

"He told me he was a fraud and a cheat. I asked him what he meant. He told me the book, the good one as he called it, wasn't his. I told him of course it was his. He wrote it, and he deserved everything that came out of it." She paused again. "He just shook his head and finally said, 'No. I stole the book. Someone else wrote it. I just retyped it, changed the title, and put my name on it.'"

I didn't know quite how to react to that, so I kept quiet and motioned for her to go on. I'd stopped taking notes by this point.

"He explained that someone had sent him a manuscript and a letter saying he was a graduate of Wheaton College and had read Will's earlier book. He'd been working on his novel for years and desperately wanted Will to read it and give him some feedback. Will told me he didn't have the time or the interest and planned to send the manuscript back with a brief note. But he read the first page, then the second, and got hooked. As he read it, he fell in love with it. He planned then to write the author back, tell him how good it was, and encourage him to get it published. But he found there was no return address on the letter. The only return address was on the big brown envelope the manuscript came in, which had long been discarded.

"Will said he'd gone to the alumni office to try to get an address for the man, but they didn't have one. He said he figured the man would contact him again about the manuscript, but he said no calls or letters ever came. Remember, this is before the days of the internet and the ability to find anybody in about one minute with a few clicks on a computer. So, he eventually made the decision to retype the manuscript, correcting a few typos, but otherwise changing nothing about the story. After the week or so it took him to do that, he knew it was great, and better than anything he could ever write. He sat on it for a few weeks, trying to decide what to do with it, then changed the title and showed it to me.

"With the failure of the next book, which was the one he was working on when we met, he couldn't get away from the feeling that he was one big fraud, a horrible writer. He felt that the money he'd earned from the book, and the life we'd had the last several years, were all predicated on a lie."

I couldn't help but ask, "How'd you feel when he told you all this?"

Betty shook her head and grimaced. "I was in disbelief at first. I couldn't believe he would do something like that. Then I was angry, very angry. I was afraid for him and a little bit afraid for myself. I just didn't want to be around him."

Betty looked away for a moment, then asked me if I wanted some water or something. When I declined, she excused herself for a minute, worked her way off the loveseat and took her cup to the back of the house. She returned five minutes later with the cup and a box of tissues. She sat back down, took a breath, and continued the story.

"He admitted that he'd lived every day since the book was published waiting for the real author to walk up to him one day and claim the book. He'd thought about what he'd say to him. He wasn't sure exactly how that would go, but he knew he'd admit what he'd done and try to find some way to make it right. He planned to go public with it and give the man every dime of future royalties, plus try to scrape up what he could of what he'd already received. He said he'd come close a couple of times to just telling his agent what he'd done but couldn't quite do it. His biggest fear, he said, was telling me. But over time the pressure just kept building, and he felt like finally he had to do something."

After a sip of water, or whatever was in the cup, she continued. "I walked out that night and didn't see him again for a week. When I could finally face him again, I came back to the house. He was a wreck. He wasn't teaching his classes, and I doubt he was eating much. He had told the department head he was sick, which he was." She studied the rug on the floor for a minute.

"We talked for hours. I told him I would stick with him, and we'd get through it together. And we did. He went back to his teaching responsibilities, but his heart wasn't in it. He got through the semester, but by mutual agreement with the college administration he resigned at the end of the year. It took a while, but we got the house sold and moved south, to Greensboro.

"He wanted to become invisible in case the man was waiting for the right moment somehow to confront him. He talked about changing his name, but never did it. No one in Greensboro knew us, and enough time had passed that the book had long since dropped off the best seller list and there was nothing in the media about it, though it was still in all the bookstores. Fortunately, the movie never got made. Writing and teaching was all he knew, so eventually he got a job teaching at a community college and I went back to work. He had a hard time at the college whenever anyone would bring up the book. He tried not to talk about it. We didn't even have a copy of it in the house.

"The few new friends we made probably thought he was quite eccentric. When they would eventually identify him with the famous book of several years ago, and bring it up or want to talk about how much they'd enjoyed it, they'd be met with absolute silence. He just refused to talk about it. I handled the many inquiries about what was wrong with him by explaining that he just wanted to put the book, and that stage of his life, behind him.

"Needless to say, we never had any children. Neither of us felt like we had the energy for that. And to be frank, we were sleeping in separate beds nearly all that time after his confession."

Betty pushed herself off the loveseat and walked to the window. She stared at the limbs of the old oak trees blowing in the coastal breeze. After a moment she turned back to me.

"Will died just five years after we moved there. He was only 46."

I debated for a moment, then decided to go ahead. "May I ask how he died?"

"No, you may not," she said, then turned back to the window.

There was a full five minutes of silence before she returned to her seat. "I'm sorry," she said. She grabbed a tissue and wiped her eyes. "It's been a long time, but it still hurts."

"I understand," was all I could say.

After another minute, and a sip to wet her throat, she picked up the story.

"I dealt with the grief and loss and tried to put his things in order. One of the things I did was open the safe we'd brought with us from Maine. He'd always kept it locked and made me promise to never open it. I'd always figured that was where he kept the original manuscript. I was right. When I opened the safe, I found not only the manuscript but also three letters from the original author.

"The first one told a little more about him, including the fact that he'd graduated from Wheaton College 31 years before Will got there. He'd been working on the story for about 10 years. He wanted it to be what he left to the world to be remembered by, as he had nothing else to leave behind. The letters increasingly demanded that Will return the manuscript. The tone got harsher with each letter, and the last one threatened legal action. Each letter had the address for the return of the manuscript. The first letter was dated shortly after Will turned the manuscript over to his agent. The second one came while he was awaiting word from the publisher. The third was dated a couple weeks before the book's release."

Betty paused to wipe her eyes, then blew her nose. When she was ready, she caught my eyes again. "As I'm sure you can imagine, that stirred everything up again for me."

"I certainly can," I said. "That must have changed your feelings about Will. At least to some degree."

"Oh, it did," she said. "But we're not going to go there."

We both listened to the wind for a moment as the tree limbs rustled and something banged against a far corner of the house.

"I decided to move here to Kinnakeet," she finally said. "That was more than 30 years ago. I'd visited here with my parents as a child. Back in the late 50s when the place was a world different than it is now.

You had to take the ferry to get to Hatteras Island, and Route 12 had just recently been paved all the way down the island. Anyway, I got a job, made a few friends, and started life over. A few people figured out who my deceased husband was. But it was easier to talk about him, and the book, and that time in my life without him around."

"I've got to ask," I interrupted. I'd waited as long as I could. "Did you ever try to contact the original author?"

She cracked a thin smile. "No, I didn't. I justified that by convincing myself that he was probably dead by then and there was nothing to be gained. I also told myself that he certainly had kept another copy of the manuscript and could have gone ahead without Will returning his copy if he'd wanted to. He just probably didn't want another copy of it floating around out there. Then I told myself maybe with the different title he never knew Will had published it."

I must have frowned.

"Oh, I know." Her disappointment in herself cut across her face. "I just made excuses. But ... that brings me back to the message in the bottle." She smiled. "Remember that? The story I just told you has everything to do with the bottle and the message inside it."

Finally! I thought but didn't say. I'd been quite enthralled with her story. "Yes, the bottle you found on the beach."

She nodded. "Well, I found the bottle during one of my morning walks on the beach," she said. "It was covered in foam and gunk near the high tide point. I wasn't sure what it was, but when I poked it with my foot, I knew immediately what I'd found."

When I asked where she was on the beach when she found it, she replied, "At one of those beach access points just north of town. I think they call them ramps now. I don't remember what those numbers are. I haven't been going there lately because walking is ... well, not so easy anymore."

She explained that she'd been walking for probably half an hour and was nearing her turnaround point. "The bottle was sealed with an old cork that was still wedged tightly in the top. After I picked it up and brushed the sand and a bunch of other old, accumulated stuff off the glass I could see through parts of it. There was something inside, though it was hard to tell what. The bottle was mahogany brown, almost black in places."

I asked how long ago she'd discovered the bottle. "I'm not sure. A long time ago. Well ... maybe not so long ago. But at least a few years now."

A mischievous grin lit her face. "I guess I should admit, I never actually opened the bottle until after the first time you were here. I tried when I first found it, but tore up the top of the old cork that was in it when I tried. I decided to just live with the mystery. I'd sort of forgotten about it. But then, after you were here, you got me interested in it again and I decided I wanted to know what the note said. So, I worked on it after you left and got it open. The cork that's in it now is an old wine bottle cork that I just stuffed in it."

I waited for her to say more about the bottle or the message inside, but she just closed her eyes. I cleared my throat which stirred her. I asked if I could see the bottle. She directed me to a wooden cabinet on the wall just behind the loveseat. I got up and stepped behind her. Upon opening the cabinet door, I immediately saw the bottle, the only object on the top shelf. I carefully retrieved it and retook my seat.

The bottle was as she'd described it. Whatever writing that had once adorned the outside of the bottle was long gone and the brown glass had turned mostly black. It was smaller than a wine bottle, but bigger than a beer bottle. I chuckled inwardly for a moment at my reference points. The cork was tight and as I turned the bottle I could see a piece of paper inside.

"Can I open the bottle?" I asked.

She nodded and said, "After listening to me all morning I think you deserve to see what's inside."

It hadn't been all morning. The time had actually gone by quickly. But then I worked on the cork and got it out in just a few seconds. I tipped the bottle up and a small roll of paper fell out into my hand. "Go ahead, read it," she said.

I unrolled the well-preserved, slightly yellow piece of paper and read the message. It was written in bold handwriting.

Cleanse your soul. Take nothing to the grave with you!

I thought that was a bit odd. I looked at her. She nodded.

"I never told anybody the story of the manuscript, the book, and the letters my husband kept hidden until now. Until you. But when I read that message a couple days ago, I knew what I had to do. And I must admit, the first part of that, telling you the story, has felt good."

I could see the relief in her face. But I wondered, so I asked, "What's the second part of that? What else do you need to do?"

After a brief cough and a drink from the cup she grinned. "I want you to help me find the original author of the manuscript."

That took me by surprise. Maybe it shouldn't have, but it did. After just a couple moments thought, I realized I could probably do a reasonable job of searching for him with the resources at my command. I considered myself a good researcher, part of my education, and almost a daily part of the job as a reporter. With the internet being what it was these days, I figured it wouldn't take long.

"Okay," I said. "If you'll give me his name and the address from the letters, I'll see what I can do." She already had these written down for me and retrieved them from a drawer in the table beside her. I returned the note to its long resting place, replaced the cork, and put the bottle back in the cabinet. I took my leave just a couple minutes later after thanking her for a most interesting morning and promising to get back to her within a day or two.

Back at my home office, I had one quick thing to do but was into my search within 30 minutes. It only took me a couple minutes to find Daniel Ellison. Or at least his obituary. He died in 1993. He was indeed a graduate of Wheaton College, in 1941. He'd gone on to serve in the Army and was a decorated WWII vet. After the war he had a career as a high school English teacher. He was preceded in death by his wife and only child, an infant daughter. His only sibling, an older brother, had been killed in the war.

I shared this news with Betty the next morning. She cried for several minutes. It seemed to me she was shedding not only tears of grief for Daniel Ellison, but perhaps also tears of remorse for actions not taken.

When she was able to talk, we agreed that there was nothing she could do at this point for Daniel. She did, however, ask me for one more favor.

Early the next morning, I helped her out to the edge of the surf beside the pier. She thought walking through the sand from the parking area at ramp 34 to the water's edge would be impossible for her. We took a moment to watch the sun rise behind the pier where several fishermen already had lines in the water. With the cork wedged as tightly into the top as I could manage, and while Betty cheered me on, I waded into the frigid water and threw the bottle as far as I could into the surf of the outgoing tide.

I wrote the article that afternoon. I told the story of the bottle and message inside found by Betty many years ago on the beach. I disclosed what the message in the bottle was, and that Betty had a most interesting story to tell relating to the message and its impact on her. I did not give the details of that story. I did report that the bottle and the message had been returned to the ocean in hopes it would find its way to another beach-walking soul in need of its message, and would provide another interesting story to tell.

Betty read the draft of the article the next day and immediately gave her permission for its publication. It was in the next week's paper. A few months later I was given an award for best human-interest story in a small circulation weekly newspaper.

I celebrated by taking Betty out for dinner. Afterwards, we threw another sealed bottle, with a message hand-written by Betty inside, into the surf beside the pier.

The House On Dory Lane

I thought at first it was an injured deer, or possibly even a bear cub. But as I got closer, my headlights lit a human form, crawling out of the ditch toward the pavement on the side of a barren stretch of Route 12 South. As I hit my brakes and slid by, the person raised an arm in an attempt to wave me down.

Once I got the car to a screeching stop, I backed up to within a few feet of the now collapsed figure, put my emergency flashers on, and jumped out. When I got close, a young woman raised her head and muttered, "Help me, please."

She was dressed in dark slacks, dressy blue and white cotton shirt, and a torn, open jacket. Even in the dim red light of my flashers, I could tell all of this was coated in sand and mud. Her face and hands were covered in streaks of blood.

I knelt to her side and wrapped an arm around her. I had thought to pick her up, but her scream, "No! My side hurts!" when I touched her, stopped me at once. At this point, I noticed the tears streaming down her face, mixing with the blood, and pulled away for a moment to reassess.

"I'm here to help you," I said, as calmly as I could. "And the first thing we need to do is get you off the pavement and into my car. Can you stand up?"

She made eye contact for the first time. "I ... I'll try." She tried to push herself with her arms to her feet but collapsed to the pavement. "Shit! My shoulders hurt too much for that. And my head is killing me!" She sat motionless for a few seconds, not so quietly sobbing.

This was painful just to watch. I knew once we got her in the car our next stop was the hospital back in Nags Head. "Maybe if I get behind you and lift you up, we can get you on your feet."

It was obvious she didn't like this idea but, after a moment, she nodded her head and said, "Okay. Let's try."

I stepped behind her, moved the coat out of the way, then put both hands on her hips over the mud-soaked pants. I counted, "One, two, three," and lifted. She was surprisingly light, and was standing, with a bit of a wobble, a moment later. She put a hand on my side to steady herself. When she took it away, I put my arm gently around her waist, then said, "Can you walk?"

"I ... think so," she said, as she took a step toward the car. We began to move slowly in tandem, and a few seconds later she was leaning against the side of the car. I punched the fob to open the trunk and got the two towels out that I'd kept in there for years. At that point I noticed she was missing a shoe.

"Here, let's try to dry you off a little bit," I said, as I handed her one of the towels.

It was probably 40 degrees standing on the side of the road at 12:30 a.m. on that chilly Saturday night in early February, but she started to take her soaking wet coat off. She grimaced in pain, then asked me to help her get it off. As I did, it was obvious that both of her shoulders or arms were injured. Almost any movement of her arms elicited groans and moans. Once the coat was off, I took the initiative to delicately pat her back and arms with a towel while she held the other one. For the first time, I noticed she was shivering. I asked her if I could wipe some of the blood off her face.

"I'm bleeding!?" she asked.

"Actually, quite a bit," I said. And she smelled like swamp sludge, but I didn't tell her that.

Without waiting for her permission, I began to delicately touch her face with the towel. The blood was trickling down from above her hairline. I wiped her face, then her bloody hands one at a time. I took the other towel from her hand and said, "Here, let's wrap this around you. Hold this one on your head, and we'll get you in the car." She nodded her agreement, and with some difficulty, and a couple of moans, we got her folded into the passenger side front seat. I threw her jacket in the floor in the back before I got in and fired up the Mustang.

"Wait! My bag," she said. "It might be in my jacket." I reached into the back and pulled a small green pocketbook out of the jacket and handed it to her. "Thank God!" she exclaimed.

"I'll have you at the hospital in a few minutes," I said with a quick glance in her direction. We were just a mile or two south of Salvo, and I figured it would take close to 30 minutes to get there.

"No. Not the hospital. Just take me home," she insisted.

"What?" I turned again to stare at her. "You're obviously pretty badly injured and need medical attention. You might need some stitches, and no telling what kind of internal injuries you might have."

"No, I just want to go home," she said, shaking her head. She lowered the towel from her head and looked at it. "I'll ... be okay. Besides ... I don't have any health insurance."

"Shit," I muttered under my breath. For a moment, I stared straight ahead while I debated the issue. I'd been there. Best case, an E.R. visit would cost thousands. Once I made my decision I asked, "Where's home?"

"Kinnakeet," she said. "Just a few miles down the road."

Against my better judgement, I hit the gas, pulled back on the road, and continued south. I turned the heat up and the fan on high. It occurred to me that with that cut on her head she could have a concussion. I knew from my first aid training that you're supposed to keep a person with a possible concussion conscious, so I figured I'd try to keep her talking. If she passed out, we were definitely headed back to the hospital. I still had no idea how she ended up in that condition on the side of the road.

I broke the couple minutes of silence with, "So, my name's Dave. Can you tell me what happened?"

"I'm ... Clare," she said softly. I could barely make out what she was saying. "And thank you for helping me. I was afraid no one would come along or stop." She used the towel to wipe her eyes and forehead. "You're not going to believe this, but ... I jumped out of a car."

She was right. That was a little hard to believe. But I realized after a moment's consideration it would explain why she was where she was with no one around. "Okay. How'd that happen?"

"It's kind of a long story, but the short version is ..." She paused for a few seconds and closed her eyes. I was thinking concussion. Then she opened her eyes and continued. Slowly, but loud enough for me to hear her. At least she'd stopped crying enough that she could talk.

"I was in Nags Head at a club with a friend. Well, actually a new acquaintance. She talked me into going to the club with her. Once we got there, she started drinking ... pretty heavily. She's very pretty, and guys kept buying her drinks and asking her to dance. I don't drink very much, so I nursed about three all evening. She may have also taken some kind of drug, I'm not sure. She went outside with a couple guys for a few minutes at some point. So ..." She stopped again and looked at the bloody towel in her hands.

"Anyway, when she finally agreed to head home, I begged her to let me drive, but she absolutely refused. She was driving ... speeding, really fast and pretty recklessly. She was weaving all over the road. I kept asking her to stop and let me drive. When we passed through Rodanthe I asked her to just let me out, but she kept saying, 'I'm fine,' even though it was obvious she wasn't." She paused and stared at the darkness out the window.

Even though there were a million stars in the sky, it was pitch black when I looked out toward the ocean. "That must have been you guys who passed me going about 80 miles-an-hour a few miles back," I said.

She nodded. "Yep, that was us." For another moment she looked out the window. "It reached a point where I figured I could either stay in the car and ride out the accident she was bound to have, and hope for the best, or jump. It may have been the second worst decision I've made lately, but I decided to jump. I thought the side of the road was just sand, so I tried to get her to slow down by yelling there was something in the road ahead of us ... She slowed down just a little, so I unhooked my seatbelt, opened the door, and jumped."

"Wow! That took a lot of courage," I said. Just the thought of her jumping from the car made me slow down. I opened the window just a crack to let in some fresh air.

"Well, by that point I had convinced myself I was going to die if I stayed in the car, so ... maybe more self-preservation, and a little alcohol, than courage. But the landing was a lot harder than I thought it'd be. My leg hit the doorframe and that spun me around. I hit the ground hard and then ... I guess I rolled into a ditch beside the road."

"Yeah," I said, "that ditch was filled with water. And the ground beside the road had a lot of gravel and shell pieces on it. I bet it was a pretty rough landing."

"It sure was. I just felt a lot of pain in my side and arms when I stopped rolling. Then I realized I was wet, and really cold."

"How long do you think you were there before I came along?" I asked. I wondered why her acquaintance hadn't stopped to help her or try to get her back in the car. I decided not to go there.

"I'm ... I'm not sure. Maybe four or five minutes. Long enough to be scared to death that I'd be there all night. Guess I didn't think that part through very well. So, again, thank you."

"No problem."

We were approaching Kinnakeet by this point, so I asked her where she lived. She told me it was in

Kinnakeet Shores; she wasn't sure of the exact address on Dory Lane but could guide me there. We took the right turn at the flag poles into the subdivision, and a minute later I pulled into the left side of the driveway, beside a Camry, in front of the three-story house. The porch lights lit up the front. "Big house," I said.

"Yeah. My parents own it," she said. As I helped her out of the car, she grabbed her pocketbook. At this point she seemed to realize she was wearing only one shoe. She stopped in front of the car and kicked it off. Then she stared at the steps leading to the door.

"Can you make it up those?" I asked.

"I've got to," she said, "There's two more flights once I get in."

I moved to her side, took her hand, and put it on my arm. "Let me help," I said as I took a step forward.

She held on tight, and we walked up the steps. Once we made the landing, she punched the buttons to unlock the door. It was a slow climb up the next two flights of stairs. From her grimacing, and the way she held her side, I figured she had bruised or cracked ribs. Once we reached the top, she flipped on lights in the living room and tossed her bag in a chair. I started to lead her to the sofa just in front of us.

"No," she said, "the bedroom." She pulled me to the left and we walked into the room after she switched on the light. She sat delicately on the side of the neatly made bed, the towel still around her, and took an obviously painful, partial deep breath with her hands on her knees.

For the first time, I could see her in decent light. Her face was smeared with blood, most of it dried. Her green-blue eyes glistened with moisture. There was caked blood in her blond hair about an inch above the hairline over the left eye. There were two small scratches on her left cheek. Her shirt was torn in a couple places, and there were three separate blood stains running down the front. Her pants were ripped, and blood stained at both knees. When I picked up her hands to examine them, they were both badly scraped and covered with dried blood.

At the same time I was checking her out, she was examining the damage as well. "I know. I'm a mess," she said, closing her eyes and dropping her head.

"Yes, you are," I agreed. It was a little hard to tell, but I would have guessed she was in her mid- to late-20s, just a couple years younger than me. It was also a little difficult to tell at this point, but she looked like she might be rather attractive once she was cleaned up.

She sat still for another minute, then said, "What I really want right now, more than anything else, is a hot bath." She paused for a moment, then turned to me with a pained expression. "But ... I think I'm going to have to ask you to help me get undressed. I can't really use my arms. And my hands ..."

I can honestly say I hadn't expected that. But it took me just a moment to realize that was the practical way to proceed ... if she really wanted to. I couldn't just leave her there like that, but I needed a moment to get myself ready.

"Okay, but how about first you tell me where I can find some Tylenol, or something a little stronger if you've got it, and I'll get you some water to wash it down."

She nodded, "Yeah. Excellent idea. Tylenol in the top drawer in the bathroom right there," she nodded to the partially open door just in front of her. "There's bottled water in the fridge. That would be good. My head is still throbbing."

I retrieved the Tylenol and water and gave her two pills and the water bottle. "That should help in a few minutes."

She popped the pills in her mouth and swallowed them with a quick drink. She took another sip, then set the bottle on the table beside the bed.

"Now, that other thing," she said as she struggled to her feet.

"I'll start the water running," I said, still stalling. A minute later I had hot water pouring into the large tub and almost knocked her over when I got to my feet. She was standing right behind me.

"I think maybe I should sit on the side of the tub," she said. I moved aside and she lowered herself to the tub. She looked at me with an awkward smile. "Maybe start by taking my shirt off."

I nodded and started on the buttons, then pulled the bottom of it out of her pants. I eased the sleeves carefully off her arms. It was obvious by her facial expression that moving her arms was painful. Several cuts and scrapes had just become visible. One just above her bra on the right side, the others a couple inches below the bra and on her stomach. There was dried blood smeared on that garment and most of her flat abdomen. She looked down and made a face. "Okay, now the bra."

I reached behind her and tried to remember how to work the hooks. It had been a couple of years, and I was never very accomplished at it. She smiled briefly at my fumbles, before I was finally successful and eased the straps down her arms. I averted my eyes.

"Don't be silly. You can look," she said. "That's the least you should get out of this mess."

I did.

"Okay. Now the pants," she said. She scooted to the edge of the tub, and I undid the belt and snap, then worked them off her hips as she lifted and rocked side to side. After I slid them down her legs and off, she said, "Now the panties." Again, I averted my eyes while I slid them down and off. "Such a gentleman," she said with a slight chuckle. Her knees were a bloody mess.

By this point the tub was nearly full. I checked the temperature and decided it was about right. I helped her turn so her legs were in the tub, then steadied her as she slid in. Her back was free of blood, but her shoulders had large ugly bruises. She grimaced, then said, "Ahhh ..." as she sank up to her neck in the water.

I got her a washcloth and said, "I'll give you a few minutes. Do what you can, then I'll wash anything you can't. I'll need to wash your hair too." I stepped into the bedroom, then the living room, and sat on the sofa.

The room was neat as a pin. There was a single book on the coffee table, the only thing in the room that suggested the house was currently being lived in. I thought about how, if not for this diversion, by now I would be snug in my bed in the chilly little cottage in Hatteras.

I was debating whether I could leave her alone after I got her out of the bath and into bed. I was not so worried about a concussion at this point, but she still couldn't move very well. She'd be sore as hell in the morning, under the best of circumstances. Probably cracked ribs, and bruised, but probably not dislocated, shoulders.

I got up and paced around the living room and kitchen for a couple minutes, then decided I should check on her. She was sitting up in the tub. The water was a deep pink color—blood mostly, mixed with a little sand and mud. I couldn't even see her knees beneath the surface. "How are you doing?" I asked.

"Feeling a little better," she said. "The hot water, and probably the Tylenol, helps." The cut I could see on her chest was clean and didn't look too bad.

"How about I wash your hair?" I said.

"Okay. The shampoo's in the shower."

I grabbed it from the stall and got on my knees. Her hair was already wet, so I poured on some shampoo and got to work. Fortunately, her hair was no more than shoulder length, and the sand and remaining blood washed out easily. I parted her hair and examined the cut. I decided a doctor might have put a stitch or two in it but wasn't sure. I knew from personal experience that the scalp bled profusely, even with a small cut, like this one.

It occurred to me that rinsing her hair in bloody water wouldn't be a good idea, so, after excusing myself for a moment, I found a plastic tumbler in the kitchen and, back in the bathroom, filled the tumbler several times with warm water from the tub spicket, and rinsed her hair as best I could. Afterward, I helped her stand up, then step out of the tub.

I grabbed a towel from the hanger on the door and began to carefully dry her. She kept her arms at her side as I patted her entire front, then her back. I did the best I could with her hair. She smelled like strawberry cream shampoo—a significant improvement. For the first time I was able to examine her cuts and scrapes.

Several of them needed antiseptic ointment and a bandage. When I asked her where I'd find these, she pointed to the bottom drawer between the two sinks.

She stood as still as she could while I applied the first aid to the several spots on her chest and abdomen, the cut in her scalp, then wiped off the blood still seeping from her knees and bandaged them as best I could. The scrapes on her hands got ointment and two bandages. The scratches on her face just got a little ointment.

Once this was done, I grabbed the blue flannel robe hanging on the other hanger on the door and helped her into it. We walked back into the bedroom, and she sat again on the side of the bed. She was moving a bit easier.

"Thank you for everything," she said with a timid smile. "I think I'll be okay now. I know you've got someplace to be, and probably somebody waiting for you and wondering where you are."

"Nope, on all accounts," I said. "No one waiting for me, and I don't think you're ready to be left alone. I'm not at all sure you're going to be able to get out of that bed once you get in it. How's your head?"

She frowned. "Still hurts, but not as bad. I think I've hurt my ribs, though. That's what hurts the most whenever I try to move."

"Yeah. Try coughing. That'll really hurt," I said with an empathetic smile. "And you're not out of the woods yet for a concussion." I picked up her hands and looked at them for a moment. No blood around the bandages. "If you don't mind, I think either you need to call someone to come and stay with you tonight, or I'll stay and sleep on the sofa so I can check on you in the morning and be here tonight if you need anything."

That made her think for a moment. I could watch the debate going on in her head.

"Well, there's no one I can call at this hour of the night. I don't really know anybody here, and my family is about four hours away."

"Really?" I said. "What are you doing here by yourself?"

"I came here to be alone and study for the bar exam. I've just been here three weeks. I finished law school a couple months ago and will be taking the bar in another two weeks." There was just a hint of pride in her voice.

"That's great," I said.

"Yeah," she said. "This little incident might set my study plan back a bit. I don't know how much I'm going to be able to study tomorrow." She turned her head to look at the little clock on the table beside the bed. "Or, should I say, today." It was 2:03 a.m.

"On the other hand," I said, "maybe you should feel lucky to be alive. You'll never know what would have happened if you'd stayed in that car."

A grimace set in on her face. "I guess you're right. I hope Nancy got home safe."

"Me too," I added. "But now, you need to get in bed and try to get some sleep. I'll catch a little sleep on the sofa, and we'll see how you are in the morning."

"I guess that's probably best. But can you help me get into some pajamas before I get in bed. That'll be more comfortable than this robe, and I don't want to get blood all over the sheets if these things start bleeding again."

We worked together to get the robe off of her, and a pair of pink flannel pajamas on her. For the first time, it struck me how pretty she was. She asked for a minute in the bathroom by herself, so I helped her get situated in front of the toilet then left and closed the door. She opened it slowly, with her foot, in a couple minutes.

I pulled down the bedcovers and sheet, and held an arm as she climbed in. She groaned a couple times as she got settled. I grabbed the Tylenol bottle and poured out two more pills and laid them beside the water bottle. "In about another three hours you should take these," I said. "If you're asleep then, just take them when you wake up. You'll need them."

She nodded. "I'm sure I will. But for right now, if I don't move, I feel pretty good, considering. Except for my head. It still hurts."

I took a step toward the door, but she spoke up. "I'm pretty sure it's going to take me a while to go to sleep. Could you sit on the chaise, or lay down on the bed, and talk to me a little?"

I debated for a moment, then sat on the chaise next to the sliding glass door to the deck. I knew sleep would be difficult for me if I'd been through what she had. "What do you want to talk about?" I said.

"Well, to start off, I don't even remember your name."

"It's Dave," I said.

"Well, again, thank you, Dave. You're literally a life saver." She turned on her side toward me, but grimaced as she did. "You've seen me naked, touched my whole body, and I don't know a single thing about you, except your name and that you're a real gentleman. That's not my usual style with guys. I usually get to know them a little better before I let them take my bra and panties off." She shared a smile that seemed both teasing and self-conscious. "How about you tell me a little bit about yourself."

I laughed for a second, and tried to think about what she would want to know. My job was the first thing that jumped into my head.

"I was headed to Hatteras when I saw you. I've been staying down there a couple days for my job but made a quick trip to Durham. I'm an oceanographer, and I'm with a team studying the Diamond Shoals off Hatteras. That's a unique point in the ocean where three bodies of water meet. The North Atlantic and South Atlantic currents meet the northward flowing

Gulf Stream. There's an incredible variety of sea life in that area, and some tremendous energy generated by the currents. We've got some instruments anchored there and are looking at whether it might be possible to harvest some energy from there."

"That's fascinating," she said. "Who do you work for?"

"Duke University, but we work mostly out of Beaufort, down the coast a ways. That's where I live. We're back in Durham occasionally, and up here every few weeks to check the instruments."

"That's interesting," she said, obviously perking up a bit. "If, and that's a big if right now, I pass the bar, I've got a job offer in Beaufort. It's one of two I'm considering."

"That's great," I said. "It's a pretty neat little town. Growing a lot."

"Yeah, I think I'd like it there. A small-town general practice. Most of my classmates are going for the big firms, a lot of them out of state. I'm not interested in that. Besides, my parents are in Fayetteville, not too far away."

I nodded. It sounded like a good plan. "And they own this house, you said?"

"Yeah, they bought it about 14 years ago, right after it was built. We used to come here for a couple weeks every summer when I was younger. And at Christmas. They rented it out most of the summer. It's never rented in the winter, which is why they let me come here to study."

"You like it here?"

"Yeah, I do. I'm the third child to spend some time here. My brother, the oldest, lived here for a year when he was stationed with the Coast Guard at Oregon Inlet. He couldn't find anything closer that was affordable since everything on the Outer Banks that people aren't living in full-time is a summer rental. Then, my sister took a year off after graduating from college to bum around. She spent the summer, and until about November, here. She worked as a server at night and hung out on the beach during the day."

"Pretty nice life."

"Sure is. I couldn't do that. Wouldn't want to. I went right from college to law school. I worked the summer between in an attorney's office."

"Then here to study for the bar after Christmas," I said. She nodded. I wanted to keep the focus on her. "So, how'd you get hooked up with Nancy?"

"Ahhh ... Nancy." She sneered for a moment. "Well, there aren't many places to eat around here that are open in the winter. I fix most of my meals here, but I met her in one of the places that is open, down in Buxton, the first night I went out to eat. She was working there and chatted me up pretty hard. Probably not a lot of young, single women come in there this time of year. We got together for lunch one day and hit it off well. The next day she called and begged me to go to the club with her. I tried to beg off, but then gave in. She said the band played good dance music, and I decided I could use a night off from studying." She shook her head and frowned. "Guess I learned my lesson about that."

I nodded silently in agreement, then yawned, only half on purpose. "Hey, look. It's time for you to try to get some sleep. Want to give that a try?"

"Yeah, I guess so." She turned slowly to lay on her back and pulled the covers up. "Thanks for talking to me. It helped me settle down a little. My head's feeling a little better too. Might get off to sleep in a few minutes." She closed her eyes for a second, then they popped open. "Oh, there are blankets and pillows in the hall closet on the second floor. Help yourself. You can sleep in one of the beds down there, or on the sofa up here. Wherever you'll be most comfortable." Her smile was immediate. And grateful.

"I'll do that. And you take that Tylenol if you wake up in a while. You'll probably be hurting." She looked at the table by the bed and nodded, then closed her eyes.

I turned off the light and pulled the door almost shut as I slipped out. After a moment's consideration, I got a blanket and pillow from the closet downstairs and settled on the sofa in the living room, after a quick trip to the bathroom. It took me about three minutes to drift off.

At 6:28 a.m. I was wide awake and peeked in at Clare. The nightlight lit the room enough that I could see she was asleep. The Tylenol was gone. I went back to the sofa and tried, unsuccessfully, to get back to sleep. So, I decided to get up and explore the kitchen. I noticed on the way her bar review materials were scattered around the dining area table. They were the only untidy feature of the house. I suspected, however, there was some form of organization to that mess that made sense to her.

The Keurig and little basket of coffee k-cups on the counter were a welcome sight, so I made myself a cup and started on it at the counter. I took a break to run down to my car and retrieve the overnight bag I'd taken with me to Durham. Back upstairs, I took off my blood-stained shirt and put on the one clean one out of the bag. After finishing the coffee, I washed my face and brushed my teeth. That made me feel a bit fresher, though there was no doubt I was feeling the effects of the long night.

I did a quick search for breakfast items and found granola and a partial loaf of whole wheat bread in a cabinet, then eggs, skim milk, and cheese in the fridge.

Besides bottled water and some butter, there wasn't much else in there. There was pasta, a box of granola bars, and corn chips in the pantry. No wonder there was no fat on her body, except in the proper places. She was probably a runner, too. I grabbed a granola bar and returned to the counter to eat it, along with a second cup of coffee.

I finished my little breakfast and figured I could get something more substantial once I got back to the cottage. Then, I went into her pocketbook and found her driver's license. I felt a little bit guilty, but copied her name, home address, in Fayetteville, and birthday into my phone. Then I found her cellphone, but it was locked, and I couldn't get her number.

Just as I put everything back in place, I heard Clare's call from the bedroom, "Dave." I was in there in a flash. She was sitting up slightly in the bed. "I think I need some help getting up," she said.

"Sure," I replied. "How're you feeling?" She looked a lot better than last night, even with her hair mussed all around her.

"Not really that bad," she said with a timid smile. "Except for the ribs. They hurt when I try to move. Maybe you can help me up?"

I walked to the side of the bed and pulled the covers down. Her pajamas had small blood stains around the knees. I didn't see blood anyplace else. She scooted slowly to the side of the bed and rose to her feet with one hand gripping my arm for support. She took a tentative step, then said, "Thanks. Give me a minute in the bathroom."

When she came out, she sat gently on the side of the bed and directed me to where I could find underwear and a sweatshirt in the dresser at the foot of the bed, then a pair of jeans from the closet. We got her pajama top off, and I got my first lesson in putting a bra on as she held her arms up just in front of her. As I did it, she said, "Thanks. There's no way I could do those hooks."

I carefully took the bandages off her cuts, reapplied antiseptic ointment, and put on fresh bandages. When I finished this task, I helped her on with the top. The bruises on her shoulders still looked pretty bad.

We got her pj bottoms off and panties on. Then I cleaned and re-bandaged her knees. The jeans went on without too much trouble. I put a little antiseptic on the cheek scratches, which were looking a lot better. Then, she asked me to get her hairbrush from the bathroom, and I got my first lesson in brushing a woman's hair. It was an educational morning.

When I finished, she smiled and said, "Thank you, again. Now, if you'll help me up, I want to get out to the kitchen."

I gave her an arm to hold on to and she got to her feet without too much trouble. She let go and walked to the kitchen unaided as I followed. Once there, I suggested she take a seat at the counter, which she did without protest. I asked her what she wanted for breakfast, then fixed her a cup of coffee and a bowl of granola with skim milk. She said today was to be grocery shopping day, but that would have to wait for a day. Maybe two.

We talked about her plan for the day, which, not surprisingly, was studying for the bar exam. Then we talked a bit more about my job as she ate. Once she finished, I washed her dishes and my coffee cup and put them away. "Where'd you learn that?" she joked.

"Just something I always do," I answered. "My mama brought me up right." Her smile this time was adorable.

After determining she didn't need anything else at the moment, we agreed she was okay by herself for the day. However, I insisted I wanted to check in on her later in the day, after assuring her I had no work responsibilities until tomorrow morning.

With only a slight protest, she agreed to let me bring her dinner, and we settled on pizza and salad. She gave me her cell number and I gave her mine. I got the bottle of Tylenol from the bedroom and put it on the counter. She smiled and said, "Yes, Dad."

After I grabbed my overnight bag and said goodbye, she got to her feet and walked to where I stood by the steps. "I'd give you a big hug, but that would hurt like hell," she said. "So instead, I'll just do this." She stood on her tiptoes and planted a kiss on my cheek. Then she stroked my arm and said, "Thank you, from the bottom of my heart. You're something special."

"So are you," I said in return, and bent to place a kiss on the unblemished cheek.

I got out the door a few seconds later and placed the shoe she'd kicked off the night before on the landing. I was quite sure she'd never find, and probably wouldn't want to find, its mate. I was back in Hatteras 15 minutes later.

Throughout the day, I thought a lot about Clare. I cleaned the mud and blood from the passenger side seat of my car, found her jacket in the back, smelled it at arm's length, then threw it away. I washed my weeks' worth of clothes at the communal laundry for the cottages, then made a quick trip to the small grocery store. I thought about calling her to see if she was doing okay but decided that might be a bit of overkill.

One of my colleagues got back in town in the early afternoon, and we caught up for a few minutes. I gave him a very short version of the story of Clare, though I omitted the overnight stay at her place. Afterwards, I took a short run on the beach, one of my favorite things to do, even in 55-degree winter weather.

Back at the cottage for a little rest time, and a nap, I took a quick shower, then turned the radio on to one of the local stations, WKIN. Before long the local news came on. There wasn't much happening on the island, except for the tragic death of a young local woman, Nancy Long, in a single vehicle accident. Her car was found, just after dawn, a mile north of Kinnakeet. It appeared, for unknown reasons, it had veered off the sound side of Route 12 and travelled approximately 50 feet through the sand and shrub thicket before overturning. An autopsy was planned to determine the cause of death. The reporter said she was not wearing a seat belt.

The news hit me harder than I would have expected. We had driven right by there and hadn't noticed anything. Probably a good thing. I immediately wondered if Clare had heard the news. If she was planning to study all day, it was unlikely she'd have the radio on. I debated whether I wanted to tell her, but decided she would hear eventually, and it would be good for her to have someone to talk to about it. She might even want to contact the Dare County Sheriff Department to provide some information. I decided I'd break the news to her sometime that evening.

I was unable to nap but puttered around until 5:15 when I phoned in our order, for a Margherita pizza and two salads, to a pizza place in Kinnakeet. I called Clare and told her I'd be there in 30 minutes. She seemed happy to hear from me and said she was doing well.

I had no idea if she was a drinker of wine, but decided a little liquid anesthetic would do her no harm if she was so inclined. Before picking up the pizza and salad, I bought a bottle of Verdicchio and some Italian salad dressing at the grocery. Then I decided a key lime pie would be a perfect dessert. I'd leave whatever we didn't eat at her place. The extra calories wouldn't hurt her.

I didn't want her to have to negotiate the steps to let me in, so when I found the front door unlocked, I stepped inside and announced, "Pizza delivery."

Clare shouted down, "Come on up." She greeted me at the top of the steps with a big smile. The scratches on her face were much less noticeable. Or maybe it was just the smile.

I shucked my jacket and dropped the dinner goodies on the kitchen counter. She caught me as I turned back toward the living room and gave me another peck on the cheek. I felt her lean slightly into me while one arm circled my waist to hold me close. I didn't mind. I returned the affection to her cheek.

After the semi-embrace, I noticed she'd cleared off the end of the dining table that was closest to the deck, and had tableware set out for our meal. There were two candles on the table as well.

She was thrilled with the wine, my choice of pizza, and the pie. She said if she'd been able to go out she would have picked up the same thing for our dinner. I found wine glasses after she directed me to the proper cabinet, opened the bottle, and made our first pour. She lit the candles.

Over dinner, we got the medical report out of the way first. She said she was feeling a lot better. The headache was gone, the shoulders were about 50 percent better, and the ribs ... well, they still hurt with most any kind of movement. She'd taken the Tylenol regularly and would be ready for another dose in a couple of hours. She had managed to get a reasonable amount of studying done.

The rest of the dinner conversation was a back-and-forth recital of the story of my life and hers. It seemed to me she'd led a pretty charmed life, and when I made that comment she agreed, with only a moment's hesitation. She summarized my background as "uneven" up to the point where I entered graduate school. I readily agreed with that assessment.

She suggested we move to the more comfortable sofa after the salad and pizza. I cleaned up the table, wrapped the left-over pizza in foil, and put it in the fridge. Then I cut the key lime pie and brought us each a piece with a refill of wine.

After we finished the pie, I broke the news to her about Nancy. She cried briefly, and I moved close to put a hand lightly on her shoulder. She admitted the tears were half for Nancy, and half for how close she'd come to her own death. We talked for a while about her fortunate decision to jump from the car, and how her subsequent injuries were, by far, the better consequences of last evening.

The conversation evolved into one about the fragility of life and the many unknowns we all face along the way. How, to some degree, one's life is determined not only by the choices we make, but also by pure, dumb luck. We both knew people who had died, or had their lives significantly and tragically altered, by accidents that were not of their own doing. One of her college friends had been in a rear-ended car accident that left her a paraplegic and in a wheelchair for the rest of her life. We agreed the lesson of the day was to make good decisions about your life, within those confines live life to it's fullest, and enjoy every moment along the way.

We managed to work our way out of that sobering topic to more hopeful ones, and as the conversation and evening continued, we became more comfortable with each other. She confirmed that she was, indeed, a runner, and I confessed to being a gym rat when I was in Beaufort. We laughed several times, though it hurt her to do so, and she tried, mostly unsuccessfully, to constrain the laughs to a charming little chuckle. I was becoming more entranced by this fascinating, bright, funny woman with each passing minute.

I don't know whether it was her or me, but gradually we found ourselves sitting closer and closer on the sofa. She got up once, about 8:45, and turned the gas fireplace on, and the other lights in the house off. When she came back to the sofa, she sat as close to me as she could and rested her head on my shoulder. I wanted to put my arm around her and pull her in, but knowing the condition of her shoulders, settled for an arm on the back of the sofa, and a hand perched lightly on her shoulder.

Since we were both obviously wearing down from the combined effects of the wine, the full stomachs, and sleep deprivation, the conversation slowed down eventually. It was replaced by a little bit of kissing around 9:15. It started out tentatively, then progressed. I was getting more turned on by the second and holding her gently in my arms by the time we separated for a breather.

Being mindful of her physical state, and our mutual fatigue, I decided it was time to make my exit, hopefully to pick things up at that point at a later date.

When I told her my plan, she sighed, and said, "Yeah, that's probably for the best. If you promise to come back. Soon." I assured her I would, and we agreed on dinner Tuesday evening.

I gave my body a minute to settle down, then got up, flicked on some lights, grabbed my jacket, and stepped to the stairs. She was right behind me, and we had one last kiss.

"Before you leave," she said, her hand holding my arm, "there's something you should know about this house."

"What's that?" I asked.

"This house has a reputation in my family."

I looked at her questioningly. She looked at me seriously.

"Both my brother and sister met their spouses while they were living here. My brother met his wife, who was also in the Coast Guard, while stationed here. And my sister met her husband during the few months she lived here. He's a surfboard designer who owns a surf shop. He was here for a fishing tournament that October she was living here. They got married ten months later and now live in Florida."

Her grip on my arm became a little tighter. "When I told my parents I wanted to stay here for a few weeks to prepare for the bar exam, my mother jokingly asked me if I was coming to the house on Dory Lane to study for the bar, or to find a husband."

I tried to study her face for a moment, but she was giving me nothing, so I asked. "And what did you tell her?"

"I told her I was definitely coming to study. But," There was a long pause while she grabbed my eyes with hers. "I said if Mr. Right showed up at the front door, with a Margherita pizza and a bottle of wine, I would certainly let him in."

I may never know if that was a line she made up, or if that exchange really happened. Maybe someday she'll tell me. But I thought about it, with a glowing feeling from head to toe, as I drove slowly, and carefully, back to Hatteras.

294

DORY
LANE

Acknowledgements

I would like to thank my wife, Debbie, my son, Cory, and my daughter, Rian, for their continued love, support, and encouragement. They have always been the biggest cheerleaders for my writing and photography. This book, and the others, would not have been possible without them.

I must also thank the many other people who have read my stories in their infancy and viewed my photographs from the Outer Banks and the many other places that have fascinated me. Angie, Vicki, Stacey, you are much appreciated. And Ken, thank you for the great story idea.

It is important to me to also acknowledge my friend and photography guru, Carlan. As much as I have learned from him about photography, I have learned more about how to lead a life of true meaning and importance. I don't always live up to his lessons, in either photography or life, but I'll keep trying.

Joe Sledge is due another great nod of appreciation. I am very grateful for his assistance with the publication of this book and the earlier *Kinnakeet Stories*. Through his kindness and support I have learned a great deal about the intricacies of book publication and been able to bring my stories to print.

Once again, I must also thank GeeGee Rosell, the owner of Buxton Village Books, for her support and encouragement. Visitors to the Outer Banks are encouraged to visit her store and buy their books from this, or their own, local independent bookstore. Support of these institutions is crucial to keeping reading as a vital part of our culture.

And to you, dear reader, please get in touch. Your feedback is more important than you know. Please visit the *Kinnakeet Stories* Facebook page or send me an email.

Bernie Lewis
Kinnakeetstories@gmail.com

About The Author

Bernie Lewis was born and raised in San Diego, California, where he first learned to love and appreciate the beauty of the ocean environment. He settled as an adult in Winchester, Virginia, his home for the last 45 years. Since the age of 20 he has been a frequent visitor to the Outer Banks of North Carolina. He and his family bought a vacation home in Kinnakeet in 2020.

Bernie graduated from Washington and Lee University, then earned a master's and Ph.D. degrees from the University of Virginia. He subsequently served the Winchester community as a clinical psychologist for 35 years before retirement.

He is the author of the first collection of this series of short stories, *Kinnakeet Stories*, the photobook *The Long Branch You've Never Seen*, and *Local Heroes: Winchester Virginia 2000-2010*.

The creative side of him has found expression in capturing photographic images and dreaming up interesting stories to tell since his teen years.

You may contact him at Kinnakeetstories@gmail.com

www.ingramcontent.com/pod-product-compliance
Lightning Source LLC
Chambersburg PA
CBHW071402300726
48976CB00006B/1955